THE BUNYAN BARTER

ADDIE J. KING

THE GRIMM LEGACY - BOOK 4

Loconeal Publishing

Amherst, OH

THE BUNYAN BARTER

This book is a work of fiction. The names, characters, places, and events in this novel are either fictitious or are used fictitiously. Any resemblance to actual events or persons is entirely coincidental.

Loconeal books may be ordered through booksellers or by contacting:
www.loconeal.com
216-772-8380

Loconeal Publishing can bring authors to your live event.
Contact Loconeal Publishing at 216-772-8380.

Published by Loconeal Publishing, LLC
Printed in the United States of America

First Loconeal Publishing edition: September 2015

Visit our website: www.loconeal.com

ISBN 978-1-940466-41-5 (Trade Paperback)

ALSO BY ADDIE J. KING

The Grimm Legacy
The Andersen Ancestry
The Wonderland Woes
The Bunyan Barter

DEDICATION

To Daniel, for making me a not-so-evil stepmother.

CHAPTER ONE

"What is that racket?" I yelled, over the sound of *thunk-thunk-thunk* outside my window. I sat up in bed and threw off the covers. As I threw open the shutters covering the windows, I saw a very large man, wearing a red flannel plaid shirt, in my backyard, chopping down a tree that was older than I was.

It was the tree I'd used to escape from the house when my stepmother had been in one of her rages. It was the tree where I'd hidden from her and her endless list of chores. I'd fantasized about that tree holding my "treehouse" because I spent so much time in its branches, even though no one ever had built me the actual house part, and I hadn't known how.

It was my tree.

As I watched, his thick shoulders slumped and the axe he was holding fell to one side.

I probably would have stopped to think about it if I'd had caffeine in my system. I would have just called the cops if I'd been thinking rationally. It was four o'clock in the morning, and I don't think rationally at four o'clock in the morning.

I'd taken to keeping a heavy iron club in my bedroom. It was one of the weapons and tools and magical whats-its my father had left me after he died. He'd left me three iron trunks full of stuff I hadn't even know he'd had, to protect me from the magical and faerie court craziness that kept popping up in my life. And why did the magical faerie court goofy always show up at dawn?

Instead of taking the rational, safe, probably smart, course of action, I headed down the stairs, ready to bash in the head of the flannel dude in my yard. I didn't care that he was bigger than me. I didn't care that he was upset and had a big axe.

After facing down the Seawitch, my evil faerie stepmother, the White Rabbit, and a Jabberwocky, a trespassing tree poacher felt like nothing.

I should have known better.

The metal club shoved under my arm, I headed for the door, fought with the locks, and threw it open as my roommate, Mia, dashed into the kitchen, yelling for me to stay inside. I ignored her.

"Janie," she called. "You don't know if there's something after you as a member of the Grimm family, after me and my dad with the Andersen stuff, after Allie," our third roommate, who trailed her, yawning and stumbling, "and her mom, and all the stuff that came up in Wonderland. What do you think you're doing?"

I ignored her and threw open the door, hefting the club over one shoulder to get ready for a home run swing. I ran out of the door and right up to the man in the yard. "Who the hell are you and what the hell do you think you're doing to my tree?" I yelled. "Who told you it was acceptable to chop down a tree without the owner's permission? Were you raised by delusional beaver lumberjacks?"

I was ready for just about any reaction except for the one I got.

"Why did they take him?" he wailed, reaching for the axe again, and hauling it over his shoulder as if about to take another chop at my tree. Before he could swing, he flinched.

I hadn't seen why he flinched, but when I turned around, I saw Mia, with one of the lava rocks from the landscaping around the back patio in her hand, poised like a catcher about to throw down a runner trying to steal second. Allie was right behind her, reaching down to fill both hands with the same purplish black rocks.

What were they doing?

Before I could ask, the man dropped and collapsed to the ground. I saw a look of utter despair and desolation. Tears ran down his cheeks.

"Sir?" I asked. "Are you okay?" I still held the club, but it was hard to maintain the anger and adrenaline rush that had propelled me outside when I saw the upset and pain on his face. I'd keep the club up until I was sure we were safe, but I was starting to believe there was more to this situation than I was seeing with my own two eyes. And something told me that not only was this situation the police weren't likely to be able to help with, they'd probably think I was cuckoo for Cocoa Puffs.

"He's gone!" he cried. "They took him, and they won't tell me where he is!"

I crept closer, hoping the neighbors weren't hearing what was going on. All I needed at the moment was a neighborhood watch commander or some nosy neighbor with an eye to being the next Gladys Kravits, the busybody who knew everyone's business. Just one middle of the night drink of water, one midnight (or rather, after midnight) pee break, and I'd have to explain why I was brandishing a club at a crying man in my backyard. Next month's neighborhood watch group meeting would be a little too interesting.

I didn't want to put down the club. There'd been just too much out there over the last couple of years that wanted to eat my face off, not including my cutthroat compatriots in our last year of law school.

There was a reason why the club was made of metal. Iron was poison to creatures from the faerie realm. More than once my friends and I had lived because we had been smart, protecting ourselves with salt, which repelled magic, as well as iron. We'd outwitted and outthought the ones who had come after us. I didn't plan to start a habit of stupid now; I'd hang onto that club until I knew that man wasn't dangerous.

As I got a bit closer, I realized he was six-and-a-half feet tall, and he probably weighed close to three hundred and fifty pounds. He was as broad across the shoulder as Mia and I combined, and the axe that lay on the ground beside him looked like something the size of a medieval weapon, something I might have seen in *Braveheart* in a battle scene. He'd be a formidable opponent, even with the club.

I decided to try a different approach. "Sir, I don't know who you are. I don't know why you're here. I can tell you that I don't appreciate you chopping down my maple tree without my permission, and I can tell you I wouldn't give you permission if you asked. Regardless of that issue, however, I need to ask why you are in my yard, why you are chopping down my tree, and who and what are you talking about?" I tried to sound calm and in control. It had served me well in the past.

He sniffed, long and liquid. Gross. He took a deep breath, and looked at me, his shoulder slumped enough to bend him almost double, but he still didn't say anything. I took the opportunity to take a better look at him, trying to see if anything about him seemed familiar.

He wore a thermal hat, and a red plaid shirt. I'd noticed the shirt before, but up closer, it looked like a work shirt, a lumberjack one from the old folk tales I remembered reading about in school. He wore jeans, cuffed at the ankles, and hobnailed heavy work boots, and there were suspenders over his button-up shirt, which was rolled up to the elbows. His cheeks were flushed, and his eyes were red from crying.

Oh my. "What's your name, sir?" I asked. "We can't help you until we figure out what's wrong." I had a funny feeling we were about to do exactly that, help him. On a whim, I sniffed, hard.

I was right.

I smelled peppermint and stale books. It smelled like my Dad, who had been a folklore, linguistics, and history professor at the University of Dayton before he'd been killed by my evil faerie stepmother. I'd learned long ago that it was also the scent of magic, which smelled different to each person, like something tempting and irresistible. *Son of a bitch,* I thought. I'd been right to have a metal weapon.

I had to swallow hard against the disappointment that Aiden wasn't here with me. He'd have known what we were facing, probably before I'd even stepped out of the kitchen door, but he didn't live here anymore. I didn't even know if I could use the term *boyfriend* anymore, but he was the one with the knowledge and training that had helped me through so many scrapes in the past.

I shoved that emotional hurt aside as the man in front of me snuffled an answer. "My name is Paul," he blubbered. "And I need your help, Ms. Grimm. I can't find him anywhere. They've taken him away from me."

Huh? "Sir, where did you get my name?" I asked, still holding the club, even though the weight of it was starting to hurt my shoulder. "You have to understand that I've got to be careful here."

He nodded, but before either one of us could say or do anything, I heard another voice, somewhere near my toes.

"Paul? What are you doing here? I didn't think you'd ever come to these parts. What could possibly get you to leave Minnesota?"

I knew that voice. I looked down.

Sure enough, it was my third roommate, a loud, opinionated,

loyal, and beer drinking frog who'd started his life as a human and went by the name of Bert.

If I'd been thinking when I'd rushed outside, I'd have asked Bert what was going on, but the brain wasn't quite functional without coffee. I let Bert take control for a minute while I tried to process the fact that out midnight trespassing tree killer knew my amphibian friend.

Paul responded directly to the frog. "They took him, Bert. They won't tell me where they took him. They just told me that I have to find the heir to the apple man and I have to turn him over to them in three days or they'll barbecue him," he wailed, the waterworks starting up again.

I was startled. "Wait a minute. Who? Who is they? And who is he? And they're going to barbecue him? That's awful." I started to feel sorry for him. Was this his brother, his friend, his nephew, his lover?

"It's Babe, ma'am. My ox," the man in plaid blubbered, the keening wail that followed in his last work punctuating his grief.

Ox?

Well, that was certainly something one didn't hear every day.

CHAPTER TWO

P aul dissolved into tears again, and I turned, to find Mia and Allie's jaws hanging open.

Babe? The ox? Who belonged to a man named Paul. PAUL FREAKING BUNYAN was the man chopping down my maple tree.

Could my life get any weirder?

Bert hopped out of my shadow and over to Paul, talking to him softly. I couldn't hear much of what he said, but the big man seemed to settle down. I heard a dog bark, not far away, and I knew that we had to get Paul, and his drama, out of the open and into the house. I wasn't sure I trusted him, but I didn't want to answer a lot of questions with the neighbors. I didn't have answers to give them, and hadn't had time to come up with a good explanation.

"Bert," I called softly.

He hopped over to me, and nodded. "It's okay. Paul's not a danger. He's an old friend. We've got to help him if we can. No matter what he just tried to do to your tree, he's not like that."

I still hesitated. "Is it possible he's been sent to get close to us, and possibly hurt us? It wouldn't be unheard of that he's a plant, or a tool, or a weapon, to get us to be lower our guard. Is it possible that he's so distraught he might have been sent to make us vulnerable, to get information on us to make us easier to attack?"

I saw Allie, our resident teenager, out of the corner of my eye, and cringed. I still had to ask the question, even though asking it in front of her made me feel bad. When we'd first encountered her, she'd been sent our way by the Seawitch. She'd more than proved her friendship, however, by refusing to help the Seawitch breach our defenses when the faerie queen had been trying to kill Mia and her father last year. Allie'd become a friend, and we'd refused to let her run away to protect us again when her past in Wonderland had come back to bite her. I saw the color rise in her cheeks, and I hated it, but it was a valid question. I wasn't asking it to hurt her, but I had to ask.

Bert shook his head. "I don't think he even knows who to go to for help. I'm pretty sure he doesn't even know who he's supposed to be looking for. He came here because someone told him you might help him, and he got overwhelmed."

I nodded. I had to trust Bert's instincts; he had been dealing with magical insanity for far longer than I had. It had been several hundred years since he'd been turned into a frog by a witch that had targeted him. I still wondered if there was something I could do for him down the road, something to let him be human again. I saw a look pass between Allie and Bert and I knew I needed to look into it further. Those two were getting plenty chummy lately. I needed to help them if I could.

And for that, I'd need to talk to Aiden, my former boyfriend, the man who had broken my heart, the one I'd decided was my one and only before things had all fallen apart.

Sigh.

I ushered everyone inside, while trying to figure out how I felt about that.

Last year, Aiden had suffered some serious health issues; he'd been poisoned by the deadly nightslip mushrooms we'd run across when we'd gone to Wonderland. The Snow Queen had appeared and helped us out. Nothing in faerie is free; we'd helped to ameliorate a bigger problem in Wonderland that she was grateful for, but Aiden, as the only half-faerie/half-human being that we knew of, had side effects from the remedy she'd provided.

Paul had quieted down, and Bert was trying to talk him into the house, as I opened the door, still ruminating on the Aiden situation. I hoped he'd be able to help, but his memory problems might keep him from helping as much as possible.

The tarts we'd come across in Wonderland had been the cure for the mushroom poison, but the side effects were startling. In humans, it caused confusion, brain fog, and memory loss. In magical beings, it could turn them into the thing they most feared. Most thought the side effects were temporary, but with Aiden's mixed heritage, no one could predict how he'd handle it. He'd temporarily turned into the thing he most feared, the Jabberwocky, but had returned to himself with a hole in his memory that persisted beyond the immediate aftermath of the whole event.

I lowered the club and gestured through the open door, pointing at the kitchen table and chairs just inside. "Sir, why don't you have a seat and tell us what happened?" I asked Paul, on Bert's assurance that he didn't pose a threat to us. "We can all get some coffee, and maybe some breakfast, since it appears no one's going back to sleep any time soon, and maybe we can see what we can do for you."

Yes, coffee. Sweet, black, live-giving liquid that would let my brain start to focus on what was going on, and maybe let me concentrate on a problem other than my own love life, or what was left of it.

Aiden and I had tried for months to keep going with our relationship, but we'd been unable to overcome the constant frustration. I'd finally overcome my commitment issues enough to realize that Aiden was the man I wanted to commit to, only to have him struggling to remember things that were cemented in my brain. He was stuck between whether to fake a memory and react in a way that he thought I wanted him to act, or telling me he couldn't remember something that was meaningful to me. which would make us feel even more distant with each other. We'd been living together before we'd gone to Wonderland last fall to save Allie. Three weeks ago, he'd moved out, asking to take some space to work on his memory issues without feeling like he was always missing something.

Everyone trudged inside. Paul sat down on one of the old wooden chairs at the kitchen table. I heard the wood creak and groan as it took his weight, but the thing held fast. I bustled around, making coffee, hearing hushed voices just outside the kitchen door. Allie and Bert had gotten past me, and out of the kitchen, just barely beyond clear earshot, to argue about something. I heard my name once or twice, and ignored them.

Mia was digging in the refrigerator for something, but she was watching me while she did it. What was she looking at me like that for? Was she reading my mind, my ruminations on my failed relationship, or just worried about me for some reason? She had complained just the other day that I'd been withdrawn. She was right.

I hadn't talked to Aiden since he'd left. He'd moved in with his mother, hoping that the familiar surroundings would help him get his bearings. I, on the other hand, was wearing my Felix the Cat flannel pajama pants with the University of Dayton t-shirt I'd bought for Aiden a year before. I was wearing a hoodie he'd left behind as well. Crap. Maybe I had been a bit too wrapped up in my own head lately.

The only thing I'd been able to agree with Aiden on was that we needed to take a break. I trusted that his mother, Doris, would be able to take care of him, and would help him fill in a lot of holes. I wondered if he'd be able to help Paul. I wasn't sure just yet who I should be worried about most, or what dangers I hadn't yet thought of. I didn't know how much of his scholarly knowledge had disappeared with his memory, as we hadn't had that kind of thing come up much since we'd come back from Wonderland. It didn't matter. I had to call; he just had way too much experience and knowledge for me to ignore.

No matter how much I wanted to give him his space.

The coffeepot beeped and Mia set out a container of hazelnut creamer and a small container of half-and-half. I poured Paul some coffee in the biggest mug I owned, something I'd brought home from the Ohio Renaissance Faire last fall, on one of the few serene days with Aiden after the debacle in Wonderland, a big ceramic thing that held four normal cups of coffee. It looked tiny in Paul's large hands, but it was the only one that I thought he'd be comfortable holding. He sipped at it slowly, and I gave him a few moments with a hot beverage to calm himself down.

I glanced at the clock. Four-thirty, with class in four and a half hours. We were in the last year of law school, with the last day of classes today. After today, we'd have a week's break for Thanksgiving, to study and cram for final exams. Of course, "final" exams are a bit misleading, because it sounds like there's more than one in each class. The truth is that one's grade for the entire semester is generally the result of one exam at the end of the semester. Those exams started after we came back from Thanksgiving break. In some ways, it was good timing; after today, we'd be able to focus on Paul's problem. In other ways, it was bad timing. We needed a full week off, with no work, no classes, no interruptions, to study nonstop, stuff our faces full of turkey, and get ready for the biggest tests of the semester. Except that sitting in front of me was the biggest kind of interruption out there.

The magical kind.

The kind I hadn't yet been able to walk away from.

The kind I couldn't schedule in my day planner with its color-coordinated highlights to tell me at a glance what needed to get done immediately and what could wait a day. The kind that made my life better, and worse, at the same time. The kind that had brought me Aiden; and had taken him away from me, as well.

"So," I said, as I poured my own cup of coffee. "What's going on, and why are you here?"

"Miss Janie, I've got lots of friends, and they've all told me you're the one that might be able to help me. I just don't know where else to turn."

Hooboy. Here we go.

CHAPTER THREE

Coffee made my brain start functioning normally again. Paul seemed to be buoyed up by getting something to drink, and Mia started making breakfast. Bacon sizzled on a skillet while she cracked eggs. Bert was on standby near the toaster, pressing down the level while she moved around the kitchen. Good thing we'd just made a grocery run the night before, stocking the pantry and fridge for study fuel.

I almost said something to Bert about being on the counter, where food was being prepared. *He* wanted to be at least at waist height rather than being on the floor where we had to talk down to him. *I* didn't want him walking on food preparation and food serving surfaces like the counters or the table. It was an ongoing argument and not one where either of us was willing to give up, or give in. It wasn't the right time to have that argument, and pushing the lever on the toaster was something he could do. There were some serious limits to how much he could help, and I knew that he sometimes felt completely useless. I'd learned to keep my trap shut and just use a lot of antibacterial wipes when he was done; having him feel useful and like a contributing member of the household was more important than my winning that argument. He'd accused me at one point about being upset at him for still being a frog; that was stupid. I hadn't had a hand in the potion that made him human again, or the magic that had turned him back into a frog. I'd be upset if any of the roommates walked on food prep surfaces in their bare feet.

"Paul," I started, bringing him a plate of toast while we waited. I had some Smucker's grape in the fridge, and when he didn't seem to know what to do with it, I spread some on his buttered toast, and handed it to him.

He crammed the whole thing in his mouth and chewed. I waited, and tried again.

"Paul, let's start from the beginning. What happened?"

He swallowed hard, and wiped the crumbs off the corners of his mouth with the back of his hand. "Babe always stays with me. You'd think he was like a puppy, even though he's a fully grown ox. He normally sleeps right beside my bed, and wakes me up in the morning by licking my face."

Ew. I fought to keep that off my face, motioning him to go on, as Mia slid a plate of eggs and bacon in front of him. He picked up the fork, which looked like a toothpick in his massive hand, and started eating, continuing his story as he ate.

"He doesn't go very far without me. We've had a few scares over the years, of people wanting to take pictures, or people who just don't understand that no means no."

Allie walked in from where she'd been talking to Bert in the hallway. "There's a lot of people who don't understand that concept, Paul. In many different ways." She picked a piece of bacon off the plate where Mia had some resting on paper towels to drain the grease and bit into it.

She'd know. Saved from Wonderland by her mother's political maneuvering, she'd found herself in Dayton, Ohio, with no ID, no street smarts, and no idea how to survive in our modern world. She'd been an instant victim, with a target painted right on her forehead for a street gang to exploit. Allie had been sold for sex over and over until she'd sought refuge in our backyard from the punks who'd treated her like property, and found herself right back in the middle of magical mayhem. In the year or so since we'd found out about her true story, Allie'd put on a few needed pounds from solid cooking. We'd helped her register for a Social Security card, and she'd earned a GED, a high school equivalency degree. All those little accomplishments were adding up quick, helping her get established in the real world, and she'd been talking lately about getting a job and contributing to rent and groceries.

I certainly wouldn't turn down the money; I was getting real tired of living on a student budget. There were only so many hours I could work while I was in school. The magical extra-curriculars weren't bringing in cash; on the contrary, they cost me money, as Mia and I supported Bert and Allie, and now we also were helping the

F.A.B.L.E.S. organization where we could with supporting all the refugees that had come back from Wonderland, including Allie's mother. The Foundation for Ancestry, Biography, Legends, Epics, and Stories wasn't a rich foundation with deep pockets; it was run on a shoestring and funded by Aiden's mother, Doris, and the rest of the members, with what money and resources they could pool together. Aiden had stopped taking a salary for his position with them the minute we realized just how much help the Wonderland folks needed. Most of them hadn't seen a car before, much less a television, a computer, or even a crosswalk.

I shook my head, bringing myself back to the problem at present. Paul was talking about how loyal Babe was, and how he was so protective of him, and how the ox was his comfort when he realized that no one wanted to be around him except to hear about cutting down trees and talking about his big feet leaving the holes that made the lakes in Minnesota.

We weren't getting anywhere. "Paul, I'm not minimizing anything about Babe. He sounds like a pretty cool ox . . ." *was I really saying that?* I thought. "But we need to know when he went missing, how it happened, and who did it."

He swallowed hard. "I don't know who did it. All I know is there was a random note. I'm supposed to find the apple heir and deliver them to the Big Rock Candy Mountain. I don't even know where that is, much less anything about any apples. Too many apples give me a bellyache."

The apple heir? *Who could that be?* Maybe Aiden would have a clue. He always did. The stabbing feeling came back at the thought of him. And the Big Rock Candy Mountain? It sounded vaguely familiar, but I couldn't place why.

"Paul, I'm going to call someone to help us. Is that okay?" I asked. Mia slid more eggs and bacon onto his plate, and he nodded as he kept eating. Allie grabbed a plate and slid into a chair at the table beside him. She put Bert on the table.

"Go call, Janie. He needs to be here," said Bert, who normally would have complained at anyone picking him up short of an emergency. I noticed, but just raised my eyebrows at him. He didn't say anything, but met my gaze. "We're good here."

I slipped into the hallway and grabbed the telephone from the hall stand, dialing Doris's house phone rather than Aiden's cell phone. If there was a way for this to stay all business, maybe that was a good thing. I wanted to give him the option. It rang twice before Doris picked up the phone, and I remembered that it was still really really early in the morning.

I explained quickly that we'd had another magical emergency, and that she and Aiden probably ought to get to our house quickly. She didn't question me; instead, she just promised to show up in the next fifteen minutes. They didn't live too far away, so I went to go brush my teeth and run a brush through my hair before they showed up. We might be broken up at the moment, but I really didn't want to see him again with morning and coffee breath and bedhead.

I pulled my brown hair back into a ponytail, the neatest thing I could think of without a blow dryer or hairspray, changed my shirt into something not related to Aiden so that I didn't look like I was desperate or heartbroken, and headed back down the stairs. I hadn't quite gotten back to the kitchen when the doorbell rang.

It was Aiden and his mother. Doris carried a big picnic basket, and I smelled cinnamon rolls. Aiden had a big cardboard box. Of course, Doris brought food wherever she went. Her baked goods were legendary, and she always seemed to equate feeding people with caring for them. I hated to see her grocery bills, but the way Paul had been plowing through the eggs and toast and bacon made me grateful that she'd stayed true to form. I smiled at her, and tried to hold the smile when I met Aiden's eyes. I couldn't read him; he looked upset, but I wasn't sure. His eyes looked wary, and he looked away again quickly, as if he was embarrassed, but he kept looking back at me.

There was another big basket at their feet, so I grabbed it, covering up the awkwardness and helping them inside. We hauled their goodies to the kitchen and unloaded, with Doris stashing some things in the fridge for later, and setting out some things for use right away. I was amazed at how much she'd brought. Paul looked bewildered at the number of people and the amount of food coming out of the baskets and boxes, and I understood completely how he felt.

Trying for a bit of levity, I joked, "Doris, did you come up with an incantation to provide enough food for an invasion?"

Paul froze, his fork halfway to his mouth. Mia dropped the spatula.

Bert even gave me an odd look. "Janie, did you really mean to accuse Doris of trying to hurt all of us with magic, *using her food?* Are you nuts?"

"I'm kidding, guys. You know better, Bert, Mia, everyone. We're here to help people." I tried to dial it back.

Paul put down his fork, looking somewhat scared. Okay, so maybe that joke wasn't a good idea. The smart thing to do when dealing with faerie court magic was not to accept any offered food or drink. He probably thought I had let slip that I was trying to trick him. I had to fix this. "Paul, it was really a joke. I'm human. So's just about everyone here. Even if we weren't, we're not here to trick you, and we wouldn't have invited you into the house to trick you. You've asked around about us. You know Bert. I made a joke because things are awkward here for reasons that don't have anything to do with you. The food's safe, I promise," I took a bit of the bacon myself, just to show him what I meant. "It just hasn't been very long since I talked to Doris on the phone, and I couldn't believe she'd had the time to put all of this food together that fast and get here."

Doris put down another pie on the kitchen island, then came over, sliding one arm around my shoulders and facing Paul. "I'm Doris, sir. I like to cook. I do it when I'm worried, when I'm sad, when I'm frustrated, or when I'm bored. My friends and I have started a small catering company. There's an event this weekend, so we had all of this ready. It's not a problem." To me, she said, "Harold and Stanley are on their way to my house to start putting together another round of this for the party. We all agreed that there was just way too much junk food last time we had a magical emergency, so it's worth the effort that we all eat healthy when we've got something like this going on. Janie didn't mean anything by what she said; she was commenting on the amount of food I have here, and how fast it got here, not accusing me of anything."

I was quick to jump in, confirming what she was saying.

Paul nodded. "Makes sense," he said, swallowing the bite of eggs he'd hesitated on with my stupid joke, and tucking back into his breakfast. I went to help Doris unpack.

She'd certainly outdone herself; a plate as big around as a beach ball was piled high with cold meat sandwiches and barely fit in the refrigerator, along with a cheese tray and a big plastic bowl that looked like it held potato salad. The big basket had four pies, including strawberry rhubarb, my favorite, along with pumpkin, apple crumb, and a peaches-and-cream pie. In the smaller basket, she had big zippered plastic baggies full of cut up vegetables and a big container of what looked like Ranch dressing dip.

She was right; we'd barely made it through Wonderland on canned and prepackaged food to avoid putting any of the memory fogging tarts into our systems, and we'd been starving when we'd gotten back. All of us had tucked into fast food tacos and hamburgers while we'd been at the hospital, worrying over Aiden's health after he'd been poisoned by those deadly nightslip mushrooms. We'd eaten French fries while the medical staff had attended to the tubing and machinery providing dialysis, attempting to filter the poison out of his kidneys and liver from the mushroom poisoning, but it hadn't been keeping up enough to save him, and we'd had to turn to the Snow Queen. He'd barely pulled through, and he still had a sensitive stomach; still recovering from the amount of work his system had had to do to process the toxins in the mushrooms.

My stomach had taken quite a while to recover from that sick, greasy feeling that wouldn't go away, and I still couldn't eat tacos without getting nauseous. How much of that was from the junk food and how much of that was from worry that Aiden wouldn't recover, that he wouldn't be the same, that I'd lose him? I wasn't sure, and I had ended up losing him just the same, even though he'd recovered from the mushrooms that almost always killed its victims.

I couldn't blame Doris for the thought, but all that food had to cost a ton, and she was just getting her catering business off the ground. While everyone else tucked into a hearty breakfast or helped put away Doris's haul, I quietly offered her some money, so that she didn't have to eat the cost of buying everything a second time. She waved off my efforts to pay her.

"We're okay, really, Janie. We're doing the catering to keep busy, and to train some of the Wonderland folks in some kind of marketable skill. Some of them are doing really well."

I nodded at her. I'd know she'd been trying to teach them how to cook in our realm, but having varying degrees of success with magical refugees who'd eaten nothing but tarts for centuries. I was grateful for the help. She put a plate of cookies in front of Paul, who reached for a chocolate chip one immediately.

He had calmed down enough to pull a ragged sheet of paper out of his front shirt pocket, and presented me with it while he leaned back in the chair and chewed. I read it aloud.

Bring the apple heir
To the Big Rock Candy Mountain
Before the end of the artificial American Plymouth holiday
Your ox will be returned when the apple heir
Answers for the ancestor's crimes

Huh. I wondered what that could possibly mean.

And what that meant for the next week.

CHAPTER FOUR

"Artificial Plymouth holiday? That's gotta be Thanksgiving," Mia said. "Thanksgiving at Plymouth, the real first one, was celebrated earlier in the year than we do it today. Abraham Lincoln established Thanksgiving as the fourth Thursday of November." I gave her a strange look. She must have read my mind. "I learned that in school somewhere. Give me a break. It's one of those weird facts that just kinda sticks in one's brain. Don't ask me why. For some reason I got really into the whole Pilgrim and Indian thing in grade school. I thought the idea of a bunch of really different people coming together for dinner was an awesome thing."

She had a point there. We hadn't made much plan for the upcoming holiday; maybe if we got through the present situation, we'd be able to invite all our friends over for a relaxing day of stuffing our faces and watching football on television, a break from everyday life and magical stress. It could work. I shook my head. Had to get through the present mess first, I thought, shoving aside the little niggling sadness those memories could bring up. If Aiden wasn't in my life, would he still show up for Thanksgiving dinner and football games? It wouldn't be the same without him.

"I just want some turkey stuffing," said Bert, bringing up the big holiday dinner thing that hadn't been planned yet. "I want stuffing and turkey and leftover turkey. And turkey soup. And scalloped turkey. And turkey a la King. And turkey burritos. I want mashed potatoes and gravy, and I want cranberries; lost and lots of cranberry sauce, and pumpkin pie. We didn't have Thanksgiving when I was a kid, but we had lots and lots of family holiday dinners, with big roast turkeys and pheasant and roasted meat. I never knew leftovers could be so wonderful until I came here, to America. I want all the fixin's."

I didn't have a whole lot of those little facts that stuck in one's brain from childhood. I still had some gaps from the memory fogging that my stepmother, Evangeline, had done while she'd slowly cursed my father to his death. I had a lot of sympathy for Aiden's lack of memory because I still had holes in my own, but I'd never forgotten someone I'd cared about. I'd never forgotten how much I'd loved my dad. In fact, in some ways, I hadn't been all that upset to have holes in my memory where I'd had some really not great experiences of a sick dad and a stepmother who was at best, neglectful and forgetful, and at worst, evil and sadistic. What bad memories had I forgotten due to her memory spells? Of course, it wasn't like she'd married my dad out of love; she'd married him to kill him, kill me, and get her powers back. And it hadn't quite worked out for her in the way she'd envisioned.

"Okay," I said. "We know our deadline. We have just under a week to get all this figured out and do whatever it is that we're going to do. But who in the world is the apple heir, and what is the Big Rock Candy Mountain?"

Aiden piped up. "It's an old hobo song. It talks about a hobo's paradise, with cigarette trees and lemonade springs and hens laying soft boiled eggs. That's what I remember of it, anyway."

I thought I remembered the song too, but those lyrics were less than helpful, and I said so. "That's not a real place. Is it through a portal? Is it another world? Is there a leader? A queen or president or dictator we need to deal with? Mia and I are a week from finals, one semester after that left in law school, and this is getting ridiculous. Can't they just tell us what they want, where to go, and what to do so we can get done with whatever craziness has come up in magic and get back to our regularly programmed normal life insanity?"

Oops. A bit too much like a rant. Aiden looked like I'd slapped him. I hadn't meant it to be personal, but it was starting to feel like no matter what we did, we'd be shoveling emotional crap while we shoveled relationship crap, and I didn't really have the patience for either at the moment. Could I just have my guy back and be able to move forward in my life?

Everyone just went quiet. I looked around the room, and saw all of them looking at me, as if I'd somehow said something that I wasn't supposed to say.

"Well, am I wrong?" I demanded.

The silence didn't stop.

"I thought you liked helping people," Paul said, in a small, tired voice. "Maybe I came to the wrong place."

Shit.

I didn't mean that.

"Paul there's more emotional stuff going on here than you had any way of knowing. I'm tired, it's really early in the morning, and none of that frustration has anything to do with you, or with Babe. I do like helping people. I've just been called on a lot to do it, and so I get a little frustrated, but I will never turn someone away who truly needs my help, no matter what other messes are going on in my personal life." I was glad to realize just how much I meant that as it came out of my mouth.

Aiden, thankfully, stepped up. I just hadn't predicted how he'd do it. "Paul, Janie and I were in a relationship and things aren't going well. It has nothing to do with you. We're overdue to have another one of those long, emotional discussions, and she's a bit anxious. I am, too. It will not affect how either one of us works together in order to get Babe back. You have my word."

Paul nodded.

I didn't like the reference to our relationship being in the past, but his statement about things not going well kinda sounded more like present tense, not ancient history. It was hard not to be somewhat hopeful, but I didn't like the sound of having another one of our long discussions. They hadn't gone well the last few times, but I could be a grown-up about this.

Doris, on the other hand, nodded at Paul, and dished him up a big slice of pie. "Paul, they're the best. And they're professional. You couldn't be in better hands. My question, however, is who sent you to those hands? It's not like Janie to advertise that she helps with issues like yours. How did you know to come here?"

Paul stood up, and his head was dangerously close to the ceiling. It's not like I had high ceilings, but it wasn't exactly a small room. He made Andre the Giant look small.

"I don't have anywhere else to turn. I need help. And I asked around. The Snow Queen and Geoffrey the Tailor told me where I could find you and that you would help. I can pay for your services. I do have money."

Money. I almost hated to take it, but the Wonderland people were bleeding us dry. We'd had to buy new wardrobes for all of them, and even though we'd shopped at Goodwill and at thrift stores, it had added up. Even though Stanley and his wife were keeping many of them at his farmhouse outside of the city for now, there was a limit at how long they could stay. With no marketable skills, no assets, and no way to register to pay taxes, there was very little that could be done without a lot of time, money, and effort to do so. With Paul's money, maybe we could get a few more of them independent and living a new life in the modern world, and take some pressure off all the F.A.B.L.E.S. budgets.

I nodded. I'd been asking around as to what rates attorneys were charging in the area, and even though I wasn't necessarily acting as an attorney in this context (and I wasn't licensed yet to act as one in the mortal realm), there was certainly no way I'd charge on the higher end. It appeared that a hundred bucks an hour would go a long way to replenishing freezer meals, replacing savings spent for clothing and shoes and underwear, and for Alfred, the former Mad Hatter, a computer with a graphic design program. He'd shown a real eye for designing fashion and home décor, and I hoped to encourage him into getting a degree in graphic design to keep him from the hats whose chemicals cause him to shake uncontrollably. And that hundred bucks an hour wasn't just for me: Aiden, Doris, Mia, Allie, Bert, Harold, and Stanley would all get a piece of whatever we earned.

"That's fine, Paul, but let's figure out exactly what we're talking about. Obviously, I'd expect you to cover any expenses or costs we have along the way." That was fairly standard from what I'd seen.

He nodded.

Bert piped up. "Paul earns money from some royalties from Disney. They've done so many different children's movies involving him, that he's been accumulating money for years. Janie, he's got enough to cover it, don't worry about that. Paul, Janie does need you to pay fair and to pay promptly, but we can send you an invoice when it's all said and done."

I was glad he'd thought to put everyone at ease on the money stuff. I'd have to pick his brain later to help me put together the invoice he'd mentioned. How to do that without mentioning magic? Would it have to be in triplicate? I had the sudden irreverent thought that it should be on colored paper with the heading "TPS report". I shook my head. I needed to pay attention.

Paul began telling us that he'd woken up that morning and hadn't seen Babe right next to his bed. He'd thought that strange, as he normally tripped over the ox in the mornings, but thought maybe he'd woken up and gone to get a drink out of the water bowl, or something along those lines. He went to see, and the animal was nowhere to be found. That was when he'd found the note.

"Where was the note?" How'd you find it?" Mia asked.

"It was left on the kitchen table, next to the phone, right where I keep the grocery list."

"Is that the place you'd be most likely to see it?" Bert asked.

Paul nodded. "Are you saying that someone would have had to known me well enough to know the place I'd be most likely to see it?"

I spoke up. "Maybe, but that by itself doesn't determine that. How is Babe with strangers? Would he go quietly with someone he doesn't know?"

He thought about it for a minute. "You know, I wouldn't think he would, but if he was hungry, if they had a treat for him, one of his favorites, he might get distracted just long enough to go without a fuss."

I thought about that. It didn't mean it was necessarily someone he knew, but it would have to be someone who knew enough to know how to tempt Babe.

"What kinds of things would he get that distracted for? I had a cat once, when I was little, who had a thing for ice cream, and she would come running through the house like, well, like a bull in a china shop, if anyone got out anything from the freezer that she thought might be ice cream. Didn't matter if it was frozen vegetables, didn't matter if it was frozen meat; if it came from the ice cream place it had to be ice cream, and she'd knock everyone over to get to it, no matter what else she'd been doing." I hadn't thought about that cat in a long time; we'd had to get rid of it when we'd moved in with Evangeline, my evil faerie stepmother. Was that why I remembered that much detail? "Paul, what would Babe react like that for?"

"Licorice," Paul said, without missing a beat. "Black licorice, the old fashioned kind, the kind that used to be sold in the general stores at the lumber camp near where I found him; that was his favorite. He also went nuts for pancakes and maple syrup and blueberries."

I guess I'd never thought of an ox eating pancakes. Of course, I'd also never thought of an ox eating candy, either. Or blueberries. Learn something new every day, I guess. I'd never have thought I'd have a frog making toast in my kitchen, either. I guess my measure of weird life experiences was getting stretched quite a bit over the last few years.

"Okay, so is that something that people know?" Allie asked. "How hard is that information to come across?"

Paul shrugged. "It's out there. It's rather common knowledge that I found Babe when he was a small calf, and fed him the jerky and licorice in my pocket after I dug him out of the snow."

Jerky? Did he mean *beef* jerky? Was that like feeding a pig bacon? That was so messed up.

"That means it could be anyone who took the time to do the research," Allie said. "That doesn't narrow down our list of suspects."

"So if we can't narrow down the suspects, then we need to figure out where we are supposed to go. Maybe figuring out the where will help give us the why," Mia, the voice of reason, stated. "Besides which, we need to start getting ready for the day. Let's all divide and conquer. Janie and I have classes this morning that we can't miss. Why don't Bert, Aiden, and Allie see what they can come up with while we're gone? Aiden, I'll leave my laptop here so you can use that. Allie, Bert, maybe there's something in the library."

Doris stepped up. "I'll clean up the kitchen, and maybe Paul can get some sleep. We'll all pitch in and help. You look exhausted."

I looked at him, and she was right. ""Paul, how long has it been since you've had a good night's sleep?"

"Since he disappeared," was the answer. "That was three days ago."

"You've got to get some sleep. We're going to need you sharp. You're the one who might know the details we need to find him. For him, you have to close your eyes and get some shut eye."

He agreed.

Mia and I ran off to get ready for the last classes of the semester while the others got Paul settled in an empty bedroom, with bedding and pillows on the floor since the room was otherwise empty. Doris shooed us off, promising to mother him and tuck him in while the others got started and we got our school stuff squared away. Bert promised that he and Allie would start in on research while we were gone, trying to see what they could piece together. Aiden nodded in agreement, and said he'd help.

I was glad I had friends. I felt bad for Paul, though.

He was acting like his best friend was gone; like Babe might not come back.

We'd have to see what we could do about that.

CHAPTER FIVE

With Mia driving, we headed for the last classes of the semester while the others dug into the research and work we'd left behind. I couldn't help but feel guilty that they were working while we were running off, and I was so preoccupied with worrying about it I didn't hear her question the first time.

"Janie, are you okay?" she asked, again, when I didn't answer.

"Why?" I asked.

She parallel parked on Brown Street, just a block or so away from the law school building, put the Escalade that I'd inherited into park, and shut off the engine before she said anything else.

"Because you weren't exactly expecting to see Aiden this morning," she said. "You've been hurting. I think he has too, but you weren't expecting to have him show up at your house this morning and I think you're still worried about what he wants to talk to you about. I know you, Janie. I've known you for way too long for you to even come close to thinking this is just minor. It wasn't your choice to break up, and I don't even think he wanted to."

"Mia, I love you like the sister I never had, but right now, I can't talk about this. We've got to get through our classes and get home. We've got a deadline, and we've got to study for exams as well. I don't know how we can get it all done without completely losing our minds. Aiden and I will talk when we get a chance, but I can't risk Paul losing Babe just because of my relationship or lack thereof. I can't live with that."

She nodded as we got out of the vehicle. And she didn't ask again, which was exactly what I needed; time to put my own relationship drama on hold in my brain, to corral those feelings away from the forefront of my worries in order to focus on Paul's problems.

I waited for her to join me on the sidewalk. We passed through the cloud in front of the building, where all the smokers congregated to get one last puff in before class. I'd think that after two and a half years of walking through it every day, I'd be used to it, but I wasn't. I was coughing as we entered, the smoke tickling the back of my throat and bringing tears to my eyes.

And I wasn't prepared for what I saw.

There was a booth set up for a student group. That wasn't unusual. There were always promotional tables for everything from bar review prep courses to computer legal research databases, to recruiters for AmeriCorps, to Lexis Nexis, to Westlaw, to job fairs and interview events, and other legal marketing promotions. Different student groups were always promoting different events at the school, and it wasn't unusual for there to be some sort of upcoming holiday promotion being put up right before Thanksgiving. Law students didn't really pay attention to anything Christmas related in December, because they were too busy cramming knowledge into their heads to worry about anything other than their upcoming exams.

What caught my eye, however, was the topic that was being presented.

The Christian Law Society and the Public Interest Law Society were joining forces to organize an outreach program; they'd come up with the idea of giving people apples to show charity and compassion. Attached to the apples were sayings about charity, forgiveness, and family togetherness, as well as a packet of seeds, for saving for the next growing season, as well as apple recipes for the holidays. I took an apple, and suddenly I knew who the apple man was, even if I didn't know his heir.

"Mia, are you thinking what I'm thinking?"

She hadn't really seen it, and I pointed at the apples. She still didn't get it.

"We're in Ohio. I think it's no mistake that Paul was pointed in our direction; the apple man is an Ohio legend. There's only one legend out there about a man who spread apple seeds and apples all over Ohio and the Midwest. I even remember a song about him from church camp, from when I was a kid," I said to her.

I'd gone to tons of camps and summer activities as I'd grown up; I had lots of memories from those. I wondered if it was because I was away from Evangeline for long enough for those memories to form and stick. We hadn't really belonged to a specific church, but I'd been willing to sign up for just about any camp or sleep away activity I could when I was in middle school. I'd done horseback riding camp, church camp, soccer camps, volleyball camps, cooking camps, library programs, and just about any other kind of activity I could get away with enrolling in. Dad always said yes, and if I asked him before Evangeline heard about it, I could normally get enrolled before she'd say no. I smiled, thinking about it, as we walked away, headed for our lockers.

Law students have lockers just like high school kids; the text books are just too heavy to carry all of them all the time. We dropped the books we'd brought from home and grabbed what we needed for our first class, as I softly sang,

Oh the Lord's been good to me,
And so I thank the Lord
For giving me
The things I need
The sun and the rain and the apple seed
Oh the Lord's been good to me.

She didn't follow. Come to think of it, I don't think she was at that camp with me. She hadn't gone to as many summer activities once we became friends; her mom just couldn't afford it. I saw a shadow on her face, and felt bad. Reminding her of the things she'd gone without as a kid was a reminder of how little her father had been around, and how little in child support he'd paid her mom. It had made for a childhood where she was close to her mom, but activities like that hadn't been in the budget. I winced.

"Mia, it's Johnny Appleseed. That's the apple man. And Paul's ransom note talked about the apple heir. I think the ransom note is asking for a descendent of Johnny Appleseed, and is saying that they are trying to get some kind of restitution or payback or something, for something that Appleseed did. We've got to figure out if he had kids, and who might be his heir." I was excited. I'd figured out the next step. How in the world was I going to sit quietly in my Secured Transactions class now?

She nodded. "I think you're right. That makes perfect sense. Do you think your dad had anything at home about Johnny Appleseed?"

"Probably. If not, I'm sure Aiden would know where to look. Maybe he knows the woman who took over Dad's position at the university, and would know how to ask the question without making it look weird."

Dad had taught folklore, linguistics, and history at the same university our law school was at; the University of Dayton. Aiden had been studying here, as well, when he'd met my father, long before I'd ever met him, and he'd been trying to continue his studies part time while he'd worked with the F.A.B.L.E.S. group. He'd taken some time off after his memories had failed to come back following the Jabberwocky incident, but he still knew people in the department that I didn't. Dad hadn't been one to mix his business and his family life. I still wondered how much of that was to protect me, and how much of it was some instinct that Evangeline should not be allowed to run amok with people who studied, well, beings like her. Yet again, I wondered how much Dad had figured out, and how much he knew during that final illness.

Mia smiled at me. "I think you're right. We've just got to figure out what that means to us. We've got to figure out who is the real target, but at least we have a better direction now. That's huge."

I agreed.

We walked to class, and got to our seats just in time for the lecture to start. I had a hard time concentrating on banking regulations and days to clear transactions, and I struggled to at least look like I was paying attention, and take enough notes so that I could look them up later and be prepared for the exam in a week or so. My brain was otherwise occupied, working on the puzzle that had started when I'd seen the apples and the seeds.

The apple heir.

Johnny Appleseed.

I was convinced it had to be someone local. Johnny Appleseed had spent much of his time in the area just north of Dayton, very little of it coming south. He'd spent time in Pennsylvania and Indiana and possibly other states in the area, but over the years, many people who had lived in rural areas around the state had moved into Dayton during the industrial boom years. Of course, they'd also moved away as factories closed and manufacturing jobs had gotten harder to find, but I had a hunch the person we'd be looking for was closer than we thought.

After all, Mia had been right under my nose when we'd been looking for relatives of Hans Christian Andersen. Allie'd come to Dayton. I was right here, the last living direct descendent of the Brothers Grimm. It made sense that strange things kept popping up right in my own back yard; that's the way things had been happening. Why wouldn't the apple heir be right there under my nose? Of course, I also had to keep in mind that just because it had happened three times before, didn't mean that it would happen again just like that.

Rather than casting a wide net, it made sense to start with my closest friends, the ones who had been with me through thick and thin. I knew many of their backgrounds, and many of their families. Not all of them, but most of them.

We needed everyone on deck, because I thought I knew who it was. I was almost sure of it. There was one person who was a friend, who had been on magical adventures, who seemed to take things with a lack of shock, one who had been a help and a friend. And I was pretty sure they had no clue as to their own heritage.

I had to be absolutely sure before I said it and turned my friend's world upside down. I wasn't sure if they'd told others, but now wasn't the time for being coy, or about worrying about how it made anyone feel. My friend was in danger, and needed to face their heritage.

Luckily, we only had three classes. I had a hard time not saying anything to Mia, because I knew she'd want to know, but that was awkward. She must have chalked it up to preoccupation with the coming conversation with Aiden, but no matter how worried I was on that score, this was bigger.

I just had to keep my mouth shut until I could get home and double check my own conclusions.

CHAPTER SIX

Our classes seemed interminable. I couldn't wait to get home and do some digging of my own. Mia asked if I minded if she called Jonah, her boyfriend.

"Why would I mind?" I asked.

She shrugged, as we packed up all of our books from our lockers, taking everything home to study. Not all of it would fit in our backpacks; we each ended up carrying two or three thick legal tomes in our arms while our shoulders carried the weight of everything we could cram in the backpacks. It was going to be a long studying week, if we were able to get everything solved. I was hopeful; we seemed to have a good start, even if I wasn't showing all my cards yet.

"Because of Aiden," she explained.

I knew what she meant. She didn't want to throw her successful relationship in my face, in light of all the troubles I'd had in mine. Mia and Jonah had been taking it slow; much slower than Aiden and I had when we'd been together, but Mia had her own issues about commitment, many of which were related to her father being absent for most of her life. Jonah had been patient, and they'd slowly built a relationship that seemed pretty open and honest and solid. She was a good friend, though, and didn't want to remind me of what I no longer had; what I no longer could claim as my own.

I loved her for being concerned, for asking, and for thinking about it, but I couldn't ask her to put her life on hold because mine was. "Mia, we've had this conversation before. Aiden and I have had our issues, but that shouldn't stop you from living your life. You live in the house too. Besides, Jonah has been helpful in the past. Another set of eyes and ears and another intelligent brain isn't a bad thing. I was going to ask you to call him, anyway. He's in the loop enough, that he should be there." I was relieved she'd asked to call him. I was a little concerned that maybe they were having problems themselves since he hadn't been around much, and I had some questions for him.

She shrugged. "There's no reason for you to be uncomfortable in your own house. We didn't want to push. We'd love you and Aiden to get back together, and make it all work. You two are a great couple, but if that's not going to work, then we want you two to be able to move on and still be able to work together. Aiden's a good guy. You are my very best friend. I want the two of you happy, whether that means you're together, or not."

She was going to make me cry. I told her so. "We've got too much on our plates at the moment, Mia. I can't concentrate on fixing me and Aiden if we're going to help Paul and get prepped for exams. I'm happy to work with him, because I think we're going to need him for his experience and knowledge. I actually think working on something like this will be good for him, and for his memory, in the long run. Whether we get back together or not, we have to learn to work together, and I'd like to continue to count him as a friend, if nothing else." That *hurt* to say, but it was the truth. I didn't want him out of my life.

We piled our belongings in the Escalade, and I got behind the wheel. We headed back to the house, and I thought about her concern. Boy, if she thought I was concerned about my personal life getting in the way of helping Paul to find his ox, her mind was going to be blown by what I'd figured out that morning.

On the way back to the house, I had Mia go ahead and call Jonah, asking him to meet us at the house. "While you're at it, Mia, call your dad," I said, as she hung up the phone. "You just never know how much he knows, or how much he can help. Do you know if he's in town?"

Mia's dad, Tobias Andersen, had been pretty absent most of her life, and she hadn't had much of a relationship with him for a long time. In the last couple of years, as she learned about my magical heritage, her father came out of the woodwork, and shared with her the real reason why he'd been absent so long during her childhood; he was the magical world's equivalent to some mix of Rambo, Van Helsing, and that Bruce Willis character from *Die Hard,* minus the cigarettes, of course. He was their boogeyman, the one that protected the human realm from magical realm beings who crossed over and exposed their magic or endangered humans. He wasn't a scholar, but he was experienced enough to be a smart choice to add to our group of brainstormers.

She dialed his number as I drove, leaving him a cryptic voicemail about popcorn on Sunday. When I asked after she hung up, she told me that he insisted on coded messages. Popcorn on Sunday meant a magical emergency. Pizza on Thursday meant a personal emergency. Ice Cream on Tuesday meant that she was just calling to say hello.

"It's not like I can leave him a message with all of Paul's information. Dad wants us to be careful when we're talking about magical stuff. He doesn't trust cell phones, and he doesn't trust that someone's not trying to figure out his location by triangulating his signal."

I couldn't say Tobias was wrong. He'd made a lot of enemies over a lot of years, caused a lot of magical and faerie court deaths. He'd made himself scarce while Mia was growing up so that she couldn't be a target for his enemies, and she'd only started to understand just how bad it was in the last couple of years. It would take a significant amount of time for all the scars to heal, for all the missed ballet recitals and softball games to lessen in importance, but Mia was a grown-up. She had seen first hand just how dangerous all of this was, and she'd started building a relationship with him all over again.

And she'd been the one to insist that we start taking some self-defense classes at the local YMCA.

Neither one of us was going to become Jackie Chan or Bruce Lee overnight, but knowing a little bit more about how to protect ourselves with some of the scrapes we'd been in, wasn't a bad thing or misplaced worry. And it was great stress relief when school got to be too much.

Luckily, though, those classes were on hiatus over the holiday. It was one less thing to deal with in an already insane week coming up.

As we pulled onto our street, I asked her how long it normally took for her father to call her back. "Depends," she said, "on what he's doing at the time. It's normally not more than an hour or so."

I nodded as I pulled the car into our driveway, parking it right outside of the detached garage that Aiden had once taken over as a workspace. I hadn't gone into the garage myself since he'd moved out. I'd have to come up with the guts to pull the car inside later, but I couldn't handle confronting the last remaining reminder of how at home he had been in my home. I had to draw some lines in order to start moving past the wreckage of my personal life and be professional here; Paul was a paying client.

We hauled in our books, calling out for the others as we came in the door. "Hullo, anyone home?"

"We're in the study," came Aiden's voice.

Mia and I stashed our stacks of books and backpacks in the dining room, and hurried to my dad's old study to see what they'd found out.

We walked in to a familiar scene.

Books and papers were scattered all over the place, while Aiden was typing on Mia's laptop. Bert was looking over a map, and Allie was on her knees on the floor, looking at books on the lowest shelf, the ones I probably hadn't realized were even there. I kept meaning to catalogue all of Dad's academic stuff, but I kept putting it off, thinking Aiden and I would do it on a school break, but when break came, I was normally either working or he was, and now he wasn't around full time to help make it happen. I'd have to do it on my own.

That hurt. I met Bert's eyes, and I think he noticed. I took a deep breath and looked down at the floor, fighting to get a hold of myself.

A statement from Doris, excited and flustered, brought me back to reality. "Janie, I think we've figured out the where. There really is a place called the Big Rock Candy Mountain. It's in Utah. It's a tourist attraction. If that's the place that the ox-napper took Babe, we don't have to go through any portals or cross over into any magical realms. That's good news, isn't it?"

"Utah?" I asked. "That doesn't have anything to do with Paul, or with Babe, or with any American tall tales that I'm aware of."

Aiden gave me an odd look, and he knew I was holding something back. Shit. He knew me too well. I hoped he'd chalk it up to the awkwardness between us, but I had a funny feeling he knew I'd figured out the target. I hoped my staying silent on it would tell him that it was something that I wasn't ready to share.

I shook my head at him, and moved on. "Well, I don't think we leave immediately, but we need to start researching how to get there in a hurry, and without spending a ton of money. How long would it take to drive it?" I was already counting gas money in my head, and wondering how to fit everyone in the Escalade. I wasn't sure everyone would fit.

Doris spoke up. "How many are you planning to have join us?"

I shook my head. "I don't know. I assume you, Aiden, me, Jonah, Mia, Allie, and Bert. Plus Paul is going to want to be there, and I think he should go. Is he still asleep, by the way? Will Tobias want to go? What about Harold and Stanley? I hate to not invite them, but someone's got to stay behind and look after the Wonderland folks."

Doris nodded at me. "I think I should stay behind, as well. I could stay at your house, and keep an eye on the place."

"Doris, that's a great idea; you'd be here if we needed to call back for an answer on something in the study, and you could use the kitchen here to re-prep some of the food you brought over. You'd have more counter space here."

She nodded, happy. I think our adventures in Wonderland rather scared her, and of course, we'd come back with her son in critical condition. I wondered how she felt about him going back in, facing the fire again, so to speak.

Before I could say anything else, Aiden stood up. "If you all would excuse me, I think Janie and I need to talk before we get too deep into any of this, and we need to talk before Paul wakes back up."

Mia took over at the computer. "Let's see if I can map out a good driving route. That mountain's not too far from Salt Lake City, according to that paper map that Bert's looking at. Let's see if we can figure out how long it would take us, and how much time we have to figure things out."

It was the right practical decision; but I so wasn't looking forward to the conversation I was about to have.

Bert met my eyes, and I could see a look of concern, but how to respond? I didn't know.

I stepped out the door, following Aiden, and waited to see what he had to say.

CHAPTER SEVEN

I waited for Aiden to start, but he looked at the closed door to the study, and said, simply, "They'll be listening in if we don't go further away from the door."

He was right. I appreciated the attempt to make this less awkward, especially if he was going to officially call it quits. I took a deep breath and pointed toward the kitchen. "Lead the way."

He cleared his throat and headed for the kitchen. I remembered mornings making breakfast for him before he headed to the former F.A.B.L.E.S. headquarters. The building was owned by Harold, but the utilities were astronomical; it was cheaper to close it up and stop using it as a meeting headquarters. Last I'd heard, Trusty John was still living there, to watch over the portal to the faerie realm inside, but heating only a former office space used for living quarters saved a ton of money for the group, and moving all of Aiden's computers out also saved on electricity.

I wondered if he'd set them all up in his mother's basement. His own childhood bedroom in that house wasn't very large; and he'd have to have room to set it all up to use it well since he used multiple screens and computer towers. Instead, I asked, "So, how's the day job?"

Aiden had gotten a factory job through a temp agency right after he left my house, stating he had to start living like a normal human again. "It's okay. It's boring, but it's good money."

I noticed a bruise on the back of his hand, and two fingers had flesh covered bandages over the tips. "How dangerous is it?"

He shrugged. "It's not bad. My job is basically pushing a big cart of parts to the assembly line. The carts are heavy, but they don't really get away from you easy. The assembly jobs are more dangerous because of climbing in and out of the cars going down the line. I had to figure out how to work the carts, but I haven't gotten hurt in a while. This," he pointed to the busted up fingers "happened the first week or so, until I got the hang of the carts."

"Oh." What could I say? Aiden was a natural klutz, always dropping things, tripping over his own feet, and otherwise being a walking menace to breakables everywhere. His car was constantly in the shop, his medical bills were always a part of his budget (and not small), and he'd been fired from many jobs just because of his kamikaze nature. I worried about him working in a factory where there were many sharp, mechanical, and, well, dangerous, moving parts.

"Do you like it?"

"Not especially, but it pays decent, and if I stay long enough, it comes with benefits. I'm trying to be more responsible."

Read, more human. One of the things that bothered him so much was his mixed heritage; human mom and faerie court dad meant that his arms and legs didn't always work together as a whole to keep him from slipping on banana peels that weren't actually there.

"How are you doing, staying with your mom?" I asked. Maybe a change in topic would make this easier.

"Janie, stop treating me like I'm a guest, or like I'm going to break. I'm working on my memory. I spent a couple of days in the faerie realm with Dad, and the Snow Queen and I talked about my memory issues. That's part of what I wanted to talk with you about. There might always be some holes, but a lot has come back."

I wanted to hug him, but I wasn't sure that was allowed anymore. I didn't know what the protocol was. I did give him a big smile, though. "That's awesome. It's what you wanted, right?"

He nodded, but still looked unhappy. "I did. A lot has come back, and I'm still processing it, and I've been wondering a lot about us."

"What do you mean?" I leaned one hip up against the counter, and crossed my arms over my chest, hugging myself to try to prevent the hurt and pain of our failed relationship from showing, or in penetrating any further. My heart banged in my chest. It hurt, but I didn't know how to make it stop beating out of control. I felt a bit light headed, waiting for him to figure out where to start.

Aiden ran a hand through his red hair, making it stick out just a bit. He'd cut it shorter than usual, but it was still long enough to be unruly with his motion.

"Janie, sometimes I wonder if we would have gotten together if we'd hadn't met during a magical emergency. Would we have been in a relationship if it wasn't for all the magic stuff? Is it a good idea for us to be in a relationship if we're going to continue to run into each other when magic comes up? This is the kind of thing we need to figure out before we get any more serious. In some ways, the memory loss issues are a blessing in disguise; it's forcing us to think about all of this."

I looked at him closely, taking in the dark circles under his eyes, the concern that shone out of them. His shoulders looked like they were carrying the weight of the world. "What are you saying, Aiden? Is this some kind of crappy test? Is this something that I have to answer a certain way or you'll walk away?"

He didn't say anything, and I had a hunch that he was actually considering something like that.

I kept going. "You want the truth? I'm not sure we'd have even met each other if it hadn't been for the magic stuff. We didn't exactly run in the same circles when we met. You know that. If we hadn't been worried about my stepmother, would we have ever even seen each other? Your mom doesn't live far from me, but she doesn't even go to the same grocery store that I did at the time. If it hadn't been for the lunches with my stepmother, I would never have gone to that restaurant where you were working; it was too expensive."

He started to interrupt me, but I didn't let him.

"You know, that kind of question is unfair. It's unfair to you, and it's unfair to me. It's unfair to our friends, and it's unfair to Paul, who we're supposed to be trying to help right now. I didn't fall in love with you because of how we met or because of what you knew about magic. I fell in love with you because I got to know you. I couldn't imagine my life without you. I actually thought about it, before we went to Wonderland. I wondered if I could walk away from all of this, to get away from the magic stuff that always turns my life upside down."

He raised his eyebrows. "What did you decide?"

I didn't skip a beat, and didn't even blink. "I wanted you. I couldn't walk away from you. I couldn't walk away from Mia. I couldn't walk away from all the people I know and love, whether magic was part of their life or not. And let's face it; I'm a Grimm. It's always going to be a part of my life, whether I like it or not. I can't run away from who and what I am, what you are, what Mia and Bert and Allie are. I didn't want a life without you. And now that I've had a taste of life without you, I can tell you that it really and truly sucks beyond all meaning of the word suck. I didn't love you for what you are. I loved you for you, for your caring nature, for your big intelligent brain, for how you always knew what I needed to hear, no matter how stressed or how frustrated I was at the time. We made a great team. Does it matter that magic was involved? I came to the conclusion that magic might have been how we found each other, but my life was always brighter with you in it, whether it was working in the backyard on the landscaping or just curling up on the couch with you and watching a Christmas movie, or watching you get excited that you got your hands on a vorpal sword."

I saw something shift in his eyes, but I had a full head of steam, and I wasn't going to be stopped. I wouldn't let him. "I had my own commitment issues, and you know that. I didn't even have to tell you what they were all about, because you knew the dynamic between my father, my stepmother, and how I still don't really know what happened with my mother. How could I explain all of that to anyone else and have them not only not think I was nuts, but listen to all of it? Even if I could, would there be real understanding? How can you explain your dad? We both have issues in our backgrounds. Does that mean we shouldn't be able to understand them, all the twists and turns of those pasts, because we shouldn't have a shared and trusted experience with magic? If that's the case, then I wish you luck in finding the person you're going to share that half-life with. You won't find someone who understands you half as well as I do. I love you, and that's not ever going to stop. I want you back, and I want to work on all of this, but right now, Paul needs us to pay attention to him, and to help him."

The doorbell rang before he could say much of anything else. Call me a coward, but I was kinda happy to hear it. I was holding onto all of my emotions with everything I had, and I just didn't know if I could be effective at helping Paul if Aiden fully broke up with me as we were just getting started. I almost didn't want to hear what he had to say next, so I ran for the front door.

He caught my arm. "We're not done here."

"I know." I pulled back, walking away from him before he could keep the conversation going. I couldn't spend a week mourning that relationship all over again; there was someone depending on me, and, well, life that demanded my attention.

But we were done for the moment. It was time for the moment to be about someone else.

And when I answered the door, that someone else was right behind it.

CHAPTER EIGHT

It was Jonah, showing up in response to Mia's phone call.

"She's in the study, with everyone else. Come on in," I said, Aiden at my heels.

Jonah looked at my face, then Aiden's. I'm not quite sure what he saw there, since Aiden was behind me. I had no idea if the two of them exchanged some sort of signal or question and answer, but they had become pretty good friends over the last couple of years. Jonah looked back to me and nodded. If I didn't know better, it almost looked like there was disappointment on his face.

I ignored their unspoken conversation. I didn't really want to know what they'd been talking about behind my back. I led them to the study, where everyone else was waiting. Mia came up and gave Jonah a big hug when he walked in the door.

"Mia, have you heard from your dad?" I asked.

She nodded. "He's on his way."

Sure enough, the doorbell rang again, just as everyone got settled again in the study. I had no problem volunteering to get the door again; activity kept me moving, and not thinking about what Aiden had brought up.

Tobias Andersen was at the door. He had a black eye, and a split lip, but otherwise, the same sardonic smile on his face that I was used to. He'd always reminded me a bit of Bruce Willis's character from *Die Hard,* the cop who always went on a one man campaign against the bad guys. The reality wasn't far from that; it wasn't like he had a whole lot of back-up to call in if things went bad, and from the look of that shiner, he'd been involved in something that didn't quite go the way he'd wanted it to. I hoped that was the extent of his injuries, but he was moving a bit stiffly, as if he had some bruised ribs or a sore back.

"Hello, Janie. Is everyone okay?" he asked. "What's the magical problem?"

"The short version? Someone ox-napped Babe the Big Blue Ox, and Paul Bunyan came here to ask for help. There was a ransom note. We've been trying to decipher where to start while Paul gets some rest."

I don't think he was quite prepared for that statement, but what statement would he have been prepared for? I didn't want to ask.

"Um, okay? You guys sure do get yourself into the strangest of situations," was his eventual response. "How in the world do you guys . . .? No, I'm not going to ask. What can I do to help?"

I laughed. "That's not a bad way to put it. It's just the way it is around here, and I wouldn't have it any other way." And that much was as true as it could get.

We walked back into the study, and Mia had done the research about travel that I'd mentioned earlier. "It's going to take about 26 hours to drive straight through to the mountain. We'd better give ourselves two full days to make it if we're going to drive it. I've looked at fuel costs, and it'll be about three hundred bucks or so for gas, with the Escalade. We can't all get tickets for the bus, or a train, or anything for cheaper than that, and we'd have to deal with stops that we didn't plan. It's probably better for us to go on our own, even if we'd be crammed," she reported.

Tobias had a better idea. "I'm driving my RV at the moment. It isn't anything special, but it's a whole lot more roomy than an Escalade. How many people are going?"

After some debate, we settled on the idea that Paul had to go; the rest of our group would be Aiden, me, Mia, Jonah, Bert, Allie, and Tobias. Doris agreed again to stay behind; someone had to keep an eye on the house, and someone would have to watch out for the Wonderland folks. Tobias insisted on going and taking the RV, stating that we could take camping gear and hit a campground if we needed to take a break from driving, and that would be less costly than hotel rooms for everyone. I had to remind everyone that Paul was paying the expenses, but that it wasn't a bad idea to keep costs down. Taking our own vehicle meant that we could make sure that we could bring our own weapons or supplies without worrying about getting through security at an airport or train station. Never mind that Mia and I could take our law school books to study on the road, rather than worry about weight restrictions in our baggage. It sounded like the perfect way to handle it. That was just a lot of people to squeeze into a recreational vehicle.

I suggested we go look at it, to see if we could fit everything. We all went outside. The thing wasn't new; it was at least ten years old, but it was in decent shape, to my untrained eye. Tobias took us through it, showing it off like a proud homeowner at a housewarming party. I noticed it; no question about it then, he lived here, and he was opening his house to us, and to his daughter, who had never seen where he lived.

She asked him about it.

"Well, I stay pretty mobile. Bought this thing used about five years ago. It's easier to move from place to place if I don't have to pack up stuff. I keep a couple of rental units in different cities in different parts of the country, and have a motorcycle or something like that in each, so that I have easy transportation other than this thing, but for the most part, all of my stuff is right here. I was actually just getting into town when you called, and I hadn't figured out where I was going to park this thing tonight. I figured you couldn't wait for me to get it to a campground and set up before I got here, so I just drove on over, after I offloaded some of my gear from my last trip."

He lived like this all the time? I felt bad for him. It seemed lonely, but at the same time, he'd found a way to have a home without being tied down to one place. In some ways, it was probably safer than having a single home base, but I had some questions.

"Tobias, forgive me, but I've got a few questions. Obviously the Seawitch isn't a problem at the moment." She'd been locked up by the Snow Queen after attacking all of us a year or so ago at the house. "But you've made other enemies. Does this thing have a threshold?"

A human's living space, something they'd made their own, carried a magical protection just from the use and familiarity of the place. The longer someone had lived somewhere, the longer it had been a *home*, rather than just a place to put stuff, the better the threshold one had to protect themselves from magical attack. I'd had to learn the hard way not to invite people past a threshold if they could be a danger, and my house had started building up a protective threshold not too long after Mia and I had started making it a home, after all traces of my stepmother were gone.

Tobias laughed at my question. "Good for you, Janie. You're asking the right things. First of all, this place has been my home for about five years. If it gets parked in a campground, I immediately spread a salt circle around it just to be sure, but it does have some threshold protection because it's where I live. Not as much as, say, your house, but it does have some. Secondly, the vehicle part itself has steel structure supports, and I had a contractor friend help me remodel the inside of the place before I started living here. There's a layer of iron reactive paint underneath the finishing that contains real metal particles."

He'd been thorough; I had to give him that. And it looked ten times nicer on the inside than on the outside. He had satellite television and flat screen TVs installed in the bedroom and the living room area of the vehicle. There was even a gas cook top and oven, a stainless steel refrigerator, and plenty of storage.

It was kinda impressive. And while it would be a bit of a tight fight, it was still doable for a couple of days' trip out west. It wasn't like it was a pleasure trip, so we weren't going for comfort and relaxation.

Besides, it was time for me to talk to the others about my 'eureka' moment from that morning.

I waited until everyone had stepped outside of the camper, and told them that we needed to not only plan the trip, but we needed to figure out who the apple heir was, and that I had an idea about that. We also needed to see what we could find out about the Big Rock Candy Mountain, and figure out what all we needed to take with us, pack, talk to Paul some more, and try to prepare for what was going on.

I didn't want to be caught as unprepared as we'd been on our hasty flight into Wonderland after Allie the year before.

And this time, I knew who the target was.

"I think I know who the apple heir is, guys. I'm not even sure they know they're the one that's wanted. I think this person has a heritage that they don't know, they don't understand, and it's about to slap them in the face." They all turned to look at me, confused looks on their faces.

"It's Jonah, guys. Jonah is the apple heir."

It wasn't everyday that I could surprise all my friends.

And then, there was the silence and disbelief on the face of the man of the hour.

CHAPTER NINE

"It can't be," Jonah said.

"Let's lay this out," I said, walking up to him. "You told me you were adopted, and that you don't know much about your biological family. You told me about your secret talent when we were in Wonderland."

His eyes widened. "Janie, I didn't want everyone to know that." He stole a glance over at Mia and her father, and it didn't take ESP to know what he was thinking. He was embarrassed I was telling them he had magic, magic he didn't understand, and didn't use. What was he worried about? I couldn't imagine it mattered to either of them. It wouldn't matter to me. It *hadn't* mattered to me, in the long run.

And then I caught Aiden's eye. He was unreadable, but there were storm clouds building behind his gaze. He was upset at something, but I couldn't tell if that was good or bad.

"Look, Jonah, I wouldn't have said anything, but it's important here. I think you really are descended from Johnny Appleseed. I think you are the one that's the target here. If there's anything any of us have learned, it's that we can't hide from our destinies."

Mia stepped forward. "Why didn't you tell me?"

Jonah swallowed hard. "Your dad; he's the anti-magic badass. He's the one they call when magic gets out of line. I don't use magic. I have lived my life as a human; as far as I know I am human. I don't ever live my life any other way. I don't think of myself as magic, but what would that do for your dad's reputation? Would they think of him as a softie? What would he think?"

"You know, you could have asked him," Tobias said, softly. "I've never been against people just being people, and living their lives for themselves, as long as they don't hurt others. I think I'm more upset that you didn't think we'd understand and accept you for who you are. You are the man who my daughter likes a lot, might even love, and you have been a good friend to her while she came to terms with all of this. You might have even talked to her about this."

Mia spoke up. "Dad." That one simple word quieted the rest of us down. She walked through the small crowd of people standing in the driveway beside the camper and asked Jonah, softly, "What magic do you actually have?"

Jonah's shoulders slumped, and he looked at his toes. "The only thing I've ever really been able to do is encourage plants to grow. I've never really tested it much, because it kinda scared me, so I mostly don't do it."

"How did you find out that you had magic?" Aiden asked.

"As a kid, I found out I could do it when I bought my mom a flower for Mother's Day and by the time I got it home from the store it was squished and mangled because I'd held it so tightly. Dad helped me put it in a pot, and Mom told me how pretty it was, but I cried all night because I'd wanted so bad to give her something pretty, and it wasn't pretty by the time I got it home. I went downstairs in the middle of the night and wrapped my hands around the little plastic pot and cried myself to sleep. When Dad found me the next morning, the plant had recovered, grown three inches, and had two new blooms."

Aw. That was adorable. I had to remember this wasn't my show. I'd already exposed that secret for everyone, and now he and Mia had to hash this out. I hated I'd done it with everyone around, but seriously, how had he not told her? It took everything I had not to respond, not to say anything. Aiden was his friend, maybe asking a question or two would help him tell it. I'd spilled the beans, that he hadn't wanted spilled. I needed to keep my mouth shut.

"How old were you?" Mia asked him.

The rest of us held our collective breaths.

"I was seven," Jonah said, in a small, hollow voice. "They'd just adopted me the year before, and it was the first Mother's Day that I had a real mom. I just wanted to get her something pretty, and Dad let me earn a couple of quarters helping him pick up sticks in the back yard after a storm. I had just enough to buy her a pretty little marigold. Dad told me love can heal a lot of things, and I thought at first that I'd just willed the plant better. Mom loved it."

He was right. I was having a hard time looking at Aiden. I hoped he was hearing this.

"Jonah, was that the only time something like this happened?" Mia asked, reaching up one hand to his cheek.

He sniffed. "No. The Christmas tree grew one year, too tall to fit the star overnight. I'd fallen asleep under it on Christmas Eve, and in the morning, the star fell off because it wouldn't fit between the tree and the ceiling anymore. That was when I realized there was something wrong with me."

Doris made a strangled sound in her throat. "Not to interrupt you, Jonah, but did your parents ever make any inquiries as to your background, or where that might have come from?"

He looked up. "No, ma'am. Mom and Dad had tried to have kids for years, and couldn't. They tried to adopt an infant, but every time they got matched up with a mom who wanted to give up her baby, the woman changed her mind at the last minute. They had applied for an international adoption, but the costs were too high. Finally, they decided to try with an older kid, and I was staying in a foster home. I never really asked, but I got the feeling they were terrified that if they said something was off with me, or that they had odd questions, that someone would come around and take me away."

"That's not how adoption works," I said. "Once the final papers are signed, it's done; unless there's some issue of abuse or neglect, or something." I couldn't keep my mouth shut on that one. How long had he wondered about where that had come from, and been too scared to ask?

Jonah nodded. "I know that now, but they were so happy to finally have a kid of their own they were terrified that something would come along and take it all away. I think I picked up on that somehow, and was always trying not to do or say anything that might bring that out again. When I got old enough to ask, that fear had never really gone away for them, so I didn't ask. They both died in a car accident about three years ago. I miss them, but they went together. They loved each other so much that I'm glad they're together. I guess I just got used to never talking about my background. It was habit."

I could see that. He never talked about his family, but it wasn't hard to imagine a young couple who wanted kids so badly and got rejected at every turn being terrified that something would happen to rip it all away. It wasn't much of a stretch to imagine a scared kid, who'd spent much of his life in a foster home, willing to hide big portions of himself to prevent having that dream of the family he'd barely hoped was possible from being yanked away from him. If they'd had the right questions to ask, if they'd known who to ask, maybe he'd have had more support growing up. Maybe he'd have learned more about his background; maybe he'd have learned some useful way of using his talents. But who would he have called? Who would his parents have known to call?

No one.

I couldn't think of a single place they would have thought to call that would have given them the kind of help he would have needed. Even if F.A.B.L.E.S. would have been around, they weren't exactly well thought of in academic circles; they definitely weren't set up to handle wrap around services for a family terrified to even talk about any form of strangeness. Would an adoption agency have even known where to ask? I doubted it. It was another thing we needed to put on the list of how and when and where to seek out people with backgrounds like mine, like Mia's, like Aiden's, like Jonah's; related to magic and not knowing where to look for answers. It wasn't a puzzle we could solve today, but was certainly something to consider down the road.

Jonah spoke up. "Look, I had a great childhood. I had the dream; the one so many kids in orphanages and foster homes dream of. I had a family. I played catch with Dad in the backyard. Mom made cookies and joined the PTA. I had the Norman Rockwell idyllic childhood. I wouldn't have changed a thing about it. If abilities like we've seen are the cost of having that life, I'd gladly have paid it not to have grown up without my parents. I don't use that ability, ever. It comes out from time to time when I'm not paying attention, but otherwise, it's not a part of who I am."

"Except that it is, now," Mia said. "Look, my bigger issue isn't that you might have some magical ability. We've learned there are ways humans can pull off magic, with potions, with repelling magic with salt, with being smart. Look at Janie's ancestors; they pulled off, with some help, a spell that bound Evangeline's powers for centuries. They were human. She is too. I'm human; but that didn't stop me from being the target of the Seawitch, because my many times great uncle spilled the beans about what she could do, and she got busted, locked up, and angry about it, not because we hate magic, but because it wasn't safe to have her roaming the streets and hurting innocent people. I don't think you're any less human because you have an ability. It's like blaming someone for having blue eyes; you just can't really change that on your own. The question isn't whether someone has an ability; it's what they choose to do with it, and whether or not they endanger others with it. I don't think you would ever endanger someone, you're just not that person."

Aiden watched my reaction carefully. I looked him square in the eyes, trying to tell him without words I agreed with Mia whole heartedly, but we had to start figuring out what we needed to know right now.

"Guys, I think it's safe to say you're our friend, Jonah, no matter what. None of this changes anything, and if you'd asked me, I would have told you to tell her, that she would understand. I did some checking in between classes, and did you know there's a little museum about an hour from here that is all about Johnny Appleseed? It's in a little town called Urbana, attached to a small college there. I think we need to consider whether or not someone needs to go on a quick research trek, while the rest of us start preparing for the trip."

Aiden nodded. "I think Jonah needs to go; Mia should go too. I'd like to go. Janie, what about you?"

We agreed the four of us would go in the morning, if we called and found them open for business on the Saturday before Thanksgiving. If it was attached to a college and the holiday was upon us, there was always a possibility it wouldn't be open; maybe we could get a hold of someone today, and find out, and if they weren't open, maybe we could make arrangements to get up there and do what research we needed to do.

Doris and Tobias began a discussion about provisioning the Winnebago for the trip. Bert volunteered to go inside, wake up Paul, and let him know we had a plan, but I pulled him aside, and indicated maybe he should hold back the fact that Jonah was the apple heir.

I just didn't know Paul well enough to know whether he would try to do something to Jonah to get him to the Big Rock Candy Mountain faster, in order to save Babe.

Desperate does desperate things.

CHAPTER TEN

P aul was thrilled to hear we had a plan. He was ready to pack up and go immediately, but I ended up warning him we needed to be sure we were prepared. I told him about our Wonderland trip, and the problems we'd faced because we hadn't had a map and we didn't know enough about the area. How we should have taken extra food, extra clothing, and we hadn't been prepared for the mushrooms that nearly killed Aiden. He said he understood, but he was anxious to get going, and begged me to let him help. So I had him bring down my dad's iron trunks to the living room where we could sort out what needed to go with us, and what could stay behind.

Paul reached into his back pocket and pulled out a roll of cash, counting out two thousand dollars in hundred dollar bills, and handed it to me. "There will be travel expenses, and call this a retainer. You can send me an invoice when it's all over, but this way, you have traveling money."

I looked at Paul, and I realized he'd come prepared. He wouldn't want to deal with individual receipts and bills on the journey. I'd keep them all for him just the same; but this way, he wouldn't be dealing with minutiae when he was worrying about Babe. I thanked him and offered to write out a receipt, which he accepted.

After taking care of the financial paperwork I called the Johnny Appleseed museum. They were open on Saturday morning, and agreed to have someone meet us and help us out with our research project. I threw Aiden under the bus, saying he was a student in folklore and history and needed to work on his thesis. While that was on hold, it wasn't a bad excuse as to why a bunch of students would want to come do research on a Saturday morning. The lady on the phone told me about a decent coffee shop not far from the university, located in an old train depot, and I figured it would make a decent outing for the four of us before cramming into an RV for a few days.

I asked Tobias, Aiden, and Jonah to go through the trunks Paul had brought down, and determine what needed to stay and what needed to go.

Bert asked about the camping gear in the basement.

"What camping gear?" I asked.

"Your dad had a bunch of decent camping gear, sleeping bags and a tent, some minor cooking supplies, and some other odds and ends that might come in handy on the road. If you're talking about traveling some distance, and maybe stopping at a campground, or something similar, it would be good to have it along. It's not going to take up a ton of room, and I bet Tobias would find the room for it, just to keep everyone from losing their minds on the drive," Bert said.

He and I went down to the basement, and I let him show me what he was talking about. He was right. And I did remember going camping once with my father, but it was a very long time ago; so long ago I hadn't even come close to remembering whether or not the equipment was still even there. There was a decent size tent, big enough for a couple of people without feeling they were crammed into it, an air mattress and pump, camping lanterns, ponchos, and even pie irons and a dutch oven for cooking over the fire. There were three sleeping bags, and a camp stove, all packed up together. Some of the equipment wasn't very old, either. Although, like most stuff Dad had squirreled away, a lot of it had metal or iron components. I wondered if he'd had some reason to pack this stuff away. I mean, he hadn't even tried to tell me he'd stockpiled it.

Of course, maybe he hadn't been able to tell me about it because he got too sick. He'd only been gone a couple of years. Some of this stuff looked like it was brand new. Why would he have been buying this? He'd been too sick to use it. Or maybe he'd been hoping to use it down the road? Planning some trip with his buddies, or with me? I wish I had some way to know.

I started dragging it all upstairs where I could catalogue it all, and offer it up for use on this trip. I was concerned we would not have enough sleeping room for everyone if we stopped at a campground; maybe there would be someone willing to sleep in a tent. Maybe we'd just need extra sleeping bags. Then again, maybe they wouldn't want any of it. As I got the first load to the top of the stairs, Aiden and Jonah jumped in to help.

The total was two big plastic storage containers, full of gear, one big canvas bag that held the tent and all the poles, and the sleeping bags. I unpacked the gear in the living room, where I could lay it all out and see what I had. Once I got to the bottom of the second container, I found an unlocked metal box, like the one Doris used when she went to bake or garage sales, the kind of money container I'd seen at a flea market to keep change.

Inside was a small moleskin book, filled from front to back with Dad's handwriting.

The tears threatened to come and I had to swallow and blink hard to keep them from spilling over. Instead, I leaned back, and started reading. It looked like Dad had kept a diary when I was a kid. I'd found one earlier, but this looked like more of a research journal than about his own life and happenings. There were drawings and notes, random scribbling and diagrams. It didn't read in a straight line; instead, it seemed a place where he kept his thoughts. But what about? I couldn't tell.

"Aiden," I said, quietly. "I'm not sure what he was going for here. I can't even quite tell what he was looking for. Why hide it? What would he be worried enough about to make sure it was in a box that Evangeline wouldn't look in? Why bury it in camping gear that looks mostly brand new? How would he know we were planning this kind of trip? There's no way he could know."

He shook his head, taking the little notebook from me, and pacing around the room. "I don't know, Janie. I've never seen him with this little book before, but from the dates, it looks like we were small children when he worked on it. There's a note or two here about American folk heroes, maybe something about a research trip to Pennsylvania? And something else about orchards out west? I don't remember it being one of his areas of expertise, but he apparently did quite a bit of work here. Even so, I have no idea what he was looking for."

"You're going to figure out his notes well before I do. You work on that; I'll start sorting this gear while they figure out weapons," I said. On the other hand, it wasn't like I was surprised to see him zone out on a research point that fascinated him. It used to happen all the time. I'd find him asleep on the desk after all night at work on some arcane bit of research, or whiling away hours at a workbench at some magical whoziwhatsit. I figured I'd need to leave him to it. Maybe it would help with the whole memory thing, remembering how to tackle a magical or folklore or history research project.

I repacked the camping gear, setting aside some of the things I didn't think we'd need, like the cooking gear—since there was a kitchenette in the camper—and some of the other random odds and ends, up to and including a small package of rapidly dissolving toilet paper.

I didn't even want to think about that one.

Tobias looked up from the metal trunks Dad had left. He had been laying out metal weapons and going through them, separating them using an organization system I couldn't figure out. It was good we were able to sort through all of this and get it organized. I never thought about it if we weren't in the middle of a magical emergency, and so it would slip my mind for months on end, and then something would come up and I'd wonder why I hadn't done it before.

"I'm just gonna go check on everyone. Do you want this camping gear in the RV for the trip?" I asked.

He nodded, and looked over the pile. "Maybe not all of it," he said. "But definitely the extra blankets and sleeping gear, the tent, and maybe the camping lanterns."

I picked up the now-lighter plastic storage bin I'd planned to take, and piled a sleeping bag on top of it. When I got outside, I heard voices in the yard. I put the camping gear just inside the door in the hallway, to start a pile of things to take, and headed toward the voices.

Jonah was outside, with Paul and Mia and Bert. Bert and Mia were trying to encourage Jonah to use what magic he had to try to fix the maple tree that Paul had been chopping down that morning. Jonah kept telling them he didn't think he could do it; Mia and Bert encouraged him to try.

"Jonah, you've been suppressing something that's a part of you, whether you like it or not. It's better to know what you can or can't do; it's worth trying, here, before we hit the road. This is in our own backyard; it's not on the side of the road somewhere. It's not in an atmosphere or environment we can't control. This is the time, to see what you can do. I'm not angry. I'm not upset. I love you. You can do this," Mia encouraged him.

Bert pushed in a much more urgent way. "You need to figure this out now, when there's no emergency, no stress, and no pressure to perform in a way that you're not used to. Do it here, where you feel safe and loved, and it will come easier when you're scared and alone."

Practical advice from someone who cared. Encouragement that magic didn't mean the end of friendship.

I wished Aiden could see this. Maybe he'd see that life with magic didn't mean a life without love, because I was starting to believe he didn't think the two could go together. With Mia encouraging him, Jonah placed both hands on the tree, one on either side of the gaping hole Paul's axe had left. The tree wasn't damaged enough to fall over, but there was a huge chunk missing out of the trunk, enough that I'd been convinced I would need to call someone to remove the tree, because it would die.

I smelled it; stale peppermints and old books, the sweet and dusty smell that meant magic to me, as it unfurled from the direction of the tree. Jonah's eyes closed, and he laid his forehead on the tree. Nothing happened at first, and Mia laid her hand on his back.

I couldn't see if it was working from where I was standing. Jonah's body blocked my view. I knew that the smell of magic grew stronger, and Tobias came running out of the house with the metal club I'd had that morning in his hand. He stopped, and dropped the club when he saw it was Jonah.

Doris was right behind him with a big metal serving spoon, and Aiden had come out as well, chasing his mother. All of us watched Jonah, who stood, unmoving, in front of the tree for a few minutes. Everyone put down whatever they'd grabbed that contained metal, whatever they'd snatched up to use for self-defense.

No one said a word.

And then Jonah staggered backward. The tree wasn't fully healed, but the missing chunk seemed smaller. I saw green shoots coming out of the cut section of the tree. It seemed like progress, but I didn't know a whole lot about trees. I looked over at Jonah, who had stumbled backwards into a sitting position on the grass, with Mia rubbing his shoulders and displaying concern as well as praise. His eyes looked unfocused, and he shook his head, as if trying to dislodge water out of his ears, like a dog after swimming.

I glanced back at the tree, and the wood was healing itself right before my eyes. It was slow, sure, but the tree had to be at least fifty years old, if not more, and was almost as high as the third floor attic windows. The thing had been big enough when I was a kid for me to climb all over and hold my weight without even trying; I was pretty sure it would still hold me now.

That was a pretty big amount of magic. And even though he'd been dizzy, it was good to know what he could do. I wondered if the reason he was wanted, the reason the "apple heir" was wanted, had to do with this ability somehow. I could see all kinds of ways a power like this could be used unwisely; encouraging plants to grow and choke someone, or to grow in such a way as to trap someone in a house, or in a castle? Or was it something more sinister? With the power to make things grow, what if he made a seed grow after a person had eaten it? What if there were no plants around? I had more questions than answers at this point.

I wondered if he was limited to trees and plants and flowers. What could that kind of magic do to heal a heart that felt like a chunk had been stolen out of it?

CHAPTER ELEVEN

Doris had been busy in the kitchen while we'd all been about our tasks. She'd searched through my pantry and freezer and made up a few casseroles we could bake in the RV oven; so the cost for food on the road wouldn't be all that bad. She packed up much of the food she'd brought over, but had set out the sandwiches and potato salad to feed everyone while we ran all over the house, running laundry, packing weapons, sorting camping gear, and in general, looking for whatever we might need. I hoped we'd be able to get going tomorrow or Sunday in order to make good time on the road. I wanted us to be able to get there, get Babe, keep Jonah from danger, and get back in time to study for my first final, and maybe have a good turkey dinner with all the fixings.

Of course, whatever gets planned and whatever actually happens doesn't always match up in the end. Especially in my life.

Mia brought Jonah in to sit down, and he complained of a headache. Allie went to get him some aspirin. Bert told him to close his eyes and take long, deep breaths. I knew it was meant to relax him, but it wasn't working. Jonah didn't like any of this; he didn't like using magic. He didn't like putting others in danger, and he didn't like that he didn't have a cooler power. I made sure to stop by and talk to him like a person, rather than like everyone else, but he was someone with a dangerous secret.

Speaking of secrets, Paul came downstairs just as everyone was getting settled back in the living room. It was probably a good idea to keep him out of the backyard so he wouldn't see that the damage on the tree had been healed; because who knew whether he'd be able to put two and two together and figure out Jonah was the key to getting Babe back.

I didn't think Paul was a bad guy; just desperate. And I wasn't yet sold that he might not have another motive. Someone might be threatening him with Babe's safety to get reports on all of us. As someone who wanted help, he was in a position to learn a lot of information about us, our friends, and families. I'd just have to keep my eye on everything and see what happened.

Everyone ran around the house, looking for different odds and ends. Aiden began packing up a first aid kit. Tobias sifted through the camping gear and the weapons. Mia headed for the laundry room, running a few loads to have clean clothing to go; we normally left that chore for Saturdays, so we were a little low on clean options at the moment.

Paul looked confused at all the activity. "Is any of this going to matter? I mean, if I've hired you to get Babe back, and we think we know where he is, then why don't we just go bust him out? I've heard stories about you guys. I've heard you defeated Queen Eva. You've defeated the Seawitch. You've befriended the Snow Queen, and you got rid of the White Rabbit. If that's the case, why do you need all of this *stuff?*" He spread his arms, indicating the piles of supplies piled up inside the front door to go to the camper, the piles of things I was going through on the coffee table, and all the items in front of Tobias on the floor.

I stopped what I was doing and looked up at him. "Because we didn't beat any of them with magic, per se. We did it mostly by being smart, by being prepared, and by being willing to 'talk truth to power'. I forced my stepmother to admit to her crimes before her court through legal argument and logic. We bested the Seawitch by being smart enough to ward the house; with the house warded, we had the time to negotiate with the Snow Queen to help us. The White Rabbit? Well, he kinda got trapped as well, in a trap of his own making. You see, we don't want Babe to wait any longer than necessary, but we also don't want to risk him being hurt because we ran in unprepared. Preparation has done more to help us get what we wanted or needed than anything. There's only a few of us with actual magic, and much of that takes preparation and foresight. We're getting prepared. We're still going to be way ahead of the deadline, I promise."

He nodded, but he didn't like it. "I just want him back. I don't like thinking of him as cold and hungry somewhere that I can't help him."

Something occurred to me, and I figured I'd better ask now. "What are you willing to do for that, Paul? Are you willing to sacrifice whoever the apple heir is to get Babe back? What if the ox-napper wants to kill them? Is it worth doing that to save Babe? How far would you go?"

He paused.

I was glad he paused. It made me think that even though he was definitely frustrated at the delay, and would have liked to have just gone running in there, guns blazing, he had enough humanity in him to realize someone could pay a price for our actions. Someone could get hurt helping him. Someone could get dead. I could see thoughts flying across his face. Finally, he said, "I don't want anyone to get hurt. But I don't know why Babe has to get hurt to save someone else. This isn't and wasn't our fight. I wish I knew how we'd gotten into the middle of this. I didn't hurt anyone, and neither did Babe."

"I understand that feeling, Paul, and there's nothing wrong with that thought. It's true. You and Babe probably don't have anything to do with the apple man, the apple heir, or any crimes they may or may not have committed. Come to that, why do we assume they actually did commit crimes? The only statement of that is from the one thing that DID commit a crime by kidnapping Babe."

His eyes widened.

I went on. "Look, I'm not saying we write Babe off. Obviously, I'm not planning to just let him rot there. But it's worth thinking about; the kidnapper's target is the apple *heir*. The ransom note said something about the ancestor's crimes. So, even if the apple guy committed crimes, we have no reason to believe the heir has. There's a possibility they're asking us to substitute a completely innocent being for another. That's not a good feeling, you know?"

He nodded. "I never thought of it that way. You've got a point. I don't reckon Babe would want someone innocent to get hurt. But Babe's my priority. I can't just leave him there. I trust what you're saying, and I'm glad you're trying to come up with the best way of handling this, but if we're not heading out of town in twenty-four hours without a good reason, I'm going after my ox on my own."

"Fair enough, Paul. But I'd ask for thirty-six hours before you do something rash. I'd hate to be rushing to meet your deadline and miss something. I do understand your hurry, though. I've been the target of a magic attack myself. I've been kidnapped by my own stepbrother. I wouldn't have wanted someone to wait too long to come after me. But at the same time, I wouldn't want them to get trapped with me, either." I laid on hand on his arm. "Speaking of magic, what magic do you have? We do need to know how our preparations on the trip might affect you. We don't want to make you sick on the way to go get Babe."

He laughed. "Really, the only magic I have is to make myself smaller than normal. I can do it with Babe, too. If I'm not near him, he's going to be normal sized, which means he'd be bigger than this house. It takes an ongoing effort of magic to keep us this small, which is why I don't normally worry about it when it's just Babe and I. It doesn't take as much to keep it going when it's just me. But that means he's full size right now."

"That's good to know. It means he'd be hard to hide," I pointed out. "It limits where they might be keeping him."

Paul grinned. "I didn't think of that. Maybe that's why they picked a mountain. Wonder if there's a cave or something there, or if there's some way he's hidden underground. It would take a heck of an underground bunker to hide him."

"Little things like that can be important," I said. "That's why we sit down and take the time to think about it."

He agreed to my request for thirty-six hours, and I agreed we'd leave sooner if we were ready. Honestly, I felt it would be earlier, but I just didn't feel comfortable promising that when we were still planning to head to the museum in the morning.

Aiden wandered through the living room, just as I'd said something about the little things, and his face jerked up from the dusty old book he was looking through as he walked. He made eye contact with me; I refused to look away.

The doorbell rang.

I wondered who that could be. I thought everyone was accounted for. Maybe the door had been locked? Had someone stepped outside and couldn't get back in? I wasn't expecting anybody.

The whole house went silent, as it seemed that everyone else went through the same calculus, counting heads and trying to figure out who was left.

Tobias picked up the metal club, and followed me to the front door, whispering to Paul to stay where he was at. My mind spun with the possibilities. Had someone figured out Paul was here? Had they come to attack us? Had someone else figured out Jonah's heritage? Had my stepmother gotten away from her cell? What about the Seawitch? I had to remind myself the White Rabbit was dead, as I catalogued the list of the magical bad guys who might target us, regardless of who we might be trying to help. And we didn't have a good list of any bad guys Paul might have pissed off, either in the past, or more recently.

I didn't like being unprepared. I didn't like feeling there was something on the other side of that door I wasn't going to like.

With Tobias behind me, the club at the ready, I opened the door.

A very short man, barely four and a half feet tall, and thin enough that his clothes hung on him, stood in front of me. He had a thick moustache and short brown hair, and something about him looked vaguely familiar.

Paul shouted. "It's Pete! My brother, come to give me comfort!"

Tobias and I exchanged looks of awe and wonder. If he truly was Paul's brother, maybe we'd have to make room for another person in the Winnebago.

I wondered how we were going to make this work.

Luckily, the man wasn't very large, and it looked like he only had one small rucksack of belongings slung over one shoulder. I noticed a very large ax strapped to his back as well, and wondered if he meant harm to any of the neighborhood trees.

If he did, our next block meeting was going to be very interesting. I was already dreading any complaints about chopping wood in the middle of the night.

CHAPTER TWELVE

W *hat the hell?* I wondered. I didn't remember hearing Paul had a brother. This was an angle I hadn't thought of.

Paul came barreling out of the living room, and enveloped the little man in a bone crushing, rib shaking hug, just outside the front door. He was laughing and exclaiming praise for his brother and his loyalty, for coming to support him in his hour of need, and it drew everyone's attention.

Including Bert.

Bert hopped his way to the front door, and hopped right in front of me. "Holy shit, it's Cordwood Pete! Janie, stand back."

Huh? I could probably knock this guy over with a feather, and I wasn't exactly the physical fighting sort. "Why?"

"Because he and Paul weren't exactly close growing up," he said. "It makes me wonder why exactly he's here."

"You knew them as kids?" I asked, astounded. Maybe I shouldn't have been surprised. Bert had lived a whole lot of years before I'd met him.

"Hmph, no," he said. "I got to know them after they were already grown. I didn't come to the United States until around 1900. They were already grown and weren't exactly the closest of friends."

"Why's that?" I asked. Why did I feel like asking made me look like a complete moron? I hadn't thought to read up on American tall tales; although maybe I should have done so because we are, well, in America? Talk about not thinking ahead.

"Well, Paul used to eat all of Pete's pancakes, growing up. The legend has it that Paul, the older one, grew so large, and Pete, the younger one, stayed so small, because of that. I don't know how much truth is in that, but I do know Pete always felt like he couldn't measure up to his big brother, no matter what he did, no matter how he impressed folks. They ended up going their separate ways. I met both of them, over the years. I got to be friends with Paul, but Pete didn't want anything to do with anyone connected to Paul. Before he realized I was already friends with Paul, he wasn't a bad guy. He's just a typical younger brother, who's got a bit of a complex about being in his big brother's shadow all the time." Bert shrugged. "Hard not to, when he's got such a big shadow."

Bert would know. He'd been the youngest brother in a family of four boys; and he'd been the one least likely to take the throne. From all he'd said to me, to Aiden, to Mia, to Allie, and to Doris, I got the idea he'd been pretty close with his brothers, but he'd been the easy going, smart, diplomatic one, the one who talked his older brothers down from some of their more hot headed ideas. While his oldest brother had been the one in charge, Bert was the one who'd been the voice of reason, the one everyone went to for advice. I wondered, from all of the descriptions I'd heard, whether Bert was actually the one most suited to be king, but he hadn't been interested in deposing his beloved brother, no matter how frustrating it must be to be the less respected one, because of an accident of birth.

I wondered just how much he regretted, but I was too busy watching the brothers hugging each other. Or rather, Paul hugging the stuffing out of Pete, who was turning red in the face.

Paul finally put his brother down.

Pete coughed a couple of times, and the hairs on his moustache twitched as he sucked in air. "Ma'am," he said to me, making me feel fifty years older than I actually was. "Didn't mean to cause a scene at your house. Haven't always seen eye to eye with the big guy here, but I know what Babe means to him. If someone's taken that ox, they're looking for a world of hurt from my big brother when he catches up to him."

Sounded to me like a little brother who, while he'd had problems with big brother, was trying to be there for him when the chips were down. It was a family thing Bert would completely understand, but I felt out of the loop. It was hard for me, as an only child, to understand that kind of dynamic.

"Bert, is it dangerous to invite Pete into the house?"

"Naw," he said. "If they haven't killed each other by this point, they're good. Pete'll be here for whatever Paul needs, but he'll probably make himself scarce after we get that goofy ox back."

"Goofy?"

"Damn thing tried to lick me once. If it had been full size, I'd have been a goner; probably wouldn't have even noticed me in his teeth. Paul thought it was funny. I felt gross all day."

I burst out laughing. The idea of someone, or something, licking Bert, was hysterical. I could just see him, angry and upset and ruffled all at the same time. I liked Bert a lot, but he could be prickly when he was annoyed. I wondered if he'd been prickly when he'd been human, or if it had come from the years and decades and centuries of not being able to relate as a human to another human, then I felt bad for laughing. How hard must that be, not knowing the touch of a friend, a hug, a handshake, or a kiss? Obviously I had no way to know, but it made me want to go hug Aiden. I had to hold myself back from doing exactly that.

Paul slapped his little brother on the back, and Pete coughed hard. I wondered if he'd knocked the man's spine loose with all the slapping and hugging and good feelings.

"Boys, I hate to break up the love fest, but what can we do for you, Pete? How did you know your brother was here?"

He grinned, the smile barely visible under the bushy caterpillar of a mustache. "The Snow Queen pointed me in your direction. I was asking around when word got out Babe was missing, and I couldn't find Paul. She said her courtiers had sent him your way, said you'd be able to help if Babe was in the mortal realm."

Tobias stepped outside. "No offense, Pete, but why were you looking for your brother? Is there new information?"

"Not rightly sure," he said. "I found this." He held out a burlap covered lump, and I took it from him.

I unwrapped the lump, and found a brass ring. "What is this?"

Paul's face fell. "It's Babe's. It's his nose ring."

Ew. Ew. Ew.

I had touched that thing.

With my *hands*.

Okay, so maybe I was too much of a city girl. It couldn't still have ox snot on it, could it? What kind of germs could still be on that thing? Maybe I was imagining things. The ring wasn't snotty or wet, but I couldn't help it. I didn't want to touch things that had been up a nose, whether human or bovine.

"How did you get this? Paul, did Babe have this when he was taken? Pete, was there any kind of note or other communication that came with this, or did it come by itself? How was it delivered? Did anyone else touch it?" I asked, shooting off questions before I got the answers, more for reaction than for the actual answer, although I wanted the answers.

Pete cleared his throat. "I went to Paul's house two days ago, looking for help with a personal matter. He wasn't there, and I knew he wouldn't mind, so I stuck around for awhile, waiting for him to come back. He didn't. Yesterday, this was delivered to his back door, near where Babe's favorite grazing spot was already getting overgrown. There was a note." He dug it out of his back pocket, and handed it over to me.

It was grubby, and typed with an old fashioned typewriter. I could still feel the grooves in the paper from the impact of the keys on the paper. It reminded me of some of the old documents Dad used to bring home from time to time, the kind he wouldn't touch without white cotton gloves, to preserve the document. The paper was worn and soft around the edges, unlike the paper I fed into my laser printer to print my law school papers. It read, simply:

This is not a joke.
The apple heir must be found.
The life of the ox is dependent on your cooperation.
To see the ox alive again, you must come alone with the apple heir.
Bring no metal.

Interesting, I thought. "'Bring no metal', huh? So they are magical. Which means they could have reduced Babe's size themselves, rather than hiding a really large ox somewhere. That would make more sense. It would be easier to hide a normal sized animal, rather than one of Babe's size. And they don't want you bringing backup."

Paul nodded. "If I can't bring backup, then I guess your job is done, Ms. Grimm." He sounded disappointed. "It's been a pleasure working with you, and I do so hope you can get all your things rearranged and put away with too much trouble. I guess I have to find the apple heir on my own."

I'd be damned if I'd let him do this on his own. For one thing, I wasn't sure if he'd figure out who the apple heir was, and I couldn't let him off on his own to do or say something that might put Jonah in danger. And if Jonah was in danger, Mia wouldn't be far behind. They were my friends.

"Paul, whether we go with you up the mountain or not, we are going with you to the mountain. No matter what, you are going to need our help."

He sputtered and protested. He wanted to go, and he wanted to go, *now*.

"Do you know how to drive on a highway? Do you know our money, how to fuel a vehicle and pay highway tolls? I don't know of a portal around here that would take you to Utah. Do you?" That one was a gamble but, I was sure, a good one. "Do you even have a driver's license? How about insurance? You do realize if you're pulled over in this realm for driving a vehicle without a license, you could go to jail? How would that help you make your deadline to get Babe back?"

He stared at me for a moment.

Pete jumped in. "Paulie, the lady wants to help. You'd already hired her? She's got a point. And she's got a good reputation. Let her do what you paid her to do. Even if you don't take her to the final meeting in the end, it might be worth having her with you on the way. You just don't know what other information you might run into on the way there."

Bert stuck his head out again. "Paul, he's right. Janie's good people. So's everyone else. If they say they can help you, they mean it. Let them. And there's also truth to the idea that you won't be able to travel easy in this realm without help."

I held my breath for a moment, letting Paul decide on his own. I just didn't like the idea of him feeling railroaded into letting us help. I didn't like the idea of him going out on his own. And I definitely didn't like the idea of trying to figure out how to protect Jonah without being in on whatever Paul was up to.

After what seemed like an eternity, Paul turned to me. "You

know, it occurs to me I shouldn't turn down help, from whatever source it might come from. I know I am nowhere near an expert in finding lost things, or in figuring out mysteries, and it sounds like you've done both. I still think we need to leave real soon, but I'd be dumb to turn down help from someone more experienced. And you're right about the jail thing. I'm sure that wouldn't be pleasant."

"We're in." Mia said, also coming to the door. "Let's start loading the Winnebago. We can leave tomorrow night, I think."

Sounded good to me.

I headed back inside, and made sure to invite Pete in with us. That Winnebago was sure going to get full in a hurry.

CHAPTER THIRTEEN

We spent most of the day getting the Winnebago organized. By the end of the night, Pete and Paul were both sleeping in the empty bedroom on leftover comforters and blankets. Aiden went home with his mother, promising to come back first thing in the morning to go with us to the Johnny Appleseed museum for some last minute research. Tobias insisted on sleeping on the couch in the living room, stating he'd sleep better behind a threshold just before a magical excursion. He insisted he'd be better protection for the rest of us if he was inside the house and somewhat in front of the staircase. I wondered how many good nights' sleep he'd gotten in his life; if he was always thinking about how he could place himself between his loved ones and potential danger.

I found myself sitting in the kitchen with Allie, drinking a cup of hot tea and mulling over everything that had been happening over the last day or so. The two of us sat silently, sipping green mint tea with lemon and honey, and just soaking in the silence of the house settling in for the night.

Jonah came into the kitchen, and asked if he could get a cup of tea and join us.

Uh oh, I thought. "Jonah, I'm really sorry about spilling your secret to everyone else. I need to apologize. I didn't mean to out you like that."

He filled up the teapot and put it on the burner, got out a mug, then set it on the counter before turning to face me. "Janie, look, I'm sorry, too. I shouldn't have put you in the position of having to keep a secret for me. I should have told Mia and Tobias. It was too easy to fall into the same trap I'd been in as a kid, too content to ignore what was going on in my life without thinking about facing things that could disrupt the status quo. My parents were awesome, but they were also masters at being ostriches, sticking their heads in the sand and hoping whatever they were worried about would just go away. And most of the time, it did. They got me all the way to adulthood that way, so I can't say they were completely wrong. I've learned the hard way it isn't the best way to handle things in many situations, but I still did it here."

I let out a breath I didn't realize I'd been holding. "If you'd asked me, I'd have told you Mia wouldn't have held it against you. She didn't hold the magic stuff against me when she first met Bert, or when my stepmother first started to move against me. She didn't quite believe me at first, but her first reaction was concern for me, rather than to immediately kick me out of her life. She didn't know anything about her own heritage at the time. She had no idea her father was the Billy Bad-Ass of the magical world; at the time, she just thought he was a deadbeat. And she was there for me every step of the way. She's been my best friend since high school. I could have told you she's as loyal and nonjudgmental as they come."

The teapot started to whistle, and he reached for it, but I jumped up to stop him. "It's an antique. I got it at a garage sale, and there's a spot on the handle where you can burn yourself real easy. Grab a potholder or something."

He grabbed a cheerful potholder with sunflowers on it. The teapot was a fat painted metal pig. I'd purposely bought kitschy and mismatched random things, to well, NOT coordinate with my wicked stepmother's matchy matchy designer kitchen and her high end serving pieces when we'd moved in. That meant that most of it was garage sale and flea market finds. Yeah, I had the nice stuff boxed up in the basement. I figured one day I might need something nice for a dinner party or some such, or needed to do something impressive. Until then, there was no reason to mess it up, and I liked the quirkiness of the cheaper stuff, but that also meant that I sometimes had to compensate for that quirkiness with extra caution.

Jonah brought his tea over and sat down at the table with Allie and me. We all sat in silence, sipping hot, relaxing liquid. I wondered if he had something else he wanted to say, but I didn't want to push him; I'd pushed him enough today.

He blew across the top of his mug, then took another sip, before setting his tea down. "So, Janie, Allie, you've been where I am now.

What do I need to know about being the target of a magical bad guy?"

I smirked at him. "You don't actually know it's a bad guy. It's easy to assume, but you always have to think of all the possibilities, especially when you don't know what the real answer is."

Allie spoke up. "Even when you know the who and the what and the why, you still have to keep on your toes. It's way too easy to assume what's going on when you think you have the answers, because you can still be wrong." I wondered what she'd been surprised with in Wonderland. She hadn't really talked about it all that much. There had been a period of time when she'd been trying to connect with people she'd known as a child, before we'd found her there.. Who had changed? Was it one of the refugees who had come back with us?

"Either way, we'll be taking some research with us, and we'll go to that museum tomorrow morning and see if there's anything else we need to know. Regardless of what we find out, you're still you, and you're still our friend," I said. "Don't forget that. Don't try to run away from your friends because you don't like something about yourself or your background. We'll come after you. We've done it before." I winked.

Allie snorted.

Jonah laughed. "I know you guys better than that. Heck, I helped you do that with Allie. I just have to keep reminding myself not to try to hide from it. It isn't easy to do, when I've spent my life doing exactly that."

"On a more serious note, however, Paul might have some idea it's you, even though we haven't told him about you. My biggest fear, though, as we get closer, is that he might get desperate and try to do something desperate. Keep an eye out. Don't go anywhere alone. Don't go unarmed. And definitely don't trust anyone who might have a magical agenda."

He nodded, the joking demeanor gone. "I'll keep it in mind. What about Mia? Should she stay here? I don't want her to get hurt. And someone's gotta watch the house."

I frowned at him. "Don't do that to her. Don't make her sit here and worry about you and prevent her from doing anything to help. That's a sure ticket to making her mad at you. She'll be madder about that than about you not telling her you had a magical ability. Besides, Doris volunteered to stay here and water the plants." Even though we had no plants to water. Oh, well.

Bert hopped his way in. "Any beer in this joint?"

I sighed. Bert hadn't had much to drink in the last several months, after his incident with drinking wine from Wonderland. He barely drank anything these days, and so I was a little surprised at the request. I thought getting blown up to the size of a dump truck and getting shrunk back down would have taught him the dangers of drinking. Never mind the hangovers and headaches and vomit in the past. I could live without ever cleaning up frog vomit again. I'd wondered if he'd actually hit alcoholic, but at the same time, he was a grown-up. Did I have the right to tell him no?

"What?" he demanded. "I can't have one? I thought I'd been good about it, and we're not in the middle of a magical emergency. At least, we're not in the middle of one right at this particular moment, anyway. I'm home, and I trust you guys to give me something without potion in it. What's the problem?"

Allie laughed.

I blinked hard. He was right. What was so bad about one? As long as he had thought all of that through, and we were behind a threshold. I went to the refrigerator, and found just one Guinness in the back, still frosty cold. It was there from Jonah bringing them over a few weeks ago, just before Aiden and I had broken up. I pulled it out and waved it at Jonah, who nodded.

Over trial and error, I'd learned that Bert preferred to drink out of a glass or mug, rather than a bowl, but at the same time, he didn't have a whole lot of arm strength as a frog to hold up the cup. I'd shopped around and found some plastic drinking containers he didn't object to. They were more like mugs, but lighter weight, and less breakable then the glasses he almost couldn't lift. I'd found them at the flea market, and they reminded me of mugs I'd had as a kid, with cartoon characters on the side, that I'd drunk milk out of while watching Saturday morning cartoons. Bert was more than fine with ones that had comic book characters on them. I'd found one with Spiderman, and one with Batman, though he'd turned up his nose at a pink one with a picture of Strawberry Shortcake. I poured about half the beer into the plastic mug, and set it on the table in front of him.

We sat and talked for a while, and Bert sipped the beer, nursing it rather than pounding it down like he would normally do in the past. I asked him if he wanted the rest of the bottle and he turned it down. Jonah ended up finishing it, and putting the empty bottle in the trash.

I was impressed. Maybe he really was moving past his alcohol phase. He and Jonah were friends, and I'd never thought that would truly be his fate, after the frog had fallen for Mia, when she didn't quite fall for him. He'd been a royal mess when his heart had been broken, which had led to some of the worst alcoholic benders I'd ever seen, man or frog.

After our mugs were all empty, Jonah went upstairs to climb in bed with Mia, although he'd expressed some reservation about doing that while her father slept on the sofa. I laughed.

"Mia would laugh as well, Jonah," I said, at his frown. "She'd be impressed you thought about it, but if she asked you to go upstairs, then she wants you to. Besides, we're leaving early in the morning. It works better if you're already here, and there's plenty of people to look out for you while you're asleep. There is, however, a back staircase, if you'd like to avoid going past Tobias."

Jonah lived by himself in a small one bedroom apartment on the other side of town. It wasn't the world's best neighborhood, and I doubted there was much in the way of a threshold. I doubted there were many houses nearby with much of a threshold; it was a pretty transient neighborhood, with people moving in and out all the time. He spent a lot of time at our house, but he and Mia were resisting moving in together. I didn't know why; it didn't make a lot of sense to me for him to be paying rent when he didn't have a lot of money coming in. He was an actor, and, generally, an understudy with a downtown theater troupe. He took parts where he could get them and did work on sets and props on the side to make ends meet. I had a strong suspicion Mia had asked him to stay more out of wanting to know he was safe, than from any romantic or physical reason. She was probably worried about him, and didn't want to let him too far out of her sight. I know I felt that way about Aiden, even after he'd moved out.

He nodded, gratefully, when I mentioned the back staircase. I pointed him in the direction of the old servants' stairs behind the kitchen. The house was old enough to have had a small servants' quarters; probably enough room for a maid and a cook. Evangeline had used a maid when she'd lived here, and some of them had used the rooms there. I never used them, but they were clear of debris.

"Follow the hallway to the door at the end. It'll open just two doors down from Mia's room," I told him, giving directions back to the rest of the house.

One of these days, I'd have to decide what to do with those extra rooms. They weren't well insulated, and they needed work I couldn't afford at the moment. I mostly kept the heat off to them, sealing it up to keep costs down.

Bert and Allie still sat at the table, even though their mugs were in the sink. I suddenly felt like a third wheel in the room. The chemistry was sparkling and crackling between them. I'd helped them have a couple of date nights at home, even cooked them dinner and served it with candlelight. They were interested in each other, but how far could something like that go when he was still a cursed frog? Then again, maybe that was why Allie felt comfortable around him; after years of victimization at the hands of men and boys, she'd been like a scared rabbit around even the safest men. Bert didn't scare her. I hoped one day we'd find a solution to breaking Bert's curse permanently, and when we did, she'd have overcome her fear issues enough to be able to have a real relationship with him.

I'd do a lot to make that happen.

I took my mug to the sink and headed to my room, leaving them some time alone. Tobias was already asleep on the couch in the living room, making Jonah's concerns moot.

CHAPTER FOURTEEN

Morning came quick.

I was up early, stuffing some clean underwear and extra changes of clothing into a small duffel bag, along with as little as I thought I could get away with in the way of toiletries. I brought my bag downstairs and left it in the hallway by the front door; the others would finish loading the Winnebago while Aiden, Jonah, Mia, and I made our research trip to the museum. I hoped we'd be back by noon and ready to head out as soon as possible. I'd like to get through Indiana before dark, and that would be several hours drive from where we were.

I started the coffee pot before everyone else was really moving, figuring it would be a multiple pot kind of morning. Our breakfast supplies had been depleted the morning before with Paul, but there was still cereal in the pantry, and instant oatmeal. I poured myself a bowl of Cap'n Crunch and set the box of instant oatmeal with the small pile of other kitchen items we'd stacked up for the trip. I laughed when I saw the bag of Funyons, remembering Alfred, the Mad Hatter, when we'd introduced him to them in Wonderland. They would always remind me of him.

The smell of brewing coffee did its magic. The others stirred and headed my way, shuffling into the kitchen as the coffee did its thing and woke up my brain to mostly functioning. Mia shlumped in first, and I poured her a mug the minute I saw her. She didn't look like she'd had a good night's sleep.

"What's wrong?" I asked. I mean, I'd had late nights before, studying. I'd had late nights after a romantic evening with Aiden, as well. She didn't look like she'd had either type of late night. Her eyes were red, and there were dark circles under them.

"Just worried. I tossed and turned all night. Jonah did, too," she said, yawning. She looked like she'd been fussing and fretting all night.

"Did you guys talk?" I worried I'd screwed up her relationship by spilling Jonah's secret. That one I was going to feel guilty about for a while.

"Yeah, we're fine. I'm not even mad I didn't know. I get why he felt like he couldn't say, but I'm not going to be fine if he continues to keep things from me. He said he understands, and we had a long talk, but I was awake even after that, listening to the clocks tick the night away. You know how you get so tired your brain doesn't want to shut itself off?"

I nodded. I'd had a few nights like that in the past. It's like the brain is on a hamster wheel and it's easier to keep the wheel going rather than to step off of it.

"You okay?"

"With coffee, I should be," she said. "You packed?"

We walked into the living room and I showed her where I'd left my bag, as her father was waking up, his hair sticking up in the back like the pouf on the top of a rooster's head. She smiled, then hid it, as she pointed him in the direction of coffee.

The others had started to stir, heading for the coffee in a steady stream, much like zombies intent on hunting brains. Then again, coffee was necessary for the brain to work, especially this morning.

Jonah came down, with the backpack he'd been leaving at the house on a regular basis stuffed to the brim and zipped up, ready to go. He saw mine in the hall, and left his beside it. Mia's bag was already there; she'd put it together the night before while Jonah and I had been in the kitchen, talking.

The doorbell rang as we were all starting to gain a bit more life. It was Aiden and Doris.

Doris came in, hugged Jonah, and went straight to the kitchen with another big basket of food. I should have known she would come with more food. I wondered where we'd put it.

Aiden carried a pastry box and a drink holder with four cups of to-go coffee. I could have kissed him, but I wasn't sure that was a good idea. I drained the mug I had, and took one of the cups from him, gratefully. I wasn't sure, but I was starting to believe I was in need of a coffee IV.

The pastry box held donuts and Danish pastries, sugary carbs that would get us kick-started into our morning. God love him.

Jonah, Mia, Aiden, and I headed for the Escalade for our research trip. The others would spend the rest of the morning packing up the Winnebago and getting us outfitted for the trip. Doris had planned to hit the grocery store with Tobias, packing food and snacks for the journey. Bert would stay at home with Allie and do some final packing of research materials and other odds and ends. The hope was to hit the road either later that day, or first thing Sunday morning. Paul seemed upset he couldn't go with us for the research on Johnny Appleseed, but I asked him to stay behind and watch to make sure Babe's treats were in the RV. It wouldn't do for us to be completely unprepared and have an opportunity to lure him away. That, of course, would be the ideal situation.

Never mind that I wanted Jonah to have a chance to see his heritage without having to guard his reactions. Jonah was an actor, and a good one, but that's asking a bit too much of a guy who spent time in foster care and didn't know his own biological parents.

It didn't take long before we were outside the city. I was driving, and we had Fergie playing on the radio. I let out a breath. I needed to remember to get out of town every once in a while, even if it was just for a quick research trip or an interesting cup of coffee. Some of the stress started easing from my shoulders. Or, then again, maybe it was just the coffee, waking me up enough to sit up straight and feel alert.

The music was just loud enough to hear and not discourage conversation. None of us said anything. It wasn't awkward; it just seemed like we all had things on our minds.

Aiden sat in the front seat, giving me directions to the small town college with the Johnny Appleseed museum. The drive wasn't long, and traffic was light on a Saturday morning.

Urbana was a small town, and the college was on the south end of town, so it wasn't hard to get to the campus. We got turned around once or twice, but still made it to the museum well before the nine a.m. appointment we had with one of the library volunteers. The lady we were meeting pulled up right behind us, and looked happy to see us show up early. She let us in, and let us wander a bit, looking at the exhibits, while she got herself figured out.

There was a big cider press; I remembered seeing one of those from some elementary school farm field trip thing. There were all kinds of pop culture references about Johnny Appleseed, and a section for kids with a great big table in the shape of an apple. It was kinda neat; but I wasn't sure it was giving us quite what we wanted.

Jonah, on the other hand, seemed, in turns, flustered, mesmerized, and lost. He wandered from exhibit to picture to display, as if trying to make sense of it all, and I didn't know where to tell him to begin.

The lady from the museum wanted to know if there was anything she could do to help, but there really wasn't. We shuffled around slowly, reading all the placards and looking carefully at the cider press set up for display. Then I saw something.

"Okay, look, Johnny Appleseed's real name was John Chapman. He had one full sister, and a ton of stepsiblings, because his dad remarried after his mom died. There are a number of documented descendants from his sister and stepsiblings, but there's no record of him having any children. Anywhere. I guess that means it can't be me, then," Jonah said.

I laughed. "Hans Christian Andersen didn't have any children; his sister did, and that's Mia's family line. It's not like there's DNA evidence out there that could prove this, Jonah. They didn't register birth certificates like that back then. If Chapman had a relationship with a woman, and moved on before she knew she was pregnant, he might not have even known he had a child. There weren't child support agencies or paternity testing back then, and there would have been no requirement he register anything like that anywhere. Now we have a place where guys can actually register if they think they might have a kid somewhere; it's called the putative father registry."

He shrugged. "Then how is this supposed to prove anything? How in the world am I supposed to believe I'm the target?"

"I believe it, Jonah. And you're talking to someone who's been around, and seen quite a lot. Let's ask how to track the descendants of Johnny Appleseed. Do you remember anything about your birth parents, or about your life before you were adopted?" Mia asked.

He shook his head. "I was in a foster home from the age of 2. I don't remember much before that."

"So we can't prove it genetically," Aiden said. "I heard the lady who let us in say something about a searchable database of relatives and descendants, but if you don't know anything about where you come from, there's no way to find out anything by that search. I wonder if there's something here that you might be able to touch, without, of course, getting any of us arrested. You might feel some kind of affinity to something he owned."

We fanned out, looking through everything yet again. Aiden had thought to bring a legal pad and pen, and was furiously making notes on everything he could think of, covering page after page with scribbles I didn't even know how to begin to decipher. It rather reminded me of the notebook I'd found of my dad's. I'd have to remember to ask him about it later. At the moment, I didn't want to get him distracted from his notes, and I was looking for anything connected to Johnny Appleseed that Jonah might be able to lay hands on.

I had a random thought, and went to ask the lady working at the museum desk. "Ma'am, is there any kind of database where we can find if there are any trees that Johnny Appleseed planted that are still around? I know there's a lot of apple trees in Ohio, but are there any that he specifically planted?"

She smiled at me. "There are trees in the courtyard that were planted from seedlings taken from the last known surviving tree planted by Johnny Appleseed. I'm sure there were plenty of others around, but that's the last known one. If you go out into the courtyard, you'll see the trees I'm talking about."

I thanked her for her time, and collected the others, telling them about the trees outside. "I think we might have caught a break," I said, leading them outside.

Jonah looked at the trees, then shook his head. "I don't know what you want me to do with them. There doesn't look like there's anything wrong with them."

Mia and I met eyes. She got it.

"Jonah, it's not about healing anything. Put your hands on the tree and see if you can sense anything," she said.

"And if I don't?"

Aiden rolled his eyes. "What are you afraid of, man? I'm telling you it's not a big deal. You're among friends. We're on a college campus during a holiday break. There's no one around. What could possibly go wrong?"

CHAPTER FIFTEEN

Jonah started laughing. "Are you nuts? You're asking me what could go wrong with magic I don't use, don't understand, and don't like? This is crazy."

I had to grin. "Look, if something happens, you can always pull back, right? You don't have to do anything crazy, but if you feel something, and if feels out of control, you can pull away. Have you ever not been able to stop? Or, if you can't stop, say something; we'll pull you away from the tree."

He looked at me. "That could work. Really. Why didn't I think of that?" Without saying anything else, he walked up to the tree in the middle, and placed on hand on either side of the trunk, spreading his fingers to make as much contact with the tree as possible.

Nothing happened, at first, or rather nothing happened that I could see. I stepped in, closer to Jonah. Mia did the same, and an apple fell out of the tree, hitting her on top of her head, just like Isaac Newton's discovery of gravity.

"Hey," she exclaimed. "Not cool."

Jonah's head jerked up, looking at Mia, or rather, looking in the direction of her voice, but his eyes were clouded and unfocused, as if he wasn't seeing what he was looking at. Another apple dropped from the tree, as if it had ripened and had chosen just that moment to fall.

Weren't we a bit late in the year for harvesting? I thought apples were harvested a month or so earlier, but I was a city girl; I could be wrong. If it was late for the apples, why were we suddenly getting apples falling from the tree? I'd think those would already be gone.

Mia picked up the apple that had hit her in the head. It was small, but just ripened. She smelled it, and put it into her bag, to be examined later.

Jonah leaned his forehead into the tree, resting it against the bark, much as he'd done with the maple tree in my back yard. I saw the tree glow slightly, as if illuminated by a setting sun, but it was still morning. The yellowish glow around the tree shouldn't be there, and I looked up. Apples were ripening before my eyes. I think we had our answer.

"Jonah, look up," Aiden said. Apparently he'd seen it, too. I was glad I wasn't the only one.

Jonah looked, and watched as about two dozen apples grew from blooms to fully ripened fruit in seconds rather than weeks. He finally let go of the tree, and the glow dissipated. The ripened apples seemed to reverse themselves slightly, their growth slowing down as he stepped away.

"Need any further proof?" I asked. "I think we've got our man."

He nodded, speechless. Mia went up to him and took his hand. "It doesn't matter," she said. "I still love you. That won't change." She reached up and cupped his face in her hands. "It wouldn't have mattered either way."

Jonah let out a breath that seemed to come all the way from his toes. "I guess I'm related somehow to Johnny Appleseed. I'm not sure I'll ever know how. But it's nice to know I belong somewhere. That's something being a foster care kid doesn't ever really give you. No matter how great the foster parents, or how wonderful the adoptive parents, there's always a sense of having something missing. I think it somehow just clicked into place. I wish I'd known about this when I was a kid. This isn't a bad heritage to have."

He was right. It really wasn't. I could think of much worse.

"Okay," I said. "So we have some answers. Let's go get some coffee and start to get back. We can come up with a plan between here and Dayton, and maybe they have some information in the museum we can take with us. I still think it's important Paul not realize what we've found, though, Jonah. I'm just worried about how desperate he might get, especially if he realizes you're the one the ox-napper is after. I'd like to know a little more about why you're wanted before we just agree to hand you over, which I'm sure Paul, or Pete, either, is expecting to do."

He nodded. The others agreed as well; not that I expected them to do otherwise, but at the same time, it was worth reminding everyone we were about to be up close and personal with someone we didn't know. Paul seemed like a good guy, and he had paid money up front for our expenses, but he also didn't need to be tempted to put someone in harm's way. He just seemed too desperate to me. And I hadn't figured Pete's angle yet.

And that worried me.

The lady inside gave us directions to a coffee shop located a little further into town, at an old train depot. We browsed the gift shop for a few minutes, and Aiden picked up a couple of books on Johnny Appleseed for research on the way. Jonah pulled out his wallet as well. They had a gavel made from wood from an apple tree planted in Apple Creek, Ohio, by Johnny Appleseed. He was careful not to touch it with his bare hands, asking the woman to wrap it up. He told her it was a gift, but I had a funny feeling it was more than that.

Did he just want something to connect him with that lost heritage, or was he looking for a more tangible memento? Did he have some plan for it? If nothing else, the thing was heavy, like a judge's gavel, and would make a decent weapon if it was used for self-defense.

And it was made of wood. Not metal. He could take it with him to meet the ox-napper at the Big Rock Candy Mountain without violating the terms of the second note.

I had a new appreciation for Jonah. It wasn't that I'd thought him stupid, but it was a really smart move to make; to have a potential magic connected weapon that might slip through a smart magical being's precautions.

Of course, we still didn't know *why* they wanted Jonah.

We piled back into the Escalade in search of more coffee. The coffee shop that had been recommended, The Depot, was a converted train depot that had all the standard coffee shop drinks and flavorings, as well as big pastries for sale and people sitting in corners, hunched over laptops and mooching the free wi-fi. I think the guy behind the counter was actually a bit surprised when I ordered just coffee, black, with no flavorings or sweeteners. Hey, I just wanted the caffeine. I didn't need the sugar buzz, and I'd gotten fairly used to drinking most of my coffee black. The frou-frou stuff was nice every once in a great while, but mostly unnecessary in a grad student budget.

We got our coffee and headed back to the car, ready to head back to Dayton. No one talked, and I hadn't yet turned on the radio. Unlike the quiet drive here, the silence was getting a bit awkward.

"So, Jonah, are you okay?" Aiden asked.

I was glad he asked. I'd wanted to, but I was afraid of sounding like a fussy busybody. And I still felt kinda bad for outing him the way I had. I didn't regret that Mia now knew; I just kept thinking that I should have pulled him aside and talked to him about it one on one before saying anything in front of everyone else. But I didn't have any idea how I'd have pulled him away without telling everyone else why I had to talk to him alone. And if I had, Mia would have insisted on following. Maybe I was just overanalyzing something I felt guilty about, but I still didn't feel good about the way I'd gone about it.

Jonah took a few minutes before answering. "It's weird, you know. I mean, I always knew there'd be things I'd never find the truth to. It's part of being a kid in the foster system if you don't know much about where you come from. I just kinda always assumed it would be things like what my medical history might be, or when my family might have immigrated to America, or what nationality my grandparents or great-grandparents came from. I never thought it would be something like this. How do you even process this?"

I laughed. "Jonah, I knew my last name was Grimm, even knew I was descended from the Grimm Brothers. I still wasn't prepared for something like this. I don't think you ever can be, no matter if you had a written genealogy all the way back to Charlemagne. No matter how much you knew, or didn't know, how could you be prepared for magic to sneak its way into your life?"

"But I knew about the magic," he said, looking down at his hands.

I saw the glance in the rearview mirror as I drove, glancing up to check on him. "Jonah, we knew our family histories, but not about magic. You had the opposite. Do you think it was really that different?"

Mia chimed in. "It wasn't. I was in the same boat as Janie in some ways, and in the same boat as you in others. I thought my dad was just a deadbeat. Who knew he was the Rambo of the magic world? My name's Andersen. Who'd have thought I was related to Hans Christian Andersen? I didn't have a clue about that either. I knew about magic, because I'd been there with Janie when she'd had all these crazy magic things happen to her. I'd met Bert. I'd seen magical hair growth. But until the Seawitch came for me, I still didn't fully believe it was all real. Be glad you found a way to confirm it without danger breathing down your neck in the same second."

He nodded.

We all fell quiet again. What else could we say? There wasn't much, except to let Jonah have some peace and quiet to let it all soak in.

CHAPTER SIXTEEN

We got back to Dayton, and found the RV closed up in the driveway. Tobias had started up the grill on the patio, and everyone was eating hamburgers and hot dogs and relaxing. Even Paul seemed relaxed. I wondered what had happened, but I was just happy there didn't seem to be any awkwardness or strangeness amongst anyone. It would be a long trip across the country if people were timid or awkward. The RV had more room than we'd have on a train or a bus, or a car, but there was no way we'd be able to avoid each other in cramped quarters if someone had a beef with someone else. And I was worried about the dynamic between Paul and Pete from Bert's description of their relationship, but they were getting along just fine.

Tobias pulled me aside, purportedly to ask me some question about cleaning up the gas grill. We went outside, and he closed the door behind us. We stood in front of the grill, facing away from the house, and he asked how the trip went. I don't think we were fooling anyone, but it was worth having a quiet conversation.

"Not a lot of definitive answers about his heritage, but some confirmation I was right." I told him about the tree and its reaction to Jonah. "I think it was a good trip, for Jonah's sake. He's still reeling from the idea that he's somehow the target this time; he never really thought he was connected to anything like Mia and I. He's still in some shock. We still can't figure what crimes the ox-napper seems to think Johnny Appleseed committed. He was a good man; religious and giving, and he was all about helping to spread knowledge of apples and their health benefits across the Midwest. He seemed to have a knack for getting things to grow in soil that hadn't been real receptive to other crops, or had been uncultivated wilderness in the past. That seems to be the biggest thing, maybe some indication that his ability really might be genetic, but there's no definitive proof; no way to know."

"So we still don't know quite what we're talking about?" Tobias asked.

I could hear the disappointment in his voice. "No, we really don't. But there are so many things that came to mind. Johnny Appleseed is a folk name; the man's real name was John Chapman. He ended up owning a lot of land. There were a lot of orchards and such he was responsible for. I wonder if there was a land deal or other such problem that went sideways. Some of the materials in the museum seemed to indicate Chapman maybe wasn't as good with money as he could have been, underselling seedlings, or just not properly recording deeds Or, maybe there was some dispute over a boundary? There was something about using his profits to rescue and care for horses whose treatment he might have objected to. Was there someone out there who believed that he stole their property? And there was some statement he might have left a decent sized estate to his sister, but no idea what she did with it. Who knows? The problem, I see, is that we just don't know what kind of magical being he might have pissed off, and we just don't have a way to ask."

Tobias thought for a moment. "Does Aiden have a way to get a hold of his father?"

"I don't know. I think Doris has a way to get a hold of Geoffrey; she did when he was sick last year, right after we got back from Wonderland."

"Didn't you say Paul hired you for this job, and he was referred by the Snow Queen? And haven't the two of you talked in the past about some kind of diplomatic relationship, to help with transitions between the mortal realm and the magical worlds?" he asked.

"Yes, but nothing's formally settled. I don't have a way to ask that, and you know what it is to ask a favor of a magical faerie queen. I'm not prepared to take on a debt to her, especially when we still don't have an idea of what to ask for."

Favors don't come cheap in the magical realm. Nothing is free. There's always a barter system, with favors owed, or some exchange of goods or services. Even knowledge comes at a cost. I'd learned that the hard way. It wasn't worth the cost unless you knew exactly what you wanted to ask.

"But it isn't your favor to ask for; it's Paul's. There's nothing wrong with having him go ask before we leave," Tobias said. "Didn't you negotiate for him to pay your expenses? Isn't this an expense?"

"I'd rather see if there's some wiggle room first. I'm not sending Paul into a faerie realm by himself. I don't trust him completely. Something about all of this worries me enough to say that we really shouldn't let him too far out of our sight." I watched through the sliding door as Paul got up from the table and served himself another hamburger.

No one was really paying attention to us outside, but I still leaned down to reach under the grill to shut off the valve to the propane tank. It was already off, so this really was just a ruse for Tobias to try to get a read on whatever we were facing. Whatever he and Mia were building between them as father and daughter, when he put on a game face to try to figure out business, he was as smart as they come, and yet he didn't want his daughter stuck in the middle of dishing information regarding strategy and tactics when it involved her boyfriend. I had to give it to him; he was trying very hard to do what he knew how to do without stepping on her toes, or making her feel disloyal or uncomfortable. I almost wished he'd been around when I'd been dealing with my own family drama, but Mia had been my own rock to lean on when all of that had happened.

"What do you think Paul might do?" Tobias asked.

"I think he might try to grab Jonah and run off on his own. He thinks we're moving too slow if we know where the meeting place is. I just think we better not give him any opportunity or temptation." I watched Jonah gathering the dirty dishes from our lunch and stacking them up next to where Mia was loading the dishwasher. "How close are we to being ready to leave?"

Tobias followed my gaze, watching the two of them in domestic chores. "We're ready. But is Jonah ready for whatever might come next? Is he ready to know the truth? Whatever that truth might be?"

"Are we ever going to have the truth? I mean, there's no record, anywhere, of John Chapman ever having children. He never married; he had no heirs. So when they say 'apple heir' I'm not sure anyone could actually be, in a legal sense, I mean. Of course, there's always the possibility Chapman did have a child, but one he never knew about. He did travel a lot. If the mother never told him about it, then the connection was lost to history. If some woman did have a child by Chapman, maybe she passed it off as her husband's, or married someone to cover a pregnancy. It did happen in those days, and wouldn't be unheard of.

"He did have a sister, and she had children. Most of those descendants seem to be recorded, but again, it's possible one or another of them could have had an unplanned or unwanted pregnancy that ended in adoption, and that information would not have been recorded for Johnny Appleseed posterity. So, it's possible, even likely, Jonah might be related to Chapman somehow, either through some unnamed child lost to history, or through his sister. He also had quite a few younger half-siblings, and he was close to them. They haven't been very public, mostly kept to themselves, not a lot known by way of easily available genealogy records."

Tobias was silent for a moment. I was, too. The two of us both had long, detailed, and known family trees; and they hadn't come without a price. But to be held accountable for a history that isn't known, and couldn't be verified? That was a hard one to swallow. And yet, here we were.

We had no way of filling in those holes for Jonah without a time machine, and meeting up with the right people who could, and would, tell the truth about whether or not he was related to the man who was Johnny Appleseed. But the reaction of that tree to Jonah's touch wasn't a small thing; it was proof of connection, of rightness to the wood and the plant itself.

And someone, somewhere, wanted to make Jonah pay for the deeds of a long dead possible ancestor.

Could I use it to my advantage to not be able to prove such a thing through birth records or family trees? I did file it away in the memory banks for later. If I could argue my way, or rather, Jonah's way, out of a pickle by arguing an inability of proof, I'd do it like a shot. But what if they had proof we couldn't put our hands on?

It wasn't something Tobias and I were going to be able to solve in a single conversation, much less one held over the pretense of turning off a gas grill so cold it was almost a joke. We needed to head back inside before someone made a stink about how long we'd been outside.

We came back in to a rather heated conversation about whether or not to take more weapons. Aiden was arguing for taking more books. Paul wanted us to take more weapons; which was moot, in my mind, because no way could Paul handle any of our metal or iron weapons if he was using enough magic to remain small enough to say within the confines of the camper itself. Never mind the fact we weren't supposed to bring weapons to the meeting to get Babe back.

As for books, I pulled Aiden aside, and told him to only take books about American history, Johnny Appleseed, or other American folklore we might run into on the way, but anything unrelated needed to stay behind.

Tobias stopped that from turning into another argument. "Guys, we don't have to take everything. Janie, Doris is staying here, right?"

I nodded.

"Aiden, if you thought of something that you'd left behind, do you think you could tell her where to look, over the phone?" he asked.

My head jerked over to look at Tobias. "I thought you didn't trust phone lines. You've got some elaborate signal system with Mia, but we can call back and forth with research on a trip that might or might not be dangerous, with all of us along? That doesn't make any sort of real sense."

He laughed at me. "I don't trust cell phones. Landlines are way more secure, because people don't have police scanners picking them up out of the air. They're less like to be bugged. This house is warded against magic, as is, I'm sure, Doris's house. I can't imagine anyone would be able to predict ahead of time where we stop for toilet breaks and gas breaks and where we might or might not need to change drivers. How in the world would they even know what route we'd be taking? How would they know which phones to bug?"

When he said it like that, it did make sense. Even though we'd planned our route, there were a few places where we could deviate unexpectedly and still stay on course and on schedule. Especially if we found we were being followed.

So why did I have a bad feeling about this?

CHAPTER SEVENTEEN

And we were off, like a thundering herd of turtles.

Four hours after I'd hoped to hit the road, we were finally on the highway, heading out of Dayton, heading toward the final goal, the meeting ground of whoever it was that had gotten us to start on this journey.

Not three hours outside of town, we had to stop. The Winnebago was overheating; probably from the amount of weight it had to haul. I said so, and Tobias laughed.

"There's a small hole in a radiator hose. I haven't been able to find which hose. I was under the hood this morning and still couldn't find it. This might actually be a lucky break to have found it so soon into the trip." He laughed, took a toolbox from under the front driver's seat, and headed out to look at it. Pete and Paul went with him, and Aiden and Jonah did, as well. Jonah ended up being more of a help than I expected, and he shrugged when I said something about it.

"He's had the spare part for a while. It was the top radiator hose that had to be replaced. He'll have it in a few minutes, and we'll top off the radiator with some water, and get back on the road."

He was right. Luckily we'd stopped at a gas station, and the owner allowed us to use the water hose behind the station to refill the water in the radiator. I pulled out some of the cash Paul had paid me with, and we topped off the gas tank, spending some money at the station to pay them back in some small way for letting us hang out in the parking lot and make our repairs. The whole stop had taken less than thirty minutes, and it had allowed all of us to stretch our legs while the guys had been so absorbed in parts and engines and hoses and fluids.

I still had a bad feeling about this. If ever there had been a bad portent to a trip, this had to be it. I had a sinking feeling we'd all regret this trip sooner or later. Something was hanging up in the pit of my stomach, and it just didn't seem good.

We all loaded back into the RV, and silently headed off into the evening.

An hour or so later, the sun was going down, and we were all quiet as the camper rolled down the highway. As it got darker, with the miles disappearing under the wheels, some of us started yawning. Paul and Pete retired to the bedroom in the back, and we heard muffled arguing for a while, before they finally quieted down, and then we heard dueling snores coming from that room. Aiden and Bert clambered into the front passenger seat, squinting at the maps and discussing which exits and which gas stops and where they might take the next break.

I caught myself yawning as well. Allie had lain down on the couch and was sound asleep. Mia and I climbed up into the forward sleeping compartment over the driver's cab, and lay down. Jonah grabbed a pillow and lay down on the center of the floor, stretching his long legs toward the bathroom, with his head near the driver.

It was funny how we'd all just settled in, I thought, before I realized there had probably been some conversation about all of this before I'd come in from my grill discussion with Tobias. There had probably been some agreement to prevent awkwardness between Aiden and myself. And so much the better for them.

I listened to the hum of the tires on the road, the pavement whooshing past us under the Winnebago, and wondered if I'd be able to have a conversation with Aiden about anything other than research, or our mission. I wondered if I'd ever have any kind of good conversation with him about anything other than magic. Was that what he'd meant by his concerns yesterday? What had he been leading up to?

There was no way I could read his mind anymore, or at least, I didn't feel like I was doing so hot at it. We used to be so close that we'd finished each other's sentences. We seemed to be on the same page without even discussing how we'd gotten there when we'd been in Wonderland. After that, things had stopped being so easy to predict, and had gotten harder and harder to figure out. I had no idea what was going on in his mind, but one thing I did know; he was thinking hard enough down there to keep his own inner hamster wheel spinning away for the rest of the night. That hamster was showing no signs of stopping any time soon.

Mia slept beside me, and my eyelids were getting heavy as well. Tobias dimmed the lights in the interior and the awkward silence we'd all been listening to slid into a contented, sleepy quiet, lulled into relaxation, I finally fell asleep.

I have no idea how long I was out. I dreamed of a vacation on a beach, with salt water around to keep the magic craziness away. I dreamed of wearing a white linen sheath dress and standing barefoot in the sand, with Aiden right behind me, his arms around my waist. Would he have a problem with that much salt, given that he was part faerie? I didn't think he would, given that he'd helped me spread so many salt lines in the past. I could almost smell the salt air, the slight fishy smell coming from the water, as I watched the moon over the beach, clear and bright.

I woke up with a start, hearing someone yell a loud curse word.

"Holy ratshit! Hold on everybody!" Tobias yelled, and then he stomped on the brakes, hard.

I grabbed the side of the bunk, and braced myself. Mia, deeper into the bunk than I was, didn't have much of anything to hold on to, but she did try.

The Winnebago slid, the brakes squealing as he tried to stop faster than a vehicle that size was supposed to stop. Something must have been in the roadway. I couldn't figure any other reason why he'd have stopped like that, but I couldn't see anything from my perch in the forward compartment. The camper finally came to a stop, but it wasn't pretty.

I couldn't see anything, so I climbed down from the bed, helping Mia down so she didn't step on Jonah as she climbed down in the semi dark.

"What happened, Dad?" she asked.

Before she could say anything, Paul barreled his way back to the front of the cab. "What the hell, guys! I almost fell out of bed!"

"Where's Pete?" I asked. "Is he all right?"

"He's fine, but he's a bit banged up from rolling across the bed and smacking his face on the dresser. He'll have a big black eye. He's in the bathroom, trying to see how bad it is."

If that was the extent of the injuries of all of us, then we weren't too bad. There were a few other bumps and bruises, but nothing too crazy. Allie had stepped on Jonah, jumping up when Tobias yelled, and she'd cracked her elbow on the kitchenette counter when the momentum had thrown her backward, but other than a good knock to the funny bone, and Jonah's sore ribs, Pete's black eye appeared to be the only major injury.

So why were we stopped?

I peered out the window, where Tobias and Aiden were looking. Aiden had been buckled in, and he'd grabbed hold of Bert when Tobias had hit the brakes, so both of them were fine, as well. But what was outside?

I saw a person, but couldn't tell if it was a man or a woman. A cowboy hat was pulled down low over a face, and a heavy poncho covered whatever else they were wearing. It reminded me of something out of an old Clint Eastwood western movie, where the protagonist would just show up, in time to stop an injustice or get into a duel.

Who in the world would just stand in the middle of the road like that? Were they trying to get themselves killed? If so, it wasn't a bad way to get that accomplished.

There wasn't much other traffic on the road, and suddenly I had the thought maybe they were waiting for us. The hair stood up on the back of my neck, and all of us drew in a collective breath.

I started for the door, and everyone cried out at once, yelling at me to stop, not to go out, not to go anywhere.

I grinned at them, and turned around, grabbing a frying pan from the kitchenette (the closest thing made of metal), and opened the door. I ran outside, followed closely by all the others, heading for the person standing in front of the RV.

The person's head was bowed, as if they were looking down at the ground. They barely looked up when I came toward them, frying pan in my hand.

"What are you doing?" I asked. "You almost got yourself killed!"

"He's dead," she (and the voice, even though husky and rough, was definitely a she) muttered. "Can't bring 'im back no matter how much I drink."

I looked at her hand, and sure enough, there was a flask there, covered in leather, with a strap, like one would use if they were riding on a horse in an old Western movie.

Who in the world could this be?

"Gotta get back to Deadwood," she muttered. "Maybe it'll all be a dream, and he'll be sitting there, a' playin' cards with McCall, and no one woulda shot 'im."

Deadwood? McCall? Cards? Who shoots people over a card game anymore?

Aiden grabbed at my sleeve, and I brushed him off.

"Ma'am, do you have someone we can call for you? A friend, a daughter, a husband? Is there someone who can take care of you?"

The hat shifted slightly in front of me. "Don't got no one now he's done been shot. Daughter ain't with me no more, never really married, he was my on'y friend. And he's gone."

Aiden plucked at my sleeve again, harder.

I shook him off again. "Ma'am, do you know anyone around here? Is there somewhere we can take you?"

She shrugged. "Don't rightly know where I am these days. Wouldn't know where to go even if I did."

Something wasn't right. Aiden grabbed my arm. "Janie," he whispered.

"What?" I asked, turning around. "Kinda busy here."

"Yeah, I get it," he said. "But I know who that is."

"Who?"

Bert hopped to the doorway and filled in the blanks for all of us. "Holy shit," he said. "It's Calamity Jane!"

I guess you could call standing in traffic a calamity, I thought.

CHAPTER EIGHTEEN

I got a little closer, and identified why something seemed off about her; she was drunk. And, it seemed, she'd been that way for a while.

We talked her off the road, and got her to sit down in a folding chair Tobias had hidden in the camper somewhere and brought out to make her comfortable. I tried to ask her what she was doing. It came out garbled, in bits and pieces.

"Well, I was mindin' my own business, see, and then all of a sudden, I was here, with these weirdo roads, and big things whooshing right at me. I kept trying to get 'em to stop, and they wouldn't, so I don't rightly know where I'm at or where I'm a'sposed to be."

Between the drunken slurring and the strange vernacular, it was hard to figure out what was going on, but it appeared Jane was a heavy drinker, who forgot for long stretches of time that her best friend, Bill, was dead.

"He 'us shot, playin' cards. I tole him and tole him that he shouldn't be out a'playin' cards with that rabble, and he did anyway and some no good gold digger shot 'em. Funny joke on 'im, though, is that Bill didn't have nothin' in his pockets to take, and no one took kindly to the shootin'."

What was she talking about?

Aiden stepped forward again. "Am I right, ma'am, that you're looking for your friend, Wild Bill Hickock?"

"Have you's seen 'im?" she slurred, apparently forgetting he was shot, or so she'd said a few minutes ago.

"I haven't seen him, ma'am," I said, and it was the truth. Wasn't Wild Bill Hickock some kind of Wild West show man from the 1800s? And if so, what in the world was she doing here?

She grumbled a bit, and took a swig from her flask. Was there a way I could take the flask away from her without a fight? As drunk as she seemed, she also looked like she could handle herself, and I really didn't want to find out the truth of that by trial and error.

I was pretty sure it would be a major trial, and that fighting her would end up being my error.

"Will y'all tell me if you see him? I miss him so bad . . ." She trailed off into a deep snore.

We all looked at each other. What were we supposed to do with a drunk Wild West legend on the side of the road? We had a deadline. We had to go save Babe. We had to get moving.

But we couldn't just leave her there, could we? I mean, I'd never forgive myself if we left her behind and something happened to her, and I knew the others would feel the same. But could we just pack her up and take her with us? And was she magic? Was she dangerous? Was she somehow booby trapped to cause us harm? Was Tobias willing to invite her into the RV, since it was his home, and technically his threshold?

I didn't know what to say; thankfully Tobias had a better idea. He pointed just down the road, and it took me a bit to see what he meant, but he was a genius.

There was no traffic around, and a small, gravel section just off the road. It looked like a place where farm tractors or semi trucks might pull off to rest a few hours. It wouldn't be a bad thing for our driver to get some shut eye, himself.

Tobias jumped into the RV, started it up and moved to the gravel pull-off area. Paul lifted Calamity Jane, chair and all, and carried her just down the road to where Tobias and Aiden were putting blocks under the tires and Jonah began setting up the tent we'd brought along. Once the tent was up and sturdy, Paul moved Calamity Jane and her chair inside the tent. At least if it rained during the night, she wouldn't get wet.

Aiden and Tobias pulled out canisters of salt, pouring a circle around the tent, as well as around that Winnebago.

"Why are you pouring salt?" Paul asked.

We all exchanged curious glances, but it was Jonah who stepped forward. "Salt repels a lot of magic, Paul. I think we'll all sleep better if we have some kind of magical barrier. We just don't know if something is out to get us. We don't know if the whole purpose of this was to get all of us out of Janie's house, out of town where we're all comfortable and protected, or if it's on the level. Was Jane," he pointed to the tent, where we could hear deep, unladylike snores coming through the open flap, "sent to waylay us, to stop us and keep us here long enough to be a target? Is there something coming for us?"

Paul's mouth hung open. I guess he hadn't thought of it.

"Paul," I said, "are you using any magic at the moment?"

"Just the magic to stay small. If I stop using it, I won't fit in the camper," he said, and shrugged "I can't use anything else. I just don't have that ability."

I looked at Bert.

The frog shrugged as well. "I've never noticed a problem with being behind a salt line, even inside a salt circle. It's a protective thing, not an undo-the-magic thing. If the magic that keeps me a frog isn't affected by the salt circle, I can't imagine Paul's magic would be affected by it. It's the same kind of magic; transformative rather than harmful."

It made me wonder if there was a way for us to undo Bert's magic. I saw Allie looking at him, and I recognized the look on her face. It was one of love.

I'd made that look at Aiden at one point, and I wondered, would I still look at him that way now? I saw him on the other side of the RV, pouring salt in a thin line, and not paying attention to me. I shook off the thought, and tried to think about something else. Paul seemed satisfied with the answer, and ambled off, helping Pete put up the awning on the side of the Winnebago and pulling out a few more folding chairs.

They were planning to sit up for a while. As much as I was tired, the activity and dealing with Calamity Jane had me wired. Apparently, I wasn't the only one feeling that way

Tobias pulled out a couple of cans from his fridge, and offered them around. I accepted a Coke, but Bert, Jonah, and Aiden all took him up on the beer. Mia turned up her nose at alcohol and caffeine, and decided to go inside and go to sleep. Allie joined me with caffeine; she wasn't twenty-one yet, so she wasn't legal.

We sat quietly outside, looking at the stars and sipping our drinks. It was peaceful, in a way that living in the city can't always be. One by one, the others started to head inside, the length of the day and the adrenaline rush finally ending, with slumber not far behind. Allie went inside, then Paul and Pete, then Bert headed inside, with the stated purpose of curling up beside Allie on the couch. I yawned big enough for my jaw to pop.

"I think I'm done, as well, guys. It's been an awfully long day."

The guys all nodded. The snoring from the tent had settled down some, but I could still hear that Calamity Jane was down for the night. I headed inside, but left the door open. It seemed stuffy to me inside the camper, and I figured the guys would lock up when they came inside.

I climbed up into the forward sleeping compartment with Mia, who was already asleep, and got comfortable, the pillow wedged into exactly the right spot under my right ear. I was curled up on my side, nearly asleep, when I heard them start talking again.

"Man alive, Aiden, have you talked to her yet? You guys have been so miserable. You gotta do something." It was Jonah's voice.

While I was glad he was focusing on something other than his own situation, I wanted to hear whatever Aiden might say next.

"Dude, you know what I want. It just hasn't been the right time. I can't distract her right now. You know that. She needs everything she's got to keep going, everything she's got to keep her mind on figuring this out. I can't screw that up, for you, for Paul, for everyone."

"You say that like you think you know her response. I thought you'd made up your mind." Jonah said.

Tobias wanted to know what they were talking about. Quite frankly, I did too.

"It's nothing. It's personal stuff, about our relationship," Aiden said, refusing to elaborate. "I'm trying to keep this all professional, and I'm struggling."

"Guys, you two have some incredible women in there, and as not all of them have dads that are here and able to say this: make them happy. If you can't make them happy, don't hurt them. I'm not sure what you guys are talking about, but there's no question in my mind you two care for them. I'm just a dad, but I can tell you this magic crap has gotten in the way of too many relationships in my life. I will always regret leaving Mia's mom, and Mia, as well. Maybe there was a better way to protect them. Maybe that was the purpose of all the attacks that kept showing up; to get me to leave them and to burden me with regrets when I did. If that was the case, then the bad guys won on that one. I will always wish I'd fought for a normal life."

There was silence for a few minutes. I desperately wanted to hear what Aiden or Jonah would say next. Aiden broke the silence. "I don't want to hurt her. But it's also about timing. I can't jeopardize everyone else. I can't do that to her."

Oh God. He was definitely going to end it. He'd made his decision. It felt like I'd just been stabbed in the gut with white hot spears. I'd figured it was coming, even expected it, but hearing him say it was more than I could hear. I buried my head in the pillow and cried, trying to control the shaking and the wailing as best I could. Somehow, I managed to get that initial reaction out without waking up anyone inside.

Or so I thought.

I got control of myself as best I could and looked out of the compartment, trying to see if they had started to come in. When I did, I met Bert's eyes.

He sat on Allie's shoulder as she slept on her back, his eyes barely opened until he saw me peering out, but at the same time, he wasn't asleep. I saw his eyes widen the rest of the way, as wide as they would go when he saw my face.

I wondered how bad I had to look when he saw it. I didn't know what I looked like, and I had no words to answer questions at the moment, so I pulled back into the compartment, pulled a blanket around myself, and curled up into a ball.

Somehow, I fell asleep, to dreams of losing everyone and everything I cared about.

CHAPTER NINETEEN

Morning came faster than I would have liked. As much as the dreams of the night before had been bad, my eyes felt gritty and dry and puffy when I finally opened them enough to face the world.

Coffee.

Someone needed to make coffee.

And they needed to do it immediately. Or someone might get seriously hurt.

The others were all outside, and no one was in the kitchenette. Heck, no one was in the camper, for that matter. I heard voices, so I knew they were still around, but there was absolutely no way I could put a brave face on anything until and unless I was caffeinated. I found the coffee maker and the Folgers, and dug until I found a coffee filter. A couple of bottles of water were in the refrigerator, and even though I hated to use bottled water for it, I had to get coffee inside of me as soon as humanly possible.

I stood in front of the machine as it whirred and whooshed and gurgled, waiting not so patiently for the sweet, brown, life giving, liquid of sanity. The machine was old, and leaked a bit of water, but at the same time, it kept enough inside to create a somewhat drinkable wake-up cup. I poured some in the cheap white mug I found in an overhead cabinet, and sipped enough to get the blood pumping before I headed for the bathroom to see if I could do anything with my appearance.

Sleeping in one's clothes doesn't do much for the appearance. My eyes were as red and puffy as they felt, and my hair was greasy and lank from not having washed it for a couple of days. I wondered how the others were feeling, because I just felt gross.

Not much help for it, I thought. I ran a comb through my hair, trying to tame it into a decent ponytail. I grabbed a stick of deodorant and used it, hoping it would help me feel less disgusting.

Another cup of coffee poured, and I headed outside to the rest of the group eating cold cinnamon rolls Doris had sent along. The sight of coffee in my mug sent Tobias and Aiden inside after their own caffeine, to the amusement of Allie, who wasn't a complete coffee addict yet, and Jonah, who was more like to grab a Coke on the go than wait for coffee to brew. I grabbed a cold, sticky cinnamon roll, hoping carbs and sugar would make me more alert and less emotional. The overwhelming crash of last night's emotional roller coaster had to get shoved onto the back burner before I could keep going, so I'd take cinnamon and icing if it helped. I hoped Doris had packed us lots of baked goods, because I was going to need every gooey, sugary bite to get through this trip without losing my mind.

Bert watched me fairly closely, but didn't say anything. I was grateful, because I didn't want to talk about anything at the moment, especially with him about last night.

I was saved from wondering how I was going to start the morning when Calamity Jane came bursting out of her tent, yelling about kidnappers, and demanding her guns.

I didn't remember she'd had guns last night. I said so, without really thinking about it.

"I don't go nowhere without my guns. If I didn't have 'em last night, you musta stole 'em from me. Give 'em back, thief!" she yelled, barreling right at me.

Tobias grabbed her by the waist, yelling at her to calm down. She was cussing and spitting and flailing at him, and he almost lost his grip on her once or twice. When he didn't let go of her, she tried to bite him.

He threw her to the ground, and put a knee in her stomach to keep her there. Jane yelled and kicked and tried to hit him, but he hung on. It looked like a rodeo rider trying to tame a bull by wrestling it to the ground by the horns and sitting on it, but in this case, the rodeo rider had about thirty pounds and ten times the patience as he hung over bull.

Jane eventually stopped fighting him. "Get off," she panted, out of breath from the fight. "I won't hurt 'er. Get off."

"Promise?" Tobias asked.

"I keep my word," she grunted, and he stood up, letting go of her as she stood up stiffly.

Her hat was missing, and the poncho was off, as well. I noticed that, as dirty and scruffy as she was, she was actually a pretty woman, probably ten years or so older than I was, but definitely a woman who had seen a hard life. She had fought hard against Tobias, maybe even gave him a run for his money in that short wrestling match, so she wasn't weak, and likely had some experience at fighting, especially against those who weighed a bit more than she did.

"Whatja want with me?" she asked. "I didn't do nuthin' to ya."

I cleared my throat. "Look, we almost hit you. You were in the middle of the road, almost like you were sound asleep on your feet right where you'd get hit. We saw you in time, and stopped, and after you fell asleep, we made sure to move you just down the road with us so we could make sure you were safe. I honestly didn't see any guns on you last night. Are you sure you had them before we showed up?"

She thought a bit, and I saw her eyes squint up at the way too bright morning sun. "Thought I did. Maybe not. But why would they take my guns, but not my flask? And they left me alone?"

"Who is they?" Jonah asked. "Was there someone you knew who might have done this to you on purpose?"

She shook her head. "Don't know. I 'us drunk last night. Don't remember much once I drank the bottle."

"Bottle?" Bert piped up. "What bottle? We didn't see a bottle. Don't you know how dangerous it is to drink out of a bottle you didn't bring yourself?"

He should know. I think the donuts and wine he'd gotten into from Wonderland had been the last straw that shocked him mostly sober. No amount of vomiting in the sink or hang-overs had done it. But being blown up to the size of a dump truck in the living room, and being shrunk back down to his normal size just for eating and drinking things that weren't meant for him had been just the wake up call he needed to start getting his brain back on straight. Come to think of it, I didn't think I'd seen him have more than a single beer at one sitting since then. Sounded like he had it under control now, but I wondered if he'd always react like this when someone around him got drunk. Maybe seeing Jane like this was a good reminder for him of how far gone he had been at one point.

Jane shrieked. "I musta lost my durn mind. Is that a frog? And did it just talk to me? Am I still drunk?"

"Ma'am," I started, trying to take the polite route. "I never saw your guns. But you said something last night about suddenly finding yourself here. Can you tell me what happened? And, yes, that's a frog. His name is Bert, and no, you're not drunk anymore. At least I don't think so."

"Well, Mr. Bert," she said. "I've never met no talkin' frog before. You'll excuse me if I just don't quite believe my eyes."

He shrugged. Whether she believed him to be real or not, we needed to hear her story. She told us she'd been riding a horse back to Deadwood when a twister came up and blew her off her horse, and she'd found herself by the side of the road, with a full bottle of whiskey, and no real way to know where she was. She hadn't known what the cars and trucks were, but she had known that something wasn't right.

"Maybe I hit my head?" she asked. We couldn't answer, but I didn't see any injury to her head, and said so.

Did magic actually move people back and forth through time? Had some time traveling cyclone picked her up, stolen her guns, and left her alcohol? That didn't sound like anything I'd ever heard of before. The look on Tobias' face told me this was a new one for him as well, but she wasn't acting like she was used to technology, in the form of cars and trucks and pavement. What in the world had happened?

Tobias and Aiden were arguing about the best way to move forward. We obviously couldn't just leave her on the side of the road when she was so lost. If we did, there was no way to know whether or not she'd be able to keep herself safe. But if she was actually magical, could we take her with us in the RV? No good answers. Finally, Aiden said he had a magic detector in his backpack, one that had to be switched on before it would work. If she passed the test, and wasn't using magic, then maybe we could take her with us.

No one could really argue with his logic. He went to get his bag, and brought out something that looked like a musical tuning fork, with a switch on the side. He switched it on, and started waving in around

Jane, like a security guard or police officer working a metal detector. It didn't make a sound, and he pronounced her safe for travel.

Jane's belligerent insistence at getting her guns and her whiskey quieted down with her curiosity over the detector Aiden was passing over her. She at first protested, but when she realized it was not going to touch her or shoot at her, she settled down.

"Is it a'gonna do tricks?" she smirked, crossing her arms over her chest and making a pinched up impatient face. "I ain't doing tricks for no one. Did enough of that in Bill's stupid show."

I remembered something from history class, that Wild Bill Hickock had had a Wild West show that had toured cities on the East Coast during the late 1800s, telling Indian stories and with sharp-shooting demonstrations. This was where Annie Oakley had gotten her claim to fame, where Sitting Bull had become famous, and how a lot of stories about the West had gotten distorted into the realm of tall tales. Was that how it worked? Was there power behind the telling of the tales that powered the magic of those that remained? Or did it keep the subjects of those stories alive, because they were alive in the minds of storytellers and the minds of the listeners. It was a good theoretical question for the F.A.B.L.E.S. guys, and maybe Aiden, if I could bring myself to ask it when all of this was over.

Would I still be talking to Aiden when all this was over? That hurt. I shoved it down deep, and asked Jane another question. "Jane, did you go through a portal to get here? Was there magic involved?"

She squinted at me, and I wondered if she'd been so used to the hat covering her eyes that she was flinching from the sun. Her hat was sitting on Tobias's lawn chair, where Aiden had put it after their wrestling match.

"Whatcha talkin' bout? No such thing as magic. Never seen anything like that out there before. What's a portal, then, something to dump me out on this strange road, talking to a bunch of lunatics?"

CHAPTER TWENTY

We might be lunatics at that, but since she hadn't set off any of Aiden's gizmos, and she didn't seem to be magical that we could tell, we couldn't bring ourselves to leave her behind. We had to do something with her, so we invited her along.

"Guess I better go along with y'all," she said. "I gotta find my guns, if nuthin' else. They was gifts from Bill after our first show was a hit. I can't just let 'em go if they was gifts from him, now can I?"

I guess she couldn't. I understood. She was a bit apprehensive about the Winnebago, but she got inside gamely, and sat down at the kitchenette table with Jonah. He pulled out a deck of cards and asked if she knew how to play blackjack. Aiden and Mia joined in, and soon they were into a poker game, leaving the blackjack behind, and playing for pennies. Jane kept winning over and over before they finally got wise and took the deck away from her, insisting that someone else deal.

We crossed the state line into Nebraska around noon. The Winnebago was fairly quiet, with Tobias doing the driving. The quiet was broken up by the sounds of a fairly serious poker game going on, with players rotating in and out. I had to give them credit; they weren't keeping the winnings, but divvying it all back out after every game evenly to whoever had tossed in money, only to start up again.

I declined to play and holed up in the forward sleeping compartment with my Secured Transactions textbook and at least trying to give the appearance of studying. I read the same case three times before I realized it just wasn't working. My brain was still poring over the possibilities of what was going on.

"Hey Jonah, can you toss my backpack up here?" I asked. "There's a book in it I want." I handed him the textbook from my perch.

He put down his cards, steadying himself with the table as he stood up, weaving with the bounce of the RV's tires and the bumps of the road. "Which book did you want? I'm not heaving that whole thing up there. I don't know how you guys carry that many books around. Those things are heavy."

I knew he wasn't a wimp; he did a lot of work on sets at the Schuster Center, and filled in the gaps between bit parts and understudy with part time jobs, including construction, but it takes some getting used to, hauling a big heavy bag of textbooks. My backpack could weigh as much as sixty pounds when fully loaded with books, laptop, notebooks, and other odds and ends. I was used to it, but then again, I didn't toss it up over chest high. I slung it over my shoulder and trekked across campus.

"The one with the yellowish-tan cover, the paperback," I specified.

He pulled out the book, a biography of Johnny Appleseed, and handed it to me, one eyebrow quirked in question, but he didn't say anything.

I smiled at him. "Can't concentrate on studying, so I'd thought I'd see if I could get my brain clicking on something else. Sometimes that helps me concentrate,, switching back and forth into different topics or activities."

Allie looked up from where she was sitting on the couch and watching the poker game. "Hey, I've heard of that. Wasn't there a documentary on TV the other night about your brain and your attention span? I heard something about how if you changed position or changed what you were doing every fifteen minutes or so, you retain more information."

I nodded. "It does actually work sometimes." I opened the book to where I had a worn index card marking a spot I'd seen earlier. "If I'm having trouble concentrating, nine times out of ten, changing tactics a couple of times will help kickstart my brain into being productive."

Mia gave me a horrified look. "I can't imagine doing that. It would make me even more distracted. How can you concentrate when you're in the middle of doing more than one thing? It makes me feel scattered."

Aiden laughed. "I'm like Janie. I seem to get more done, the more

I've got going on. I guess different people have different learning and productivity styles."

Paul had joined in the poker game, and was watching the conversation with interest. It didn't look to me like he'd seen the title on the book I was planning to dig into, and that was probably a good thing. I knew I didn't want to tip our hands too early that we'd figured it out, but how else was I going to do research? I wasn't sure how long we'd keep a handle on it.

I didn't think I had anything to worry about at the moment, though, because he turned back to the game as if nothing major had transpired.

"I'm like you, Mia," he said. "I like to do one thing at a time, get it completely done, and done right, and then move on to the next. If I have to do more than one thing at a time, I feel like I'm not making any progress. I think that's why I liked working in the woods. If you were cutting trees, you could see the progress you made as you went. If you were floating logs, you could seen them coming down the river with you. If you were chopping firewood, you could see the progress as the pile got higher. If I did each log separately, I'd lose my mind, because it would feel like it was taking forever. I like seeing progress."

She nodded. "Like checking things off a list."

But don't you have to know what was on the list before you checked them off? I wanted to ask. Instead, I curled into the bed with the book, vaguely listening to the conversation below. Jane was fairly quiet, but then again, she wasn't drinking. Instead, she seemed to be drawing Paul out about Babe, and about his stories about the ox, listening carefully, and patting his hand every few moments, encouraging him to keep talking.

She had a quiet, comforting way about her, I thought. I bet she'd have made a good nurse, or home health care worker; she seemed to enjoy helping others, and was a good listener. Paul eventually started wondering about what to do when we got to the Big Rock Candy Mountain, but no one had any real answers to give him.

Tobias called back from the driver's seat "Paul, don't think we aren't going to be prepared. We've talked some. Everyone is working on this for you. We haven't had a whole lot of time to figure things out. But we're early for the exchange. We've got a long drive to go. And we're not there yet. There's time to figure this out."

"No offense, sir," Paul said, softly. "But it's not so easy being patient when it's your loved one."

Tobias was silent for a moment. "That's why it's even more important. You want to make sure you don't jump into something in the heat of the moment when it would be better thinking things through, and not getting your emotions involved."

Paul was quiet for a moment, digesting this, before I saw him nod, and turn back to the card game. Mia picked up the deck again, shuffling awkwardly before beginning the next hand.

The conversation turned back to the poker game. I turned back to my book, trying to concentrate on Johnny Appleseed's early life.

Chapman had been the oldest, with one younger sister. His mother had died in childbirth along with her third child, and Chapman's father had remarried. His stepmother had had multiple children, and the whole family had lived in a very small house in Massachusetts. He and one of his half-brothers had taken off for a while on their own when they came of age, and eventually, Chapman had gone his own way, taking his religious beliefs and charity on the road. So far, all very normal and human and non-magical.

It appeared Chapman had accumulated a sizable amount of land by planting and raising apple orchards, selling tree seedlings, and teaching others about using apples and raising them in a time of land grants to people who were willing to work the land. Because he cultivated crops, the land became his, due to the state of the Midwest at the time; it was still fairly primitive, and not well settled yet. He didn't seem to have any major wants or needs, and few material goods. He just floated on the wind, going where the spirit seemed to move him, spreading Swedenborgian (I'd never heard that term before) Christian beliefs of charity and giving.

I couldn't find a single reference to him being involved in a relationship, but it wasn't out of the realm of possibility he had a friend in a remote location, a widow or an older woman alone, who might have welcomed the company and been too far out of civilization for anyone to know of their relationship. In fact, I was rather betting this had been the way it happened; the way that Jonah came to be, many generations back. It didn't seem like Chapman had every really said anything against marriage, nor did he ever say he was looking for it. For a man of his time to be really uninterested in a long term relationship generally meant he had a secret, and one that no one really talked about; and there was no one around that we could ask.

So what had Chapman and his brother gotten into while they were on their journey together? What caused them to split up? Was it just that his brother had gotten old enough to go his own way, or had something happened? The history didn't explain why they had gone their separate ways, but it did indicate their father and the rest of the family also moved to Ohio some years after they had first gone exploring. What were they leaving? Why? Had something happened in the farming community where they'd been born, or was it too crowded, or too overtaxed after the Revolutionary War?

I wasn't sure there would ever be a good answer. And there was no real answer as to how far the brothers had traveled, but there were also no apple orchards linked to Chapman as far west as we'd gotten in just a day's driving. We were already further west than the brothers had traveled, together or separate. So, as much as I was learning about the man behind the Johnny Appleseed legend, what made it special? What made it such that someone would target him, or any descendants, who were apparently so unknown as to be hidden from history?

CHAPTER TWENTY-ONE

As the day dragged on, all of us were getting restless. Not used to being cooped up in such a small space, we all felt a bit grimy and cranky. When Tobias said something about knowing where there might be a truck stop with shower facilities, I begged him to stop, and the others chimed in.

We were somewhere in the midst of driving through Nebraska, and I was feeling more and more like the bottom of a heavily worn shoe. Even Bert was getting cranky. Tobias insisted on staying with the Winnebago while we sent a group inside to clean up; Jonah and Bert stayed with him. The rest of us grabbed our bags, heading for whatever facilities we could find.

I enjoyed every moment of that shower. I didn't want to get out, because that meant getting back into the RV and heading back down the road again. I'd never been one for minding a long road trip. In fact, I normally liked them, but at the same time there was a serious limit to what one could handle with the high tension level, the secrets, the emotional stress, and the sheer proximity to that many people in that enclosed of a space without losing one's mind completely. I was quickly reaching my limit.

Finally, I couldn't delay any longer, so I shut off the water, and toweled off as best I could. I hadn't brought a hair dryer, opting instead for ball caps I could hide my hair under, letting it air dry to save time and packing space. I ran a brush through my hair (which was getting too long again, but nowhere near the magically induced growth of a couple of years ago), and pulled the cap on, yanking my ponytail through the hole in the back. I put on fresh clothing, and waited for Mia and Allie to finish up their own ablutions before we headed back to the camper.

As I waited, I saw something odd in a corner, underneath one of the sinks. Only the three of us were in the ladies room, and it didn't look like anything I'd brought inside with me.

"Are either of you wearing any jewelry?" I called.

Allie came out of her shower stall, her hair still wet, but fully dressed with her t-shirt clinging to her back in damp spots. "I don't own any jewelry. You know that. I've borrowed yours, but I've always given it back."

I leaned down, and there was no question; it looked like a pearl out of someone's ring or necklace. "Wonder what this is. Mia, how about you?"

She was lacing up her sneakers, almost ready to leave. "I don't own any pearls. The only jewelry I have that's really worth anything is my high school class ring, and it's got my birthstone in it; a sapphire, not a pearl, and it's right here on my hand." She held out her right hand, showing me the stone in its rightful place.

I wasn't wearing any jewelry, either. I had a strand of pearls at home which had belonged to my mother, but I never wore them. In fact, they hadn't been out of my jewelry box in years. I'd never get rid of them, but I never really had anywhere to wear them.

I wondered if the pearl was real. I decided I'd go ask the attendant.

On our way out of the showers, we stopped in the convenience store, and bought a couple of cases of pop and some chocolate and gummy bears. Doris had packed all kinds of healthy meal stuffs, but the cranky of all of us crammed on top of each other wasn't going to be fixed with a veggie tray. I wanted chocolate, damn it.

Well, what I really wanted was to know what was going on with Aiden, and to have him back, but it didn't sound like I was going to get that.

I stood in line to pay for our loot, and when we got to the front, I paid with cash, out of the money Paul had given me. The attendant was friendly, but she looked tired and frazzled. The shop was busy with traveling families, truckers, and locals making fun of the first two groups. The line was consistently long, and while we'd had the shower facilities to ourselves in the middle of the day, the regular restrooms were doing a brisk business, with a short line outside of each. I showed her the item I'd found in the restroom.

"Looks like just a rock, lady," said the attendant, a blond woman whose nametag proclaimed her to be Cynthia.

"I'm not sure it's just a rock. Has anyone reported missing a stone from a piece of jewelry? Maybe a missing stone from a ring or something?"

She barely looked at it, focusing instead on the line of customers waiting to check out. "Lady, I appreciate that you're not trying to hold up the line, but no one has reported anything, and it doesn't look all that valuable to me. If you want to ask around a bit that's fine, but there's too many people waiting for me to talk about it at the moment. Can you step aside so I can take who's next?"

I could tell she wasn't trying to be rude; she looked tired, and no wonder. She was the only one working the cash register. There was only one other employee present, and he had out a mop and bucket, heading toward the back of the store. There were probably fifteen or so people in line, and there was no way I was going to be able to get much help from her.

"Should I leave it here with you?" I asked, again trying to do what I could to get property back to someone. It looked valuable to me, and if it was real, I didn't want to just leave it on the bathroom floor or take off with it. I hated the idea someone might be looking for something like this.

"I don't want anything to do with it. We don't have a lost and found, and we don't take responsibility for anyone's personal items." She pointed to a sign behind her which proclaimed the management of the facility wanted everyone to keep their own items with them at all times and they were not responsible for any lost or stolen items. I shrugged, and stepped out of the line. She wasn't the one in charge. It wasn't worth it to make her miserable, and there was no real reason to hold up others. Instead, I worked my way down the line, asking the waiting customers if they had been in the showers, and whether they were missing any piece of their jewelry.

All of them thanked me for asking, and all of them stated they had not been in the showers or lost any jewelry. One lady specifically looked down at the rings on her hands to make sure before answering in the negative.

Mia and Allie went back to the Winnebago to allow those left behind to have their turns in the showers while I kept asking patrons.

The line finally thinned out and the lady working behind the counter took a moment to look again before turning back to the cash register tape that needed to be replenished.

"Look, lady," she said. "You've gone over and beyond makin' sure nothing happened. I'm not allowed to hold items from customers; they're real strict about that. If you want, though, I can take your phone number and if anyone comes in looking, I can pass it on."

I thought about it. Maybe that was a good idea. I gave her the house phone number, back in Dayton; remembering Tobias's discussion about the safety of a landline over the safety of a cell phone. My cell phone was in my pocket, but it was turned off, like all our cell phones, to prevent a magical bad guy from finding someone who could use GPS to track our movements and come after us. We'd call Doris on a regular basis, anyway, so I figured it would be better to leave a phone number of someone who might actually answer their phone. Tobias, Mia, and Allie left to find a payphone to give Doris a heads up that she might get this phone call, and some of the others took the opportunity to stretch their legs before we loaded back up in the Winnebago.

My good deed done for the day, I headed back, feeling slightly better, and definitely more cheerful after removing the outer grime layer. The Winnebago had been parked at the far corner of the parking lot, and just beside the edge of the pavement was a chicken coop and enclosure. Jane was waiting outside, clucking under her breath softly to the chickens on the other side of the fence. A big rooster was in the back of the pen, watching her warily, as she cooed and clicked at the chickens who reached their beaks toward her as if she was about to feed them.

"Jane?" I asked. "How are you doing?"

She looked back over her shoulder at me. "I'm doin'. I guess I don't rightly know why I'm here, or what I'm a'sposed to do, but I sure do feel bad for that Paul feller. He talked about his ox like he's a dog though. You know that?"

I nodded. "I know that. But he's pretty close to Babe. I get it. I wouldn't want to see an animal hurt, whether it was a dog, a cat, or an ox, if I could help it."

She nodded. "What about people?"

I didn't follow, and I told her so.

"What if you had to choose between an animal and a person? Which would you choose?" she asked.

I felt a presence behind me, and I didn't know who it was, but I decided it would be smart to be safe, rather than sorry. "I don't know, Jane. I think it depends on the situation. If it's a difference between a small child and an aggressive dog, that's different than a loving animal and a mean man who is picking on that animal. I wish I could give you a good answer on that, I really do."

"Good answer," said Paul, behind me.

I was glad I'd been diplomatic, but before I could pat myself on the back for not sticking my foot in my mouth, I heard yelling and shouting from behind the camper that had me running.

"Help, someone, help! It's got me!"

I looked around and I didn't see anything, but I knew I'd heard it.

There was a scuffle and a cry, and I heard a struggle, before I heard an odd laugh, coming from somewhere near the ground.

I looked down, and heard the voice again, yelling.

"Help me! It's dragging me away!"

I knew that voice. It belonged to a certain frog.

Aw, crap. What had he gotten into this time?

CHAPTER TWENTY-TWO

Some kind of creature had grabbed Bert by the foot and was trying to drag him off into the brush. I reached down and grabbed Bert's other foot, trying to drag him back.

"Ow, ow, ow! I'm not a freaking wishbone! You're pulling me apart!" he yelled, as the furry little thing didn't let go, and yanked harder on his leg.

I reached out with my other hand, grabbing him around his waist, and yanked, hard, digging my heels into the dirt to pull him away.

Was that seriously a rabbit with antlers? It turned to look at me and snarled, growling as it reached out at me and swiped its front claws. I took advantage of the swing to yank Bert out of its grasp, and staggered backward with the leverage I'd used to pull him away. I ended up falling on my rear end, Bert in my lap, and the furry antlered scary looking thing hissed and charged at me.

"Get lost!" Aiden yelled, jumping over my shoulder and swinging the metal club.

I ducked my head, narrowly avoiding getting whacked in the head as he swung. Leave it to Aiden to make the big gesture and leave someone with a concussion, or almost a concussion, anyway. I smiled as I leaned sideways again, staying on the move to keep my head out of the way. The furry thing hopped sideways, just missing getting whacked with the club.

Aiden lost his own balance as he swung and missed, but kept his feet, and didn't drop the club. That was a step up for him, with his normal clumsiness almost guaranteeing that someone would get hurt by the end of the day. I was glad not to have that metal club upside of my head, but I also was glad that whatever that thing was, it wasn't going to drag Bert away.

The furry frog-napper slid into the grass on the side of the road, away from where the Winnebago was parked at the far end of the parking lot. There wasn't anything behind where the parking lot pavement met grass, other than more grass and a wide open lot that went on for miles. The chicken coop that had fascinated Jane was at the front of the Winnebago, in the opposite direction, and not blocking any view of the nothingness that went on behind where Bert's attacker had disappeared. We were truly out in the middle of nowhere. I watched for a while, making sure that thing was really gone, before scooping up Bert and heading back around to go inside the Winnebago.

I could see why Bert had decided to get out of the Winnebago and get some fresh air where he didn't have to worry about someone seeing him and flipping out about the big frog, or catching him doing something distinctively human and potentially exposing magic to unsuspecting humans. He was always very careful not to do anything (or say anything) that would destroy the illusion that real life was mundane and not magical, because humans just don't generally understand magic. The F.A.B.L.E.S. organization, and Aiden, had both told me that human military, police, and government just wouldn't understand how to handle a magical threat, and the fallout from handling it badly would be devastating. The magical world didn't want to be exposed, because the small amount of interaction they had would be impossible if humans knew how to protect themselves from magic. It would fundamentally change how the world worked.

Would one talking, beer drinking, NASCAR-loving frog be enough to expose it? I didn't know, but Bert always said he didn't want to take the chance. I wondered how much that cost him, though, in human interaction; because regardless of the curse that kept him in a frog's body, he was still a human at heart. And he had a normal human's need for interaction with others, for feeling needed and wanted and loved. I hoped his budding friendship and potential involvement with Allie was helping with that; he seemed less depressed lately than normal. I wondered how much this incident would set him back.

I set him on the table. His leg, the one the antlered rabid rabbit had grabbed, was raw and bleeding. Without a word, I pulled the first aid kit Aiden had packed before we'd left home out from under the sink in the kitchenette, and found a skinny roll of gauze that would work for a loose bandage. I found some antibacterial ointment, and insisted on dabbing some onto the raw open spots on his leg before wrapping the gauze a couple of times around his leg.

He put up with my doctoring without much comment, and stared off into space, barely wincing when the ointment touched his sore skin. He stared out the window as Aiden stood outside the door, watching for the others to come back and talking to Paul while giving me the time to get Bert cleaned up before Allie could get inside and see him. Not much I could do about the scrapes, but I was able to get the dirt wiped up. It didn't make it look much better, but all of the scrapes and rough spots gave him a rather rakish and tough guy exterior look.

I smiled at him. "Chicks dig scars."

He laughed.

That was the point, so I smiled back at him again. "Let her fuss over you. Stay in the Winnebago if you're alone; don't go outside by yourself while we're here. Do you know what that thing was?"

He shook his head. "Paul might, or Jane. I've never been west of Minnesota. I found people that made me happy in Ohio, and I stuck around. I've never dealt with anything involved in non-European tradition faerie courts or outside of the realms we've already dealt with. I've never had much to do with American tall tales or Wild West folklore other than what magic Paul uses to not be enormous. I should have realized there was more out there, but I just didn't, until he showed up at your house. I'm sorry, Janie. If I'd thought about it, maybe I'd have asked more questions. "

"Bert," I said. "You live there. It's your house, too."

"Call me old fashioned, but I don't feel like it's mine unless I pull my own weight, and I don't feel like I do."

I started to protest, but he shushed me pretty quick.

"Look, I know there are things I contribute to, but it's nowhere near enough to call me self-supporting. If you were to ask me to buy the groceries, I couldn't do it. Ask me to do the laundry? I can't reach the knobs and switches, much less haul the baskets and fold the clothing. If you ask me to cook dinner, I can't do it. I can't even get a skillet out of the cabinet without help. I can't hit the button on the security system panel in the hallway; it's too tall. I know there are times you guys let me do what I can do, even if you could do it faster, and I appreciate it, but how'm I supposed to let Allie get attached to me when I can't support her?"

I crossed my arms over my chest. "You think that's what life and love is all about? That you can't be happy unless you can support the woman you love financially? Are you nuts?"

He opened his mouth, closed it again, then opened it to answer. "Of course it is. That's the way it was with my parents, with my brothers. Look at Doris and Geoffrey. They couldn't keep it together because he couldn't work enough to support her in the human realm. Look at what Aiden's doing. You think he *wants* to work in a factory?"

I seized on the last part of his statement. "Bert, you're nuts. Aiden working in that factory has nothing to do with a relationship; as far as I know, he's not in one. His mom isn't worried about money, she wants him to get his own brain on straight, and whether we are together or not, I do, too. Doris and Geoffrey couldn't keep it together for lots of reasons, not just about whether or not he was working or supporting her. You're going to have to learn that women in today's world don't think like that. I don't think like that, and Allie's lived in this world long enough to think the way we do as well. She's used to fending for herself, and she's done incredibly well doing it. She will go on doing that no matter what you're doing. As I will. As Mia would, if she wasn't with Jonah. Doris did the same, and it looks like she and Harold are getting closer, but it's not about whether he can support her financially."

Bert looked at me skeptically. "Then what do women want? If they don't want a provider anymore, what's a man, or a frog, supposed to do? What else are we good for?"

How was I giving him relationship advice? "Bert, women want men who support them emotionally; who are there to hug them and hold them when life gets stupid. They want men who aren't afraid to let them go their own way, to let them reach for their own dreams. If Allie came to you tomorrow and told you she was going to be an actress, and she had just landed a role in a movie paying her millions of dollars, would you feel threatened because she was making more money than you were? Just because she makes more money than you doesn't mean she needs you any less. And bringing in less money isn't the issue, if you aren't just mooching off of someone. You're not. You do help. And you help to the best of your ability."

"How am I supposed to show her I love her if I'm not doing things to provide for her? If she doesn't need me, then why is she with me?" he wailed. "And 'the best of my ability' kinda sucks."

"What are you going to do about your ability, Bert? You became human once, and you traded away all kinds of things we wouldn't have agreed to because you wanted it. I'm sorry to be blunt about it, but Bert, we know what you can and can't do, and no one holds it against you. Would it be any different if you were in a wheelchair, or if you were seriously injured? You contribute what you are able to. No one expects you to do things you're physically incapable of doing.

"Why is she with you? Because she loves you, for you. She loves how you talk to her. She loves how you support what she feels is necessary. You see, when you were human, at least the first time, there were very defined gender roles; because there had to be. Men went out and did the hunting because it was dangerous, and women were more vulnerable because they were pregnant or needed for breastfeeding, or for caring for really small kids. Now, it's different. Those are things that both parents can do. So men can do things other than just providing for a family. They can chase their own dreams, and care for their families rather than just hunting down buffalo; they don't have to be pigeonholed. Women can, too.

"You have to talk to her. You have to figure out what she wants out of a relationship, because it looks to me like you're already in one. You have to figure out what works for the two of you, in a world that doesn't require day to day struggles just to continue the human genome." I rubbed my hands over my face. "I sure didn't mean to get philosophical, but it's true. She does need you; *you,* not just what you can provide. It's not about just opening jars and grabbing the stuff from the top shelf."

He wrinkled up his nose a bit. "Not quite sure how to handle that one."

"Then ask her." I looked out the window, seeing Aiden stare right back at me. The walls of the Winnebago weren't exactly sound proofed. He'd probably heard every word of that conversation, and I wasn't sure what to say about it. It probably sounded like I'd been on a soapbox. I didn't care. It was true. I hoped he hadn't gone to the factory just to show he was capable of supporting a wife. But did that mean he had a new girlfriend? As much as I was all about partnership in relationships, not everyone was. Did he have a new girl in his life that wanted him to support her? Was that what he was leading up to talking to me about? I could put him off with the best of them. I resolved to keep finding ways out of the relationship conversation until this trip was over. This might be the last such trip we got to make together. I was going to enjoy whatever I could of it.

Allie wasn't far away, heading back to the Winnebago with Tobias and Mia after calling Doris to inform her of the clerk having the phone number to call about any messages regarding a lost pearl. She was laughing, her long blond hair straight down the middle of her back, still slightly damp from the shower. She looked young; something I hadn't thought I'd see. She'd always seemed so much older than her actual age. Then again, with everything she'd been through, it was no wonder she looked more mature than she was.

Aiden caught her on her way to the Winnebago. I watched them talking through the window, but I couldn't hear what they said. It sounded like the garbled voice of an adult in the Peanuts cartoons, the "whah-wu-whah-whah" of speech with meaning. I had the sudden irreverent thought hearing it like that meant I was Lucy, and I didn't like that idea, although maybe I did need a sign that read "Psychiatric Help 5¢".

I just hoped no one was going to pull the football out from under us as we tried to figure out the puzzle of what was after us, how to rescue Babe, and how to keep Jonah safe throughout.

CHAPTER TWENTY-THREE

Doris hadn't been home at the time, and they had left voicemails both at my house and at her own. I wondered if she was at her catering event, the one whose food she'd brought to my house. At the thought of food, my stomach growled, and I stumbled over a number of bodies to get to the kitchenette and dig out the large platter of sandwiches she'd convinced us to take. If nothing else, a good sandwich would fill the stomach and we wouldn't have dishes to do later. There was no dishwasher in the Winnebago, and I had a funny feeling no one would want to do dishes later, when we finally got to where we were going. Until we hooked up to a water source, such as at a campground, there wasn't much water to use.

I knew I didn't want to wash them.

I passed the sandwiches around, feeling Aiden's eyes on me the whole time. I tried to ignore it. Allie was, as predicted, fussing over Bert, and treating him as some wounded warrior, taking one for the team. Paul was smiling again, and making comments about being happy he'd hired us. Was it because Aiden and I had jumped in to save Bert? Because of my comments to Jane? I didn't know.

Jane, on the other hand, acted less and less scared at the movement of the Winnebago. She shoveled food into her mouth, but didn't let it stop the conversation as she asked about Bert's injuries and our research. She wanted to know more and more about what we were doing, and was coming uncomfortably close to figuring out Jonah was the person we were protecting. I wasn't sure I wanted Paul in on that one just yet. I liked that he seemed more confident in us, but I still was worried he'd find a way to get Jonah away from us and take his chances, and the closer we got to Utah, the easier it would be for Paul to do exactly that. I think Jane finally got the hint. She stopped asking questions when the answers got shorter and shorter, and started asking more about the food we'd brought. She was hungry. I wondered how much of that was because we hadn't given her alcohol with her lunch.

Aiden, on the other hand, wasn't really taking part in the discussions of the group. He sat in the front seat of the Winnebago, looking at maps. While Tobias drove, the conversation in the back kept going about whether mayonnaise or mustard was the right condiment to go with turkey and swiss, or on roast beef on rye. Aiden and Tobias didn't talk much, other than a word or two about direction, or the next highway exit. I offered them both sandwiches, which they took without saying much of anything. Tobias asked for a Coke, and the others passed it up from the refrigerator.

"Anything else?" I asked. "Tobias, I'm sure one of us could drive if you needed or wanted a break at some point. You don't need a special license to drive this thing, do you?"

He chuckled. "No, you don't, but I'm used to it, and you guys aren't. It's no big deal. I'll say something if I get tired, but I feel pretty good behind the wheel of this thing. I've spent a lot of years doing this, and doing it alone. I rather like the distraction of listening to the conversation, regardless of the topic, rather than being stuck with my own mopey thoughts."

I guess I hadn't expected him to use the word 'mopey', but I got what he meant. It had to be lonely, on the road, not knowing for sure if your family was safe, but knowing they were probably safer with him on the road, away from them. He had to know being on the road was hurting his relationship with his daughter, but how much worse would it have been if he'd stayed behind and something had happened to her? How hard of a life was that? And yet, he and Mia had been piecing together what they could of a father-daughter bond, given the decisions he had made to keep them safe by his absence.

I wondered if I'd have been able to make the same decision.

I sat down on the couch next to Allie, who had Bert in her lap. The frog was sound asleep, probably the best thing he could do at the moment, giving his battered body a chance to recover and relax. She looked at me, and mouthed the word, "Thanks."

I grinned at her, and looked up at the rest of the group. Jonah had asked if anyone minded him taking a nap in the bed, since he'd slept on the floor of the camper the night before, and Mia had gone with him. From the snores coming from the back room, they really were sleeping. Jonah probably had a deviated septum or sleep apnea or something, because he snored like a diesel engine, grumbling and whistling as he slept. I didn't know how Mia slept through it, but she had to be used to it. He slept at our house a couple of times a week, depending on his stage schedule and her study schedule. It wasn't the first time I'd heard his whistling rumble. This time, though, it reassured me. It was something normal and very Jonah.

Pete and Paul were trying to join into a card game Jane was goading them into. It looked like some rowdy form of slapjack they were trying, and failing, to keep quiet enough to let people sleep. It didn't matter how loud they got, though; Mia and Jonah couldn't hear the game over Jonah's snores, and Bert was just wiped enough to crash through it. I think a dump truck could have plowed through the Winnebago parked at a nitroglycerin plant and Bert would have slept through the whole thing.

All of a sudden, I had a thought.

What if the ox-napper we were driving cross country to meet wasn't going to kill Jonah for any "crimes" committed by Johnny Appleseed? I wondered, suddenly, if there was an angle that I was missing in all this. We were assuming they meant him harm, as opposed to just wanting him to do some bit of magic for them. Or maybe there was another angle.

A line out of the biography I'd been reading jumped out in my brain. The apples from Johnny Appleseed's trees actually weren't all that great for eating. I remembered reading he was very religious, very into charity and animal welfare. We'd learned at the museum he followed the Swedenborgian church, and their beliefs weren't about accumulating material things.

The apples his trees produced were small and tart, and not edible. They were, on the other hand, perfect for making alcoholic beverages, and Chapman had gained his huge tracts of land before his death by planting and maintaining those orchards. Those trees had made him a rich man. How much more materialistic could one be than accumulating vast tracts of land?

So was this about the alcohol? Plenty of teetotalers had been angry and insistent over the spread of alcohol throughout our country.

I remembered something about the Whisky Rebellion, moonshine, Prohibition, Carrie Nation, with her axe, chopping up barrels and barrels of alcohol as if this was the answer to all of society's ills; as if preventing people from having a drink would magically make everyone happy and industrious and perfectly Christian, regardless of their own personal beliefs or thoughts.

Or was this something even more sinister? Was it about something more simple than the spreading of alcoholic beverages and distillation with the word of God? Was it about the land itself? Was it something about the land? Had Chapman used his trees to keep it out of someone else's hands? Was it a way he could prevent something magical from taking root in America, like faerie magic had entwined so much in European legends and fairy tales?

I didn't have a good answer, but I was starting to think I was on the right track.

So who—or what—would have been that mad at a man who had spent most of his life nurturing plants and animals and people, and telling stories to children, spreading his religious beliefs and talking about the simple life, the life he lived on his own, without imposing on anyone else?

There was a piece I was missing somewhere, I was sure of it. But where would I find out?

I didn't have a good answer. Instead, I watched the road go by in a wheat field haze, with very little breaking up the view. A farm house here, a barn there, otherwise, nothing but wheat fields, end to end.

The card game finally quieted down, and I lent my mp3 player to Pete, who said he'd used one before. Luckily, the ear buds I had in my backpack were long enough that Pete and Paul could each use one. Pete began playing disc jockey to his brother's ears, which weren't used to the kind of music I listened to for studying; Celtic rock and heavy metal were my go-tos. Apparently Paul hadn't heard popular music in a number of years; he'd asked what Elvis was up to lately. He was heartbroken to her that The King was dead, and had been before I'd even been born.

I never would have thought of Paul Bunyan as an Elvis Presley fan.

And then I heard a noise.

"Hold on!" I heard Tobias yell.

I grabbed the side of the couch, and held on as Tobias hit the brakes, sliding us into a stop as the brakes squealed and I heard two thumps coming from the back of the Winnebago.

CHAPTER TWENTY-FOUR

A few more bumps and bruises, the Winnebago's inhabitants were none the worse for wear, but the RV had a monster of a flat tire.

Luckily, we were right in front of a campground, where we could pull in, find a phone Tobias felt comfortable using, and set up for the night. There were shower facilities available for the morning, grills available near each campsite, and a crusty old guy running the place who reminded me a lot of Quint from *Jaws,* the boat captain who whistled at Brody and Hooper when he thought they were nuts. The guy had a big four wheel drive truck with enough horsepower to pull the Winnebago into the closest empty campsite. He was willing to drive Tobias into town to find a payphone and a tire dealer who might be able to either patch the tire or replace it so we could back on the road as soon as possible. Aiden and Jonah went with him. They rode in the back of the truck, planning on a few odds and ends to cook a decent dinner on the grill outside, and to stock up on extra salt. The rest of us began making plans to spend the night at the campground, giving everyone a chance to get a good night's sleep before we hit the road again fresh in the morning.

Luckily, the campsite we had didn't face anyone else. The place wasn't that crowded, and people weren't hanging out much in the common area of the park. It was on the chilly side, but we put on extra layers and piled out of the Winnebago, glad for the opportunity to stretch legs and try to put the place back to rights. Ten beings in a camper did not make for a fun drive. We were all crammed in on top of each other, with all of the stuff we'd brought making it an even tighter squeeze. Mia and I put together the tent, while Allie and Bert tried to make sense of the printed directions in the fading sunlight. It started to get dark, but it wasn't downright cold. We had sweatshirts and even jackets along, and moving kept the blood pumping, so we weren't thinking about the cold.

Jane and Paul and Pete weren't much help, making suggestions about the tent. None of them had ever put one up before. Mia and I weren't exactly experts, since neither of us had been camping in the last ten years, but we at least had some semblance of a clue of how it would go together. It ended up being a fairly large tent, with two sleeping areas. We set the sleeping bags up inside and had the tent secure by the time the guys got back with charcoal and lighter fluid, hot dogs and chicken breasts and buns, and condiments, for a quick and easy dinner. Jonah grinned as he opened a bag with corn on the cob and parmesan cheese and butter. Aiden had picked up the makings for s'mores: graham crackers and Hershey bars and jumbo marshmallows. Tobias had decided we all could use a night to relax, and had picked up a case of beer and a couple of bottles of wine for those of us who weren't beer drinkers.

They hadn't forgotten the supplies we'd need to make sure our campsite was completely secure. They'd bought out the store when it came to salt and had found a couple of containers of cheap thumbtacks. Allie and Jane began the circle of salt around the Winnebago, going far enough around us to include the picnic table at the campsite and the tent we'd set up, to give us all a bit more breathing room through the night to sleep.

The charcoal was lit, and heating up the grill. Tobias and Jonah left to straighten up the Winnebago, especially in the bedroom where Jonah and Mia had been hurled out of the bed and knocked over items that had previously been tossed there to get them out of the way. Paul was given the task of grilling hot dogs, something he was enthusiastic to learn, and Jane stood next to him, expertly cooking the chicken breasts.

"I cooked over a fire a'plenty in my time," she said. "Ain't anythin' new ta me. Don't know what you're doin' with those white things but we can cook meat on a fire anytime."

Aiden and Mia took charge of cleaning the corn and putting them on the grill. They'd decided to use cheap wooden skewers to spear the cobs and make it easier to grill them, butter them, sprinkle the cheese, then eat them. It was a good thing they'd gotten paper towels as well; as much as we'd made this a fairly dish-free dinner, we couldn't help the melted butter from getting on hands and faces.

The corn was perfect; the hot dogs and chicken on buns with ketchup and mustard weren't exactly gourmet, but I couldn't have asked for better at the moment. Plastic cups went around with cheap white wine, and Tobias shared around cans of beer. If an outside observer were to see us all sitting in folding lawn chairs and at the picnic table, seated on blankets in front of the Winnebago, and fussing with the tent, the grill, and passing around drinks, they would think it just a group of friends on a late fall camping trip—not a group of worried people running to save someone or something from magical danger.

I wasn't a big drinker, but I accepted a full cup of wine anyway. I figured it would help me to sleep. I hadn't slept well lately, and I didn't just mean the last night or two in the Winnebago. I hadn't been sleeping well since Aiden moved out. I watched him as he cleaned up the grilling supplies and packed away the leftover meat and buns for lunch on the road. He used the remaining skewers to start roasting marshmallows over what was left of the fire in the grill.

Jane and Paul had never eaten s'mores and they dug into them in earnest, the sticky white marshmallow all over Jane's face; a smear of chocolate on Paul's cheek. Pete was having way too much fun laughing at his brother enjoying the almost-too-sweet snack. He'd had them a few years ago in a lumber camp when one of the other loggers had enjoyed a visit from his daughters. Pete told a story about the little girls with marshmallow in their hair and everyone laughed.

"So, Janie, did you eat s'mores as a little girl?" Paul asked, with a grin on his face.

"I think so," I said. "I remember camping with my dad from time to time, but I don't remember a lot of details. Little things come back from time to time though, the longer I'm away from my stepmother. She used to try to suppress my memory so she could hurt us more. I'm still working on it. But I don't remember the first time I had s'mores. Either I was too little to remember, which was before Evangeline married Dad, or I'd had them enough at camp when I was a kid to not remember when I'd first seen them. Either way, they always make me smile."

Paul's grin faded slightly. "I'm sorry. I didn't mean to bring up bad memories."

"It's okay, Paul. Memories of my dad are good memories. Memories of camp are as well. The tent was Dad's; which is part of what makes me think I did some of this as a kid. Those aren't bad things. And I keep remembering things I didn't realize I knew. Time keeps healing those old wounds. I keep wondering what Dad would think of all this. I think he'd be in his element, once he wrapped his head around it, but you'd have to be firm with him, or he'd be asking questions about all kinds of things, forgetting you weren't a subject of his research, rather than a person who had a goal and a plan."

I sipped the wine. It wasn't something I drank a lot of, but it helped to dull the chill of the evening, and I really didn't want to go inside the Winnebago any earlier than I had to. I was feeling a bit relaxed, my stomach full, the wine making me warm and somewhat sleepy, the sugar in the s'mores making me a bit sick, but in a pleasant way, reminding me of childhood and campfires and Dad.

I noticed Paul and Jane starting to get chummy; he put his arm around her shoulders and she didn't yank away or act like the gesture was unwelcome. Bert was perched on the picnic table, with a thick towel over and around him; as a frog he was cold-blooded, and didn't have the ability to keep himself warm outside like the rest of us. Allie didn't have any of the alcohol, but her eyes were drooping. Tobias was nursing a beer while keeping a fatherly eye on Mia. She stood, with Jonah's arms around her waist, laughing and joking and telling stories about our teenaged escapades. Aiden listened while he cleaned up the remnants of our dinner.

We were all relaxed and full, lulled into complacency by the security of a salt circle and a good dinner, good company and good times. Several of the antlered rabbit things were just on the other side of the salt circle, growling and hissing. Bert saw them first.

"Get inside! They're back!" he yelled. "Allie, get me inside. I'm not going to be their midnight snack!"

I could see why he was panicking, but they weren't crossing the salt. Allie took him inside, putting him on the kitchenette table where he could see out the window, but where he couldn't be at risk for the rabbit things to grab him again. Tobias stood at the ready with the metal club Aiden had used earlier, ready to swing if they crossed the salt, as the rest of us packed up the tent and the rest of our belongings that were outside of the Winnebago. So much for having some extra room for sleeping inside of the camper, we'd all be crammed inside again tonight, with one extra since Jane was with us now.

Now that Tobias had had a chance to see the antlered rabbit thingys that had grabbed Bert earlier, he had a name for them. "Those are jackalopes," he said. "I've never seen them so angry. I've never seen them attack before. I wonder what's caused them to act this way."

"What are they?" I asked.

"Well, it's a cross between a jackrabbit and an antelope. They normally are shy, but, wait . . . I've got an idea," he said, shoving the club into my hands and running inside. He came back out a moment or two later with a plastic cup, a bottle of whisky, and a pair of scissors, cutting the top of the plastic cup off so that the cup only stood about an inch from the bottom. He poured some whisky in the cup, and set it on the other side of the salt line, just a couple of yards from where the jackalopes were hissing and growling at him. They immediately stopped growling and hopped over to the cup, fighting between them to get at the whiskey. As they fought, he cut the top off three more cups, pouring about a shot's worth of whiskey in each, and setting them just on the other side of the salt line, careful not to smudge the line as he did so. That would negate the salt line that seemed to be keeping the jackalopes out, which told me that they were either sensitive to salt, or magic, or both.

While the jackalopes were entertained by the multiple cups of whiskey, we took a moment to watch them. "Obviously, we can't just all go to bed. Someone needs to be watching to sound the alarm if they try to get through the salt line, and I think none of us will sleep unless we have some assurance we're not completely vulnerable. Bert isn't going to sleep with them out here, I'm sure, but he's hurt; he shouldn't be out here on watch," I said.

"Agreed," Tobias said. "I'll take first watch."

"No, you won't," I said. "You've done all the driving, all the details for the tire, for dinner, for all of that. You need sleep more than anyone, especially if you're not sharing the driving. Don't get me wrong, I appreciate it. I have no idea how to drive something like this without leaving the side mirrors scraped off on some road sign on the side of the road. But if you're doing that much driving, you need to take the break, close your eyes, and sleep. We can take watch, and sleep while you're driving in the morning. That's the way it needs to be."

Aiden concurred, and Mia stepped in as well. "Dad, you are incredible when it comes to getting through an emergency. But that doesn't help if you're too tired when we get to where we have to go. We're still way ahead of schedule. We can't go anywhere until we get a new tire in the morning. You've got to get some sleep."

In the face of all of our insistence, he gave in. Mia and I took first watch, insisting that Jonah and Aiden take our forward bunk, above the driver's head in the Winnebago, as Aiden had slept sitting up the night before and Jonah had slept on the floor. It took some argument to get them to agree, but we were insistent, and Aiden started yawning. They gave in slowly, but I could see the tired in their eyes as they went.

That left me and my best friend, Mia, teamed up against the jackalopes in the parking lot and any other magical mayhem that might be coming our way.

The way I was feeling at the moment, I almost hoped something would show up. I was ready to do battle against something tangible, rather than the relationship issues or the unknowing research that sent me round and round and round with no answers, only more questions.

I just wanted to yell to the skies, to whatever magical deity or being was out there.

Bring it.

CHAPTER TWENTY-FIVE

Of course that kick-butt-take-no-prisoners attitude didn't last long when nothing happened.

There was a limit to how long either of us could sit there waiting for an attack or a magical emergency keyed up and ready for battle when there was no battle to be fought.

Even the jackalopes melted off into the woods behind the campgrounds after getting their fill of whiskey, and didn't hiss or growl anymore. Nice to know whiskey had that effect on them; sure wish I'd known that when one had attacked Bert; but at the same time, Tobias hadn't been standing there to tell us what it was, or what to do. I was glad we had an answer now. We'd have to stock up on whiskey.

The rest of our crew settled down in the camper, although I was sure they weren't all asleep yet. I did hear the heavy snores from Jonah, and shook my head. "That man so needs to go to a doctor to see why he snores like that."

Mia grinned at me. "I'm used to it; but you're right. I bet he'd sleep better if there's a medical reason to be treated. Even if he had to wear one of those crazy masks to sleep with, I think he'd do better that way."

I knew Jonah was probably putting off getting checked out for money reasons, and I understood that. I'd fought my way through bronchitis last year with hot tea and honey because I didn't want to spend the money at the doctor's office and the pharmacy. I probably wouldn't have needed that trip to urgent care, but I'd thought it was just a bad cold at first. We laughed at it, and agreed we were getting older and needed to take better care of ourselves. Yeah, we'd figured that one out at the ripe old age of twenty-five. That didn't make it any less true.

There wasn't a lot of light outside; just what came from the street lights in the campground, lighting the walkways between the campers and buses so people getting up in the middle of the night to use the restrooms would be able to see where they were going. There was still some light in some of the campers, but not the ones closest to us, and those added just a soft glow to the poles and trees around them. It was peaceful sitting on the picnic table with Mia. I wished it were under better circumstances.

"So, Janie," she said, as the Winnebago quieted down, any sounds inside muffled by the chainsaw buzz of Jonah's snoring, mixed with the sounds of everyone else falling asleep. "Alone at last and with a white noise muffler, maybe we can finally talk about all of this." Apparently Jonah wasn't the only snorer; but he sure was the loudest and most distinctive. There was no way anyone inside would overhear our conversation over that racket.

I winced. "I'm really sorry you found out about Jonah that way, Mia. I should have told you. He should have told you. I'm sorry you were in the dark."

She gave me a sideways glance, telling me that my mea culpa wasn't wrong. "You shoulda, he shoulda, but the fact remains I didn't know. It makes a lot of sense now, some of the things he'd say or do, and it definitely makes some sense why he was acting a little weird when the Seawitch was around. He says he was afraid he'd be blamed since he had some magic, and he went out of his way to stay away from anything that could bring out his abilities so he wouldn't look bad. It makes me wonder what else he might be capable of, that he's hiding from himself. And yeah, you should have said something, but that's not where I was going with this conversation, either. I meant to ask if you knew what Aiden wanted to talk to you about."

I really didn't want to hash out the emotional crap now, while I still had time to spend with him. I was starting to wonder if I would see him ever again after this trip. He'd made himself fairly scarce here lately, hadn't even tried to restart the conversation we had started in the kitchen just days ago, where he'd asked about magic and whether we'd have had a relationship without it. She hadn't been there for that conversation, and I hadn't had time to fill her in. I did now, giving her the highlights.

"So, I'm pretty sure he's trying to move on with his life," I told her. "I'm trying to make the best of it, but if I'm right, then I may only have a few days left with the old Aiden on this trip before we all get back home. I'd like to enjoy the illusion that it's not the end."

She started to say something but I heard a noise out in the woods just beyond the campground. "What was that?" she asked.

It wasn't an animal. It was wind. A lot of wind. It sounded like a freight train off in the distance, and the wind was picking up, heading our way.

"Yeehaw!" I heard, in the background.

What the hell?

Some guy wearing a big broad cowboy hat, leather chaps, and honest-to-goodness boots with spurs that jangled ran right between the wind and the Winnebago, yelling at me to get everyone up and out of the camper. Mia ran inside, and I was on her heels, shaking everyone awake and yelling for them to get out of the camper and outside. People weren't exactly moving fast, but when they got awake enough to hear the urgency in our voices they moved outside pretty quickly. Allie grabbed Bert from the table and wrapped him in a kitchen towel before he could protest much. Aiden had stripped off his t-shirt to sleep, and I was distracted by him shirtless as he came outside to face whatever was going on.

Jonah wasn't wearing shoes. Tobias had on a pair of wire-rimmed glasses that I didn't remember him wearing on a regular basis. He probably wore contacts during the day and had taken them out to get the good night's sleep I'd insisted on.

Paul and Pete came stumbling out last, since they'd taken over the bedroom again.

"Bill?" Paul said, as if he knew the man in the cowboy gear.

"Hang on, cowpokes, this one's a doozy!" The man he'd called Bill took a lasso from around his own waist and started to twirl it over his head, as if he was about to rope a wayward calf. The only thing that picture was lacking was a true cow pony, a horse trained to ride into the fray under someone doing a serious John Wayne impression.

I felt the wind starting to lift my hair, and the dirt from the ground around us started to lift, scattering. "The salt!" I yelled. "How do we protect the salt circle if it all gets blown away?"

"Nothing we can do about that!" Tobias hollered back. "It's a tornado. The Winnebago can't outrun it with a bum tire, and I don't see a storm shelter anywhere nearby. If that's who I think it is, he might be able to handle it."

"Who is it?" Aiden called. "I don't recognize him from any of our books."

"It's Pecos Bill. He's lassoed twisters before. Looks like he's trying to do it again." Tobias shouted. "Watch."

He was right. Bill twirled the lasso above his head, and tossed it up in the sky, high enough to float in the air above the trees. It must have caught on something, because he dug in his heels and started to yank it down, wrapping the rope around his hand and arm to get some leverage. "Grab hold on my waist, y'all! It's a whopper of a breeze!" Bill called to the rest of us.

We ran to do as he asked, grabbing him around the waist and arms and shoulders, but being careful to keep his hands free to hold the rope. At one point, the wind started to lift him off his feet, and we all yanked backwards, keeping him from blowing away with the . . . wait, did they say *twister?* He was trying to lasso a freaking tornado?

Well, our salt line was toast. It had to be the salt stinging my cheeks as we held on tight. The Winnebago started to slide sideways with the force of the wind, and I felt wetness on my cheeks. Rain could sometimes accompany a tornado; or be part of the lead-up to one touching down. I'd grown up in Ohio, where we'd learned about tornados and sirens and storm shelters and the warning signs and symptoms as part of life. Ohio didn't get as many tornados as Nebraska and Kansas, the areas we were traveling through, but at the same time, I'd never actually seen one in person. Ohio was prone to them, so all children learned how to take shelter, and we'd hear of them from time to time. A town not twenty minutes from the house I'd grown up in was hit more than once by major tornadoes, but I'd never heard of one in Ohio that was anywhere near what I was looking at in the skies above the campground.

This was the biggest, nastiest, messiest pattern of wind I'd ever seen. It looked like something I'd have remembered from the Wizard of Oz.

We didn't have time for the house to blow away and hope it

landed on whatever witch or wizard or bad guy was involved. We didn't have transportation without the Winnebago. We didn't have a balloon or ruby slippers, and as much as I'd really like to sleep in my own bed sooner or later, clicking my heels wasn't going to wipe all this away and get me there.

Bill seemed to be getting some control over the wind, which started to die down as he reeled in his lasso. Tobias's glasses had been blown off, and Bert was yelling, all zipped up inside Allie's hoodie, so he wouldn't get blown away.

The wind gradually decreased, and the weather started to calm. It took several minutes before we could let go of Bill and he continued to draw in the tail of the tornado, pulling it down to where he might be able to contain it better. He continued to use brute strength to keep the twister from gaining more wind power, and it ended up collapsing in on itself, losing strength and finally petering out as he drew it down.

When the wind finally stopped, we were all a disheveled mess. Tobias found his mangled glasses about thirty feet from where Pecos Bill had stood, reeling in the storm. Aiden had small scrapes on his chest from the salt flying; all of us had similar scrapes on our cheeks.

"Well, y'all sure do know how to throw a party," Bill stated, with an aw-shucks grin on his face.

Jane looked up at the familiar cadence in his speech, and I think, from her expression, she was hoping it was her old friend Bill, but her face fell when she realized it was not the Wild Bill Hickock of her memories. She fled inside the Winnebago, and Paul went after her. Pete wasn't far behind his brother, making some noise about making sure things got picked up inside. I had a sneaking suspicion he knew Paul was getting attached to Jane and was concerned enough as a brother to check on them, to make sure he was okay.

I was somewhat jealous of the sibling relationship, since I'd never had one, and then I realized Mia had done almost the exact same thing for me earlier, just before the storm hit. She'd checked on me, hadn't judged me, and made sure I knew she was there for me no matter what. It meant a lot.

But no matter how much we all meant to each other, we needed to make sure we knew what was going on, and why more and more figures out of America's tall tales were showing up.

There was only so much room in the Winnebago, and if Pecos Bill was coming with us, we were running out of space. I wondered where he'd sit when we got the camper back on the road.

CHAPTER TWENTY-SIX

Bill turned out to be the groundskeeper at the campground, so he wasn't planning to go anywhere. He'd moved here years ago, when horses and wagons had been overtaken by families in station wagons and Airstream trailers crossing the country for recreation rather than pioneers heading west for a new life in the wilderness. He used his talents to keep the campground safe for travelers who probably didn't have any idea of how to watch for tornados, or when to head to shelters.

"So how often do you see jackalopes around here, Bill?" Tobias asked. "There were a couple of them earlier tonight who seemed rather angry."

Bill shook his head. "I've a'seen 'em around but I ain't seem 'em get vicious. I normally do a patrol around the place to make sure, and I ain't seen 'em around for a couple o' weeks at least. They normally go away with a bit o'whiskey." Bill pulled a flask out of his back pocket. "I carry this around all the time, and leave a bit in the woods at the edge of the woods every night to keep 'em happy, so that they leave ever'body alone. It normally works."

Well, it hadn't worked tonight, that was for sure.

Bill seemed a bit surprised to see Bert, and even more surprised when he spoke, but he looked over Bert's injuries and said he'd never seen a jackalope do such a thing before. There had to be something or someone affecting them; they normally ran away from people. The whiskey kept them tame and happy in the woods, where few people got enough of a good look at them to do more than share exaggerated tales.

Jonah had gone back inside and grabbed the last of the salt. "Not sure we've got enough to draw another circle, and if we do, it's gonna be pretty thin. Bill, do you have any salt we can put down? It's still pretty late, and we can't leave for a while. The tire shop in town will repair that blown tire on the front of the Winnebago when they open for business in the morning. We're not gonna feel safe until we have some kind of barrier keeping magic out. It worked on the jackalopes."

"Huh, never heard of it working on the jackalopes before, but I never heard as it was needed. Learn somthin' new ever day. If y'all want, you can bunk in at my place tonight. It's at least solid, and warded. Magic ain't gonna bother ya there, and it's gonna be a bit more secure than one of these prairie schooners."

Well, it wasn't the Hilton, but I didn't care if it was a corner of a wooden floor, if we'd all feel secure enough to get a good night's sleep. Tobias especially needed it; he looked like the long hours behind the wheel were catching up to him. Him being too tired to drive and crashing the RV would not only get us hurt, but get us stranded and keep us from meeting our deadline and getting Babe back.

We all grabbed our blankets and backpacks, sleeping bags and pillows, and secured what we could inside the RV. Tobias insisted on taking the metal club we'd been using as a weapon. We all trudged to Bill's cabin, hidden just a few hundred yards from our camper, and went inside.

It wasn't anything luxurious, but it was definitely solid, had more than one bedroom, a couple of couches, and a floor big enough for us to spread out our sleeping bags with decent leg room so we weren't kicking a wall or the side of a camper. A fire blazed in the fireplace taking the chill out of the room once the door was shut behind us.

Bill offered us food, and even though he was being more than hospitable, the rules about accepting food or drink from faerie beings were screaming in the back of my head. Eating or drinking something offered by a magical being could enslave you to them; make you unable to say no to their requests. It was kinda like a magical roofie; making you unable to say no even if you didn't want to do what they asked.

Everyone else politely declined without saying anything, so either our hot dogs, chicken, and s'mores were filling everyone up, or the others were thinking the same thing I was.

Tobias took one of the bedrooms, followed closely by Jonah and Aiden. All three of them were willing to bunk in together to have a bed and some privacy, and to be fair, they were the ones doing the lion's share of the driving and the navigating.

Bill offered up the second bedroom as well, and Paul, Pete, and Jane all headed that way. I raised an eyebrow at Jane as she went, and she shrugged. "Slept with a lot of guys on the trail without it bein' an issue. This is about sleepin', not about romancin'."

I grinned at her. I wondered if she'd end up going back to her own time and her own life once all this was over, but I was definitely warming to her. She could be rather coarse and undignified, but she had a directness about her that I liked, and she definitely cared about people; telling her about Bert's injury, or about Aiden's clumsiness, or about Allie's background had made her instantly ask about them, and act like she cared. It was endearing, even if it was a bit odd to hear how she spoke.

That left Mia, Allie, Bert, and I in the living room. Bert was exhausted, though whether that was from trying to recover from the attack earlier today or from something else, I wasn't sure, but he was out cold within minutes, warmed through by the fire. It seemed the chill in the air had worn him out. I hoped he didn't get sick. I'd worried about his health ever since he'd taken a chill in an unexpected soaking in a river in Wonderland.

Allie wrapped him in a towel, leaving him sleeping next to the fire while she spread out one of the sleeping bags we'd brought with us into the cabin. "He's so worried about everyone, and he doesn't do well in the cold. I'm worried about him."

"I am, too," I admitted, watching her care for him like I'd done when he'd been sneezing and chilled in Wonderland, and while I wasn't interested in Bert romantically, I had to admit to a small bit of jealousy. She was taking over in caring for him, and a part of me had liked doing things for my friend. It was so minor, and yet, it struck me yet again they were getting closer and closer, and there didn't seem to be a good answer for them as a couple.

"Allie, are you two getting serious about each other?"

She sighed. "I don't know. I think he'd like to be. It's me, though. Too many things I'm worrying about would keep me from feeling comfortable in a relationship. I really just can't think of myself deliberately depending on a man. There've been so many who've let me down in this world. I think it's probably easier for me to trust Bert right now, because he's a guy, but he's not a man, if you know what I mean."

I did; she'd been victimized and sold by a street gang for sex. When I'd first met her, she'd shied away from any man who'd even looked in her direction. Being a frog was probably a blessing in disguise for Bert at the moment, because Allie didn't think of him as a threat. But sooner or later there would come a time when one or both of them would want more out of their relationship than just friendship or caring, and I wasn't sure how that would work if Bert was still a frog. I wondered if I could talk to Doris and Harold and Stanley, who had once helped Bert become human through a potion. Could they redo the potion, or was there was another option for him to break the curse the witch had laid on him? If nothing else, he might enjoy being able to keep himself warm, and possibly taking his interest in Allie to the next level.

"Allie, he cares for you a lot. I wouldn't want to see him hurt." That came from Mia, the last person I'd have expected to jump to his defense.

Bert had once had a devastating crush on Mia, who hadn't returned his romantic interest, about the same time she'd met Jonah. Bert's use of the potion to become human had been a last ditch effort to grab her attention and show her he was a man, just trapped in a frog's body. He'd traded all kinds of things, sacrificing our security in order to do it; but he'd redeemed himself by jumping in front of the Seawitch's magic to save Mia's life, and probably mine as well. That blast of magic had turned him back into the frog we'd all come to know and love; in a purely platonic sense, of course.

Allie blushed at Mia's protective threat. "I wouldn't want him hurt, either. I care too much about him for that." She glanced over to check on him, but Bert was sound asleep, his face slack and drooling. The look on her face left no doubt about her feelings; if she hadn't fallen for him yet, she was on her way down the slide.

"Allie, he's a good guy. We've solved other magic riddles before. Let's see if we can't solve this one. Once we get back from this trip, once we've gotten Babe back, and life has gotten back to normal, then let's start seeing what we can do about fixing Bert."

She nodded, and we all started to turn in. Allie curled up next to Bert, by the fire, in a sleeping bag. Mia curled up in a battered recliner, and I took the couch. Bill had promised to keep watch for jackalopes and tornados for the rest of the night, so he was out walking the campground, giving us peace and quiet, and room to stretch out and sleep. At the moment, it was the best gift anyone could give us.

I smiled, feeling good about the world, as the house settled down for the night.

Until I heard a small voice, coming from near the fire.

"So what would normal be like?" Allie whispered, just loud enough for me to hear.

It almost broke my heart.

CHAPTER TWENTY-SEVEN

Morning came too fast, fingers of light sneaking in around the gingham checked curtains on Bill's windows. I woke up stiff and sore, sleeping too many nights in too many cramped positions. Not even stretching out on the couch last night made up for my being so used to having a queen sized bed to myself when we were at home. Of course, that bed seemed too big lately. Even when Aiden had lived there with me, it was more comfortable than cramming myself and Mia into an uncomfortable bunk in the Winnebago while we were driving down the road. There just wasn't enough room for nine full grown adults and a frog in that camper.

I sat up, and smelled coffee.

Whoever had brewed that elixir of life was about to become my new best friend. I was willing to sacrifice all kinds of things to whatever being had been smart enough to make sure coffee was forthcoming that morning.

I stumbled into the kitchen and found Aiden pouring a mug full of the stuff.

He handed it to me without a word; smart man, he knew from prior experience that getting between me and coffee was a dangerous place.

I sipped it slowly, letting the warmth and the caffeine tease the brain cells awake enough to start functioning in reasonably coherent adult-like thought processes.

Aiden waited for me to get through the first half-cup or so before making any sort of statement that required a response. Once the brain fully kicked over, I looked up at him.

He had bags under his eyes, and he looked tired, even though we'd all gotten a decent night's sleep, or so I thought. He started to ask me a question, stopped, then started again.

"Janie, I know we were short on options last night, but I'm a little concerned. I don't know Bill. I don't know his connections, or who he might be working for, and I'm just not sure I trust some guy that came out of nowhere."

I smiled at him. "You came out of nowhere for me, when I was in danger. I ended up trusting you, and it was the right decision."

He turned pink. "You still think so?"

"I do. I haven't changed my mind about that. I haven't changed my mind about anything I've said to you the whole time I've known you, and I don't intend to start. You saved my life. If we have nothing else between us, there will always be gratitude, and friendship."

"Oh," he said, and fell silent for a few moments.

We sipped our coffee, and I felt like I was missing something. I wasn't always the sharpest tack in the box, but at the same time, something was going through his head. In the interest of not speeding up the conversation I knew would come eventually, ending what was left of our relationship, I went back to his statement about Pecos Bill.

"You ever hear he was dangerous? I heard tall tales about him, his horse, and that his girlfriend rode a catfish. I never heard if he purposely tried to hurt anyone, or if he was involved with anything in the faerie courts. Have you?"

He shook his head. "I haven't. I just have a bad feeling about this."

"Keep me posted. I'm not ungrateful for his help last night, but at the same time, I don't want to make light of what you're saying. There's something I'm missing here, but I can't put my finger on what." I told him about the research I'd done on Johnny Appleseed the day before, and how I hadn't yet figured out whether there was something about apples being made into alcoholic beverages, whether there was a land deal gone bad, or if there was some other issue.

He agreed with me. "I'm not sure we're ever going to get answers to everything we want to know before we go in, but it sure would help if we knew who or what we were facing before we got to that mountain. I'm a little concerned about Jonah's safety."

Paul walked in right at that moment. "Why worried about Jonah? I'm worried about Babe. How long before we can get moving again? And what's this discussion about Johnny Appleseed?" He stopped, nearly freezing in place. "Oh, my. You've figured out who the apple heir is. No wonder you had books on Johnny Appleseed in the camper. You've been doing research and not telling me about it, even though I'm the one who is the client here. You've been protecting your friend instead of helping me to find my ox!"

Oh, shit. "Paul, we're not protecting anyone," I said, even though we totally were. "I didn't want to tell you something we hadn't confirmed. I didn't want to get your hopes up until I fully believed it."

His eyes were wide. "You asked me about whether it was worth rushing in without all the facts; and about not rushing in and endangering others without a plan. How many of those facts did you have at the time that you weren't sharing with me? Is there a plan being made that I need to know about?"

"Paul, have a seat. I'll fill you in on everything we know." I tried, but he was furious with me. He stormed out of the kitchen, through the living room, then out the front door of the cabin, slamming it against the wood frame as he headed out.

Everyone was awake now.

Pete took off after his brother, with Jane just a few steps behind him. Something was definitely sparking between them. I hoped Jane's practical directness would work in our favor, and she'd talk him down.

Everyone else came into the kitchen. "What just happened?" Jonah asked, innocently reaching for a mug to pour himself some coffee.

Aiden shrugged. "Janie and I had just gotten a few minutes to catch up on some of her research and some of the things she's figured out. We hadn't gotten into much when Paul walked in and caught us talking about Jonah. He's figured out Janie hadn't let him in on everything and stormed out."

Tobias took off his glasses and rubbed at his eyes. "I'll go after him."

Jonah spoke up as well. "I'm going with you."

"You think that's wise?" Tobias asked. I agreed with him.

"Look, this isn't just about me. He is the client here, and you didn't tell him. Yeah, you were protecting me, even if you didn't realize you were. But I want him to get Babe back, just as much as I want to figure out as much as I can about my own heritage. So, you see, he needs to hear it, and he needs to hear it from me. He needs to know I've got his back on this one, and that your research, while it might have started out of concern for me, is also about knowing what we're facing when we get there. So give it to me in a nutshell. What am I facing?"

I re-explained the things I'd just brought up with Aiden before Paul had walked in. Jonah's eyes were wide, and a bit scared, when I finished. "He needs to know it, Janie, all of it."

The two of them headed for the door, not listening to any of us begging them to stop, that it was too dangerous. Even Mia's cries for them to slow down went unheeded.

"Paul," Jonah said, calling after my client as he stomped towards the woods. "I need to talk to you for a second. Slow down."

I didn't see Pete, or Jane, anywhere, just the back of a red flannel work shirt, like the one Paul had been wearing when he'd stormed out of the cabin.

"Paul," Tobias called. "We need to talk."

Nothing. The shirt kept going, as well as the man wearing it, heading into the woods. Tobias and Jonah hurried into the woods after him.

I had a bad feeling about this.

I couldn't see Tobias and Jonah as they disappeared into the trees. I heard a roar, something I hadn't ever heard in my life, something feral and angry and, well, hungry seemed the best word.

I swallowed hard, and ran back inside for our weapons. I came back with the metal club, an old aluminum baseball bat, and a wicked looking axe.

"We gotta go after them. That doesn't sound good, and they're not armed. Let's go," I said to Aiden and Mia.

Without a word, each one of them grabbed a weapon, and the three of us ran off, yelling and hollering and whooping into the woods to scare off any jackalopes, wild animals, or other beings that might cross our paths.

Look out world, here comes the next generation of F.A.B.L.E.S. bad-ass-ery, charging off into the unknown.

God help us all.

CHAPTER TWENTY-EIGHT

We crashed into the woods with the adrenaline and fortitude of a mighty army, and the plan and foresight of a blind raging sloth.

Once into the woods, we had no idea what we were looking for or what we were doing. We charged through the tree line, looking back and forth for where they might have gone. I saw tracks in the mud, and we headed off in search of our friends.

"This way," I pointed, hurrying after the tracks that looked big enough to be Paul's feet, which were almost twice the size of mine. "Hurry."

The trees seemed to careen towards us, tilting as we ran. The growls and howling of some animal that got louder as we ran, didn't help, My heart was in my throat as we came to a cave in the woods.

The cave opening amplified every sound and every twitch as we crept in. It was dark enough to have trouble seeing..

Aiden fell forward, tripping over a body lying on the ground. Mia leaned down, yanking her keys out of her pocket, where she had a small penlight attached to them, and exclaimed when she saw the face. When I heard her cry, I knew who it was.

It was Jonah.

Mia was panicking, but I squatted down next to her, grabbing the penlight from her hand, and running it up and down his body. He didn't seem to have any open wounds on his torso or legs. There was a big bruise on the back of his lower arm, but it wasn't bleeding. He did, however, have blood oozing from a nasty looking gash on his forehead, right above a huge goose egg. He must have whacked his head on something, but with the bruises, I wondered if he'd been thrown across the cave.

"Mia," I whispered. "I don't think we're alone in here; and Paul, Pete, and your dad are missing. He's unconscious, but it doesn't look like he's badly hurt. We've got to keep going and see if they're okay. He's between us and the entrance. He's breathing on his own and," I double checked to make sure, placing my fingers on his neck, "his heart's beating steady. He's probably going to have a heck of a concussion, but we've got to figure out what's going on with everyone else."

She didn't have much time to react. We heard another growl, and some angry yipping coming from further into the cave. I still had her penlight in my hand, and I took off running in the direction of the noise, Aiden right behind me.

The penlight gave us just enough light to see where we were going without running into the walls. I heard that same animal bellowing, and a bunch of human yelling, with one long scream.

We got into the depths of the cave to find a small campfire burning. An animal wouldn't have a fire for warmth; but Paul, Pete, and Tobias hadn't been gone long enough to start one themselves. So who had started the fire? Who was out here in the woods with that animal?

I shone the light around, and something furry standing on two legs rushed at us. I felt something grab the metal club out of my hands before I could do anything; I was too busy ducking the claw that came toward my face.

Whoever grabbed the club must have swung it; it connected with a meaty thunk and I heard a bellow of pain coming from the furry thing that stepped away from me and swung its claws in the direction of whatever had grabbed the club. I heard a scream, and Aiden rushed past me with the axe in his hands, as Paul came out of the shadow with his fists clasped together over his head, pile driving the animal's head as Aiden swung the axe and struck it in the neck.

It fell to the ground, whimpering, blood spurting out of the gash in its neck, the danger over as the creature bled out into the dusty floor of the cave.

Aiden and Paul were breathing hard, but seemed to be okay. I looked to the left, in the direction of whoever had grabbed the club away from me, and my breath caught in my throat. It was Tobias.

He wasn't whimpering much, but he was definitely hurt. Bruises and bumps covered one side of his face, but that wasn't the problem.

He was covered in blood, and as I looked down, I realized it was his own. He was holding his own guts in with his hands. Big bloody gashes crossed his stomach.

"Dad," Mia exclaimed, tears in her eyes. "Oh my God, you're hurt. We've got to get you to a hospital."

"Mia," he grunted. "No time. I'll bleed out before the ambulance will even get here. Only got a few minutes here. Gotta tell you a few things . . ."

Tears rolled down her face. "Dad, it's going to be okay. Let us call for help. Just hold on. We can make this better."

"Mia," he whispered. "There isn't time. I love you. Tell your mom I love her, and I always have. That has never changed and it never will. There is a silver key in the hide-a-key under the front wheel well of the camper. The key will open my unit at the Public Storage place just off of Smithville Road. You'll find all the answers to everything you ever wanted to know about me there. My only regret was leaving you . . ."

There was blood on his lip, as if the blood came from his mouth. Mia was almost hysterical, begging him to hold on so she could call a doctor, get Care Flight to come in, bring him back, save him.

He drew in a ragged breath, then took another and let it out slowly. He didn't take another one.

He was gone.

I grabbed Mia, and she fell to pieces, crying and screaming and reaching for her father. Aiden excused himself, going back to check on Jonah, who had started to come to. Paul and Pete came up as well, silent sentinels to Mia's wailing grief.

Tobias had saved us one last time. He had come through for his daughter, for her friends, and for her boyfriend in a time of magical emergency, in a way that left him a hero in his daughter's eyes. I was sure he was likely good with how it had gone down, and would be looking down on us with the thought that if he had to go, better to go down swinging, fighting the good fight.

Eventually, Mia calmed down, but she stared straight ahead, as if transfixed by something. She sat, cross legged beside her father, and disentangled herself from me enough to take one of her father's bloody hands, holding it in her own as if she was trying to memorize the feel and shape of his fingers.

I left her with him for a few moments. Aiden had gotten Jonah back on his feet, although he was groggy and confused. Paul and Pete staggered over to us. Paul had a bruise running from his hairline to his jawline, nearly solid purple and black in the flickering light of the low campfire and the fading light of the penlight I still held.

As we sent Aiden back with Pete and Paul to find the others, to find Pecos Bill, and to determine how to call to report Tobias' death, I sat with Mia and Jonah in the dark.

If only I'd told Paul my suspicions about Jonah's heritage earlier so he hadn't stormed off.

If only we'd had the tires checked before we'd left on the trip.

If only we'd taken more time to figure out what was going on before charging into the woods.

If only . . .

One of these days, I was going to invent a time machine, so we could all go back in time and fix the things we wished hadn't happened. I just hadn't wanted to add another thing I wished hadn't happened to that list.

CHAPTER TWENTY-NINE

A long day was made even longer with calls to law enforcement, and the paramedics asking questions we couldn't answer. I'd never passed a day quite as emotionally draining, except for the day my own father had died. That day, too had passed in a blur, but like it would never end, with the endless forms and questions, and details to take care of.

Mia had asked for a phone, and privacy, when we'd gotten back to Bill's cabin. She called her mother, and I heard her crying on the phone, but I'd respected her wish for some alone time to tell her mother what had happened. About an hour later, she came out, her eyes red and puffy, and announced her mother would be calling a funeral home in Dayton and making the arrangements with the local law enforcement when the body would be released. She also told us her mother said any plans for the funeral would wait until we were all home. Even though she'd been abandoned by Tobias's occupation, she understood that some things were important enough to wait to be done the right way.

Pecos Bill had been incredibly supportive, offering us the run of his cabin, and his hospitality for as long as we needed it. The owner of the campground also offered to let us keep the Winnebago there as long as we needed, free of charge, and wouldn't let us pay for the night we'd already spent. Other campers in the campground offered us all kinds of friendship, coughing up money and gas cards and food and all kinds of camping gear if we needed it, to stay.

The police asked us how long we were planning to stay, and Mia couldn't answer them. "We have a deadline to keep, sir, some private business for one of our friends. We stopped here unexpectedly; no one could have been waiting for us because we didn't even know we'd be stopping here ourselves. We'd like to make our deadline and get back as soon as possible, so that we can proceed with making the arrangements for Mr. Andersen's services," I told them, trying to be vague, and not commit us to sticking around. We still had time to make our deadline, but we couldn't hang around here waiting on the police to investigate something we couldn't explain without sounding completely insane.

Paul, Bill, and Pete had gone back to the cave with Aiden after we'd gotten Mia and Jonah out and back to the cabin. They removed all traces of the being that had killed Tobias, even spreading around more dirt to soak up the blood and checking Tobias's pockets to be sure that anything magical had been removed. I stayed behind with Jonah, who was still acting confused from the blow to his head, and Mia, who had gone silent after the conversation with her mother. The police reported no one in the cave other than the body, and there were no superficial clues as to what had happened to Tobias. The officer in charge thought it might have been a wild animal whose den had been disturbed and n had lashed out to stop the intruder.

It wasn't all that far from the truth. Aiden pulled me aside just before the police arrived, indicating the animal in the cave strongly resembled some of the more detailed sightings of Bigfoot, the hairy, large, man-like beast rumored to roam some of the American wilderness, with excessive body hair and feet twice the size of a human man. That certainly explained the footprints I'd seen in the woods earlier that I'd mistaken for Paul's, not necessarily a wrong assumption.

"I've never heard of Bigfoot in this area before," Bill stated, when we filled him in after the police had finally left, taking their blue and red lights with them. "I've run into one before, but I've never known one to actually get violent with a random person in the woods. Of course, I'd never heard of a jackalope getting aggressive either. There's got to be something going on. Either way, I took care of your Winnebago and the tire while you were dealing with the police."

That was huge; the Winnebago had been blown off the pavement by the twister that had shown up, and had been listing sideways with the bad tire at the time. While we might have been able to right the camper on its own, the bad tire made it impossible to get the traction we would have needed to pull it off.

Jonah had been checked out by the paramedics; he had a

concussion. No surprise there, but it also appeared he had a broken wrist. Allie went with him to the hospital, and Jane had gone with them, with Bert inside Allie's zip up hoodie. Aiden had followed, with the campground owner in his truck behind the ambulance, to make sure they all had a ride home afterward. They were gone for three hours, waiting for Jonah to get his arm x-rayed and a cast put on. They all came back with strict orders to keep Jonah quiet, and to wake him every hour to make sure he was still alert and coherent.

Once they got back, I asked Jonah what had happened. In bits and pieces, with Paul and Pete filling in the gaps, we got an idea of what had transpired.

"Well, we saw Paul going into the cave, and we couldn't figure out why, so we followed," Jonah started.

Paul shrugged. "I was looking for a place to get some peace and quiet and maybe figure out what in the world had happened. I wasn't looking to cause trouble. It's all my fault."

I shushed him. "We can all blame ourselves all day long. If I had been more forthcoming, if you hadn't stormed off, if we hadn't had a flat tire in front of this campground. There's more we could do, but that doesn't fix any of this, and we still have a deadline to meet. Tobias wouldn't want us to give up on Babe just because of this. You went to find some quiet to work this through in your own head. That's not wrong. We've all needed a break now and again while dealing with these kinds of emergencies. What happened next?"

"Paul went in the cave, and I followed him, because I could tell he wasn't thinking straight," Pete, in his quiet, concerned manner, added. "I shouldn't have followed him either, because that *thing* was in there, and it definitely didn't want us there. It was angry."

Jonah started back in. "All I know is that when I stepped into the cave something came out of nowhere and smacked me, hard. I bounced against a wall, and it felt like getting hit by a Mack truck. I laid there for a bit, listening, and I saw Tobias jump over me, heading for Paul and Pete, and then I blacked out."

There wasn't much more than that. Paul and Pete had been trying to hide from the creature in whatever corner or crevice they could find, hoping to find their way back out of the cave without the creature seeing them, but it hadn't worked because Tobias had come in after them. Paul said he thought Tobias threw a handful of dirt in the animal's eyes, temporarily blinding it.

It might have been something else, something magical, but I hadn't smelled magic in the cave.

But why the Bigfoot? Why the angry, seemingly rabid jackalopes? There didn't seem to be a good answer to those questions.

We took Bill up on his offer to stay in his cabin one more night. Jonah and Mia took one of the bedrooms, and Allie insisted on going with them, taking a sleeping bag and Bert, and promising to wake Jonah and check on Mia through the night.

Paul, Pete, and Jane took the second bedroom.

That left Aiden and I in the living room, by ourselves; other than Bill going back and forth to check on all of us and maintaining a watch over the cabin.

I'd been holding in all of the emotion from the day; all the hurt and guilt and pain and fear and exhaustion. Once everyone else was settled for the night, I turned to Aiden. "Whatever else happens between us, whatever else happens this week, can you please just put your arms around me? I need it right now. No emotions, no rehashed arguments. I just need a little comfort."

He opened his arms and I stepped into them, finally breaking down myself. All the pain of the night I'd lost my own dad came flooding back, the hurt that I might be losing Aiden, the fear of what we might be facing, the confusion of why all this kept happening to us, came tumbling out as I cried. He did the perfect thing at that moment, cuddling me quietly in his arms, and when the tears came faster, murmured soft, wordless sounds of apology and comfort.

I would never forget how he was there for me in that moment.

CHAPTER THIRTY

The next morning came earlier than any of us wanted. It had been a long night, punctuated by Paul walking the hallways, unable to sleep, Mia crying off and on, the need to wake up Jonah to check on his mental state, and Bill coming in and out from patrolling around the campground. We awoke to coffee, thank goodness, and packed up our belongings as fast as we could. We had to get on the road. Already this trip was taking longer than we'd expected. Good thing we'd given ourselves plenty of time to get to Utah prior to our deadline.

We took off, with me driving the Winnebago, probably slower than it could go, but I was still getting used to driving a vehicle of that size. Aiden sat in the front, with the maps and the directions, where he'd sat when Tobias had been the one behind the wheel. Bert sat with Aiden, watching the road and insisting on being where he could see everything. I think he did it to give Allie a break, clearly worn out from worrying about him as well as Mia and Jonah.

Jonah and Mia were in the bedroom at the back of the camper as we drove. Jonah had made it through the night without getting confused or getting worse, and the doctors had told us he could sleep normally after he made it through the night. Mia was worn out, and didn't want to leave Jonah's side. Paul and Pete and Jane sat at the kitchenette table, playing a very quiet game of cards, and Allie sat with Bert on the sofa, reading the biography of Johnny Appleseed I'd been looking at earlier. No one spoke much; no one really had much to say. Nothing would fix what had happened the day before.

It was Tuesday. We had to be at the mountain, which wasn't far from Salt Lake City, Utah, before Thursday, and it appeared we'd get to the area today, after a long day of driving. We'd be able to set up at a campground and come up with a strategy before we went up the mountain, because no matter what the ransom note had said, there was no way I was going to let Paul and Jonah go up that mountain alone. Not after what had just happened when the group was split up.

I wondered if we'd be there in time to drive up the mountain. It was a tourist destination, after all. If we could get up the mountain and try to figure out the layout and the actual meeting place, maybe we'd be able to come up with a plan on how to ransom back Babe.

Paul was getting worried because this trip was taking way longer than we'd expected, but he didn't say a word about the length of the trip. In fact, I think he was still blaming himself for what had happened to Tobias. To be fair, I was blaming myself as well.

The only noise in the camper as we drove was Aiden, giving me directions or asking about the gas tank from time to time, the shuffling of playing cards, or Allie turning a page now and again.

The silence was hard to listen to; but the harder noise was the sound of Mia crying off and on for her father, wearing herself out, then crashing again. Aiden went back and checked on her as I drove, but otherwise we just stayed silent, the trip punctuated only by the sounds of her grief.

I stopped once, filling up the gas tank. We didn't stop for meals, just eating out of the refrigerator from the stash of food Doris had stocked us up with; sooner or later, we'd need more. The refrigerator didn't hold a lot when it came to feeding nine humans and a frog. And that frog had a decent appetite, especially when he was using up calories for healing the wounds from his jackalope encounter.

Aiden mentioned there was a campground right at the base of the Big Rock Candy Mountain, one that had an RV park, on-site laundry, and decent accommodations. He'd seen the listing on the guide and travel books he'd grabbed when we hit the Utah state line. By the time we'd gotten that far, we only had a couple of hours to go before we pulled into the RV park he'd found, but it was dark.

We were lucky; it was coming up on the Thanksgiving weekend, and there was still one spot left for us to rent and park the Winnebago. It was late. I was exhausted from the drive, and it was going to be a long day tomorrow. Aiden grabbed some literature from the rental office when we paid for two nights at the park, and found we could rent an ATV, an all terrain vehicle. I wondered if we could rent a couple of them, so we wouldn't have to hike up the mountain to scope out potential meeting sites. My legs were stiff from all the driving; we hadn't made many stops over the course of the last day.

Our energy was taken up by getting hooked up for utilities and power for the night, setting a salt circle, and otherwise getting ourselves set to go. Where Tobias had just taken care of these things without us asking or thinking about it, we were total newbies. Luckily, there was a retired couple in a camper next to us that was able to talk Paul, Pete, and Aiden through the steps to hook up, how to drain the chemical toilet, and get the power going without getting electrocuted. I offered them one of the pies Doris had sent along, as thanks, and they were thrilled, offering to feed us dinner.

I declined the very effusive offer, knowing they didn't realize just how many of us there were in the Winnebago and just how much food that would entail. Instead, I made Mia go with Allie and I to run a couple of loads of laundry at the park's Laundromat. We were getting a bit rank from being cooped up in the Winnebago, and I was hoping the routine task of sorting, washing, drying, and folding everyone's extra clothing would help Mia start to feel a bit more normal. I knew that when my father died, I had taken solace in the mundane tasks of running laundry for clean towels and underwear, or cleaning kitchen cabinets, or reorganizing a sock drawer.

She looked tired; for all that she'd been in the bedroom resting all day. I wondered just how much sleep she'd actually gotten, and I wondered how much rest Jonah had gotten, with his head injury, but he was acting fairly coherent other than complaining about a massive headache. Small wonder; the goose egg on his head looked swollen and painful, and was nearly the size of a lemon. He also had a black eye coming up below the bump on his temple.

We hid in domesticity for a while, before I asked her, finally, "So, Mia, how are you?"

She looked at me with a bleak expression. "I've been wondering what I was going to say when someone asked me that. I'm glad you're the one to ask. I'm here. That's about as good as it's going to get. I don't blame anyone for what happened. Dad threw himself into so many situations that, let's be honest, were probably so dangerous he was lucky that he ever came back to us again. I'm glad I got to be there to say goodbye when he did go. Not everyone gets that chance. Janie,

I know you got to say good-bye to your Dad. I know it doesn't change the fact that he's gone, but it does help to know you had a few moments with him at the end."

I agreed. I had been glad to be there at the end for my own father's death, even though I didn't like remembering him like that; sick and gasping, in pain, and ready to go. Mia's dad went doing something he was passionate about. He died protecting his daughter and people who were his friends, and innocents. It was what he was best at. I told her so.

"You're right, Janie," she said. "I'm glad he went doing what he did best. I just wish he hadn't gone at all. I wish I'd had more time with him. I think I'll always wish that."

"You will," I said. "It doesn't matter when he went, or how, you'll always wish that,"

She nodded. "You're right. There was just so much wasted time. So much time he thought he was protecting me by staying away, so much time I didn't have him around. I know now he wanted to be there. I found his pictures."

Apparently, she had found a drawer in the bedroom that contained a shoebox full of pictures of herself, catalogued by age, with notes on the back in her mother's handwriting.

"Wow, Mia. That's a wonderful keepsake."

"It is," she said.

I was a bit jealous. Dad wasn't much for the keeping of a scrapbook or a photo album. What things I had were all pieces and bits crammed in between pages, overstuffing the books he always said he meant to get back to. One of these days, I was going to have to go through them and see if there were enough notes on the back of the pictures and clippings to get them in some semblance of order. I hoped so; I hadn't been through them all since I'd been digging through for clues when Bert had first shown up and my evil stepmother had just started to set her sights on me.

The dryer beeped and we pulled out the clean clothing to fold, staying busy while we talked about subjects both of us wished we didn't need to talk about.

After a few moments, Mia put down the shirt she had been

folding and looked out the window. "What the hell?"

I glanced up to see people, yelling and staggering, running past us, as if something was chasing them. It was only then I realized that the earth was shaking under out feet, and I actually heard the screams of the people outside.

"Earthquake!"

CHAPTER THIRTY-ONE

The ground shook; worried as I'd been about Mia, I hadn't realized it at first. I grabbed her and ran to stand in the open doorway of the laundry room. Allie joined us, and we huddled there, clutching the doorframe until the world stopped shaking.

It didn't take long, but at the same time, it took forever, as we held on, hoping and praying for the safety of everyone else who had come with us. Unable to move, to check on them and make sure they were okay, was torture.

Eventually, the world stopped shaking and we took stock of what had happened. We were okay, with a couple of bumps and bruises from being knocked against each other and against the door frame, but otherwise, unhurt. We grabbed up the piles of laundry and ran back to the Winnebago.

Everyone there was fine, just a bit rattled. Someone from the campground had come around to make sure the tourist and out-of-towners were okay. Apparently earthquakes might not happen every day, but this area of the country was definitely prone to them. This was bigger than most of the ones that normally reached them, but not unheard of.

I no longer believed in every day coincidence and events.

That earthquake had something to do with whatever we would be facing up on that mountain, I was sure of it.

I took stock of everyone. There were no major injuries or other problems that would keep us from our mission. Jonah was fine, and Aiden, while he'd fallen against the side of the Winnebago in the quake, had suffered a bruise to his arm and shoulder. Paul had a bruise on his leg from falling against the kitchenette table and Pete had bruised his ribs from falling against the sink in the RV bathroom. Bert was fine; he'd been wrapped up in a towel, and while he had fallen against the wall inside the RV, he was cushioned enough that he hadn't suffered a single injury.

We put the Winnebago and all the hookups to rights and decided we needed a plan for the morning. Mia, Allie and I brought back the clean laundry, and we went, in shifts, to the showers. It was an unspoken agreement that no one went anywhere alone. It wasn't safe; even if we were surrounded by tourists wearing white socks with Birkenstock sandals, or t-shirts proclaiming that their parents or children had gone to a certain city or attraction and all they'd brought back had been that lousy t-shirt.

I went back to the bedroom, and took stock of all the supplies we'd taken with us from Dayton: all the weapons, the metal items, the books, and the personal supplies. Aiden came in with a map of all the local hiking trails. We put our heads together and planned an early morning mission to check out the trails and try to determine where our rendezvous to exchange a man for an ox might take place.

Aiden, Jonah, Mia and Allie joined me in the bedroom, where we stared at the map until we were bleary eyed, without much progress.

We decided to get up early, have a quick breakfast of leftover cinnamon rolls, which Doris had left in the fridge, cold cereal, and coffee, and then go rent a couple of ATVs to drive up the mountain in search of the ox-napper. We bunked down early, but while it was too dark to go up the mountain in search of anything at the moment, it was also too early to just crash.

I grabbed the half-empty bottle of wine out of the refrigerator and the last of the plated sandwiches before heading outside to sit on the picnic table. I drank from the bottle, took large bites from the sandwich, and studied the mountain, and the different colors of the elevation. Where might there be some place to hide a seriously oversized ox who was likely getting anxious for someone to come and rescue him?

Mia came outside, while the others lounged around the camper. She found me holding the bottle with one hand, the plastic wrap leftover from my sandwich in the other. She didn't say anything, but took the bottle from me and gulped as she swallowed. I started to say something, because I wasn't sure she'd eaten anything, but she shook her head when I tried to say something. Apparently, she didn't care.

I did. I took the bottle away from her. "This doesn't solve

anything," I said. "It just gives you a headache."

She shook her head, snatching the bottle back. "My dad's dead; we have no plan. We have weapons, but no idea how to use them. We have maps, but no idea where we're supposed to go. We have clean laundry, but no idea how long we're going to be here to deal with whatever else is going on. So I thought I'd drink a little. You got a problem with that?"

I shook my head, mute in the face of my best friend hitting the anger stage of grieving. I'd been there myself. There wasn't much that was going to help except her working her way through it. Nothing anyone could say would make it better, or get her through it faster. She just had to work her own brain through it. I shrugged, and let her keep the wine.

She took another long pull from the bottle. Jonah materialized behind her, catching her as she stumbled back against the table itself. "It's okay," he said. "She's exhausted, and she can't let herself sleep. Maybe it's a good thing she got into the wine. She'd feel better if she got a few hours with her eyes closed and her brain not clicking over, thinking about her dad over and over again."

I smiled at him. Maybe he was right.

He picked her up, carrying her into the Winnebago, with her bottle of wine, and put her in the bed. I was just behind him, and she was asleep before he'd even gotten a blanket over her legs. It was the best thing for her, I thought. We left her to her bottle of wine and slumber and headed back outside.

Everyone else had been waiting for all of us to get her settled. Paul and Pete asked if we could set up the tent outside, so that we'd have a bit more room for everyone to sleep. Aiden and I took care of it, with Jonah keeping an eye on Mia and Allie trying to put the inside of the Winnebago to rights. Too many people spending too much time in that enclosed of a space had the place looking like some sort of refugee camp.

I had an idea. I wondered if we all could crowd into the areas that looked promising for the rendezvous and make it look like a bunch of lost tourists, bumbling around with maps and big sunglasses and cameras. Too bad we didn't have cameras with us, but we did have our cell phones, and I wondered if we could pick up some disposable cameras and pull it off. There was a convenience store at the campground. Maybe, just maybe, we could pull it off.

I no longer worried that Paul would take off with Jonah, and I was glad everyone knew what was up regarding Johnny Appleseed and Jonah's heritage, but that didn't mean we were in the clear now.

My brain spun with ideas and plans, but it was time for all of us to get some sleep and see what we could see in the morning. Jane insisted on sleeping in the tent with Paul and Pete, and Jonah went to the bedroom to crawl in beside Mia and offer what comfort he could. Allie curled up on the couch, as usual, with Bert. That left one bed, the sleeping compartment above the driver's compartment. There was another sleeping space if we tore apart the kitchenette table, but that would disrupt everyone who had already settled down for the night. I looked at Aiden, the only one left without a bunk, and said, "Look, you've been sleeping in the passenger chair the last couple of nights; there's no reason why you shouldn't take the bed."

"And you were driving all day, Janie. I know you're trying to hold all this together and lead everyone, but you need a good night's sleep as well. We're adults, and we care about each other. It's been a long couple of days. It would be really nice to curl up together and get some sleep. I haven't slept well in weeks. Do you mind?"

I shook my head, silently. I didn't mind. In fact, it was the exact right thing for him to say, and exactly what I needed as well.

CHAPTER THIRTY-TWO

I woke early, but I had slept better than I had in a long time. Whether it was because we'd finally made it here, or because I'd slept in Aiden's arms all night, I didn't know, and at the moment, I didn't care. The solid sleep had chased a lot of cobwebs out of my head. I was thinking clearly, and I was ready to go see what I could see.

I disentangled myself from Aiden, and climbed down out of the forward sleeping bunk. Allie and Bert were still asleep, and the loud snoring from the bedroom told me Jonah was out cold as well. I hadn't heard movement from the back, so I assumed Mia was still asleep. A look at the digital clock on the stove in the kitchenette told me it was barely six in the morning. No wonder everyone was still asleep.

I pulled on my shoes and decided to step outside to see what the day would bring. No one moved while I got my jacket and opened the door.

It was slightly chilly. The sun was barely above the horizon, and it illuminated the layers of sediment and rock that gave the mountain its name, green and red and orange and pink stripes glowed as the sun hit the side of the mountain. I left everyone to sleep and walked to the convenience store just down the way in search of coffee.

The clerk wasn't very awake; it looked like they had just opened, but the coffeepot had already brewed up life-giving wake-up juice. I asked about ATV rentals and hiking trails, and she gave me a list of rental companies and another map of the trails. It looked like there were a ton of trails. How were we ever going to be sure we could find the right spot for the rendezvous to get Babe back? Then again, we hadn't really planned all that well for rescuing an ox. We had no means of transporting a large animal anywhere. We had no trailer and no hitch, and I wasn't sure the Winnebago could pull such a load anyway. We'd have to come up with something, although maybe Paul had thought of a solution. I'd ask him when he woke up.

I bought a couple of boxes of granola bars and some fruit snacks to take with us when we went up into the mountain trails to look for whoever we were supposed to meet. I picked up a few other odds and ends as well, including as many canisters of table salt as I could find. We were burning through salt like mad trying to keep a salt line down, and had used up the last of our supply just before the earthquake.

I headed back to the Winnebago with a couple of plastic bags worth of supplies, but also with a giant insulated foam cup of coffee. When I got back to the campsite, there was a rock on the picnic table. I set down the bags of snacks and picked up the rock, unsure of where it had come from. There was a note under the rock, on the same type of paper that Paul's original note and the ransom note Pete had found had been on; old, worn, and creased. The paper contained just a few short sentences.

Come to Zion National Park
Alone with the apple heir
Meeting today at noon
At the Zion Narrows
If you wish to see the ox again.

I didn't like that the ox-napper had not only found us, but also our Winnebago, and knew that we had the apple heir with us. I didn't like that they'd gotten that close. And I especially didn't like that we didn't have long to figure it all out.

I burst into the Winnebago, waking everyone up, and ran back outside, waking up Paul, Pete, and Jane, who were all still sleeping, curled up together in the tent with multiple sleeping bags tangled around them all.

I wondered for a split second whether Paul was putting us all on; whether he'd have planted the notes, whether he was up to something else, but in this case, it just didn't make sense. He would have had to get up before me, somehow untangle himself from Jane, Pete, and the sleeping bags without waking them up, set up the note and rock on the picnic table, then crawl back in, re-tangle himself with the sleeping bags, and go back to sleep in the fifteen minutes or so I'd been gone. Not impossible; but highly improbable he'd have pulled all of that off in time. Besides, he was too big to get up and untangle himself from the other two without pulling the tent stakes out of the ground.

So what in the world was going on? No one seemed to know, and no one had heard anything while I'd been gone. It hadn't been there, or if it had, I hadn't seen it on my way to get coffee.

Either way, we at least had a meeting place and a time. Zion National Park wasn't far from where we were at; and we had time to come up with a plan, as well as hopefully getting there early enough to figure what we were going to do.

Aiden had grabbed a map of the park earlier, when he hadn't been sure exactly what we'd be looking for. He pulled it out and used the rock to hold down one side of it on the picnic table. Paul grabbed the other end. We found the rock formation for the meeting place and had a good idea of how to get there from the main road.

"We need a plan. I think I know what to do," I said, looking at the map. "I just need to know what supplies your dad brought along, Mia. Does he have any walkie-talkies, or radios, or any other kind of device like that?"

She swallowed hard, and nodded. "I think he did. He's got a bunch of equipment in the bedroom I didn't realize he'd brought along. It makes me wonder if he already had some kind of plan for handling whatever this situation would be. I wish I'd known what it was."

Before she could get teary eyed, I gave her a task. "Mia, I need to know what kind of walkie-talkies he had, and how far their range is. I also need to know if he's got any kind of binoculars, and how many pairs he might have, and whether or not he's got any other kinds of weapons that might come in handy. I picked up granola bars and fruit snacks, but I think we might need some other food, because I have a feeling we might be out there for a bit. Do we all have sweatshirts or jackets?"

Allie stepped forward. "I think the only one without something like that is Bert, but we've got those towels he's been wrapped up in. I think there are fresh ones in the bedroom. I'll check, and then I'll figure out what extra food we should take."

Aiden looked up at Mia. "If you don't mind, I'll go through some of your dad's stuff with you. I was with him when he was packing up some of Janie's stuff from her dad's trunks. Maybe between the two of us we can figure out what we need to take with us."

She nodded, agreeing with him.

Jonah ran off to use the payphone to call for ATV rentals for the group of us. Pete and Paul and Jane busied themselves packing up the tent and sleeping bags and getting ready for whatever we might have going on.

We had a plan and a direction, something we'd been sorely lacking on this trip. We still didn't know quite what we'd be facing, but we weren't going to face anything unprepared.

Now, if we just knew what we were preparing for, I'd feel a whole lot better.

CHAPTER THIRTY-THREE

Mia and Aiden uncovered a ridiculous amount of firepower in a drawer underneath the bed. I'd known Tobias had been a bad-ass, but this was insane. He had guns that didn't quite look 100% legal; like they were assault rifles that only the military had, or rather, something only the military should have.

He had boxes and boxes of ammunition, which looked odd. The boxes themselves were old, and I wondered if the bullets were homemade and refilled in old boxes. I took the lid off one the boxes and looked inside. I wasn't an expert on bullets, but something looked off about them. I put the lid back on and turned the box over. On a thin strip of masking tape, someone, likely Tobias, had written, "fairy queen specials". I opened the box back up and took one of the bullets out and examined it. It felt heavy and it looked like there was iron on the tip. Digging further into the drawer, we found bullet molds, and a small notebook with written directions for making bullets.

"Holy crap," I said. "He was making iron core, iron tipped bullets."

All of us looked down in shock.

"No wonder he had the reputation he did," Aiden said quietly. "I'm not sure exactly what he thought was coming, but this is years' worth of work. It had to be something he was making all the time, like every single evening he didn't have something else going on."

I pulled out Mia's backpack, and my own, and dumped the law books onto the bed. We could sort them out later, but right now, we needed to be armed for the magical equivalent of bear. I scooped up five or six boxes of his homemade bullets, and shoved them down into the bottom of each bag. I grabbed two of the handguns and split them, one in each. There were also a couple of crossbows, with iron tipped arrows gathered in bundles and tied together with twine, and we took those as well.

There were four walkie-talkies and three sets of binoculars, and those went into the bags. The last thing I grabbed was a shotgun, sawed off to half the length of a normal barrel, and when I looked, I realized it was already loaded. It was loaded with rock salt.

That would sting like mad, and really hurt a normal human, but would be almost lethal to a faerie court being. There was a big bag of rock salt, and I decided we needed to take that as well, putting it into a backpack where it was hidden.

We rolled up the crossbows and shotgun into a bundle with blankets. Allie came back from another run to the convenience store with armloads of sports drinks, beef jerky, and packs of peanuts, almonds, and pretzels. Between that and the snacks I'd grabbed earlier, we had enough for an all-day surveillance of the park if we needed to.

Jonah had reserved three all-terrain vehicles, that would each fit four people. We started up the RV and headed toward Zion National Park, where we were to meet the rental people, and on the way there, I outlined the plan, as simple as it was.

"Look," I said. "The notes say Jonah and Paul have to go by themselves. We can't be right with them, or we risk blowing the whole thing and having Babe hurt in the process. So they'll go alone to the meeting place at the Zion Narrows. The rest of us will take the remaining ATVs, and split up, heading to find places where we can use the binoculars and keep an eye on the two of them."

Jonah wanted some kind of weapon, but the original letter had said no metal. We settled for giving him a baggie full of salt for each pocket. He wasn't thrilled, but he understood.

We arrived at the park, and the rental dude was there to hand over the keys to the vehicles. We thanked him and he took a wad of money from Paul, and then waved us on, telling us we had them for twenty-four hours. We unloaded our supplies into the vehicles, and found the one that we were sending with Paul and Jonah had room in the backseat.

Bert spoke up. "I'm going with them."

We all argued with him, since he couldn't use a weapon, and would be fairly exposed should something go wrong.

"I don't care. I'm strong enough to push the button on the walkie-talkie. I can be the fallback emergency call in case they get out of range of the binoculars, or if you guys lose sight of us. I can be there in case they get snatched and be able to tell you guys where they went or who might have taken them."

I had to agree it wasn't a bad idea. In fact, it was pretty darn good. With one exception. "Bert," I said. "If we let you do this, then you also are going to take my iPhone. Leave it off until and unless there's an emergency. We'll turn on Mia's if we lose sight of you, but not before. You remember how to turn it, right?"

He nodded. "And you've got Mia's number programmed in, right?"

"Yeah. Mia's number is programmed in, but don't be afraid to call 911 if it's that bad. Just don't turn it on until and unless you have to. Tobias had a real point about GPS locating. We'll use it to find you if something happens, but until and unless it does really happen, don't turn it on. Just in case they're using humans or human technology to find us, there's no reason to give them an easy heads up as to where we're at."

I tucked my cell phone into the towel and blanket wrapping that kept him hidden in the backseat area. I also tucked in a granola bar and a bottle of Gatorade for him. Who knew how long we'd be out here? I didn't want him to get sick or hungry if there was a way to prevent it.

They headed off, and we hopped into our own vehicles. I drove one with Mia and Jane. Aiden and Allie took off with Pete, with Aiden driving. Much as I didn't like the idea of Aiden driving, I really didn't want Mia behind the wheel. I didn't think she was as ready to be paying attention as she might have thought she was, and I wanted to keep an eye on her.

We veered off to the right, as Aiden took the other vehicle off to the left, taking a long way around the direct path that I'd seen Jonah take towards the Zion Narrows. About fifteen minutes later, we saw the Narrows, visible from a fairly long way off. I stopped the vehicle, and Mia raised the binoculars, looking for Jonah and Paul to approach the meeting site.

We were still an hour early, but I was okay with that. We were set up. We had weapons and food. We had drinks. We were ready to rock. Maybe I should start looking into going to a target shooting range, as well as stepping up the self-defense classes we'd started taking. I needed to know more about handling myself in this kind of encounter. We might have a plan this time, but that didn't mean we had a good one, or that we would have a good one the next time something like this happened. This was the fourth time we'd had a magical, dangerous, life-threatening emergency. And this time, we'd had an eye-opening dose of just exactly how dangerous and life-threatening it could be, because we'd lost someone.

The problem with sitting around and waiting for something to happen is the sitting around when nothing's happening. I wondered if cops on a stakeout felt the same way, but this was definitely getting boring in a hurry. My fingers itched for a book, or my computer, or a smart phone, but all of those things would take my eyes off of the rock formation where the meeting was scheduled to happen. I couldn't do that; because the minute I took my eyes off of Jonah and Paul would be the very minute something happened to take them away from us. We had already lost one person on this trip. I was determined that it would be the last loss we had.

Nothing much happened. I watched the ATV as Paul and Jonah sat there together, waiting for the meeting, but they didn't even get out of the vehicle. Instead, they sat inside, talking but not doing much of anything else.

I checked my watch, and we still had twenty minutes to go before the meeting.

Only I would be this early for a magical emergency.

CHAPTER THIRTY-FOUR

This kind of sitting and waiting reminded me of a summer job I'd had as a lifeguard when I was in high school. When the pool had been busy, there was plenty to see and plenty to watch. It kept the monotonous job of watching from being so boring that the eyes glazed over. If I'd been bored in the lifeguard chair, the day would have lasted forever, and I'd have had to fight to pay attention to what was going on. If it was a light day, without a whole lot of people to watch, I would get bored easy.

There weren't a lot of people to watch. I was getting bored pretty easy.

I opened up some Gatorade and a granola bar, handing Mia the binoculars under the pretext that I needed to rest my eyes from staring through the binoculars. She kept an eye on Paul and Aiden while I took a moment to get something to drink and eat, then rest my eyes.

"Wait," she said. "I see something." She handed me the binoculars, and I looked through them.

She was right. Something was shimmering, glistening in the sun. I adjusted the lenses and saw a woman come into focus.

She hadn't been there before.

Paul and Aiden got out of the vehicle, then stepped toward her, walking just under the rock formation where the meeting was taking place, almost out of our line of sight. I handed the binoculars back to Mia, and told her to let me know if she lost sight of the men. I inched the ATV forward, following her directions, keeping them in sight as long as I could. Before too long, however, Jonah and Paul had stepped completely past the rock wall, hiding them from sight.

I grabbed the walkie-talkies. I wasn't worried about making noise, because they didn't have the walkie-talkie; Bert did. I hadn't seen them grab Bert out of the back of the ATV. I hit the button, whispering for Bert, trying not to speak too loud if there was something there that could overhear and blow this for them.

"Bert, come in Bert. It's Janie. I can't see them anymore. Are they okay?"

There was silence for a while, then I heard Bert's voice. "They're okay, I think. They didn't say anything though. They just got out of their seats and started walking away. Something is going on. Nothing made them do it, but something's going on."

I didn't like the sound of that. "We gotta go," I said, jamming my foot down on the gas. "We've got to get to them." I asked Bert if he'd noticed any use of magic.

"Yes," he said. "There's magic here. Whether it's from the lady they talked to or not, there is magic. I don't know what magic. It's got kind of a wild flavor to it. I haven't noticed anything quite like that before." He yawned, almost as if he was bored, or about to fall asleep. Either it was really not that big a deal, or something was making him so sleepy he wasn't paying attention. Either way, I didn't like the sound of that, and I just really wanted to get there and figure out what was going on.

"We're on our way, Bert. Stay where you're at," I called, as Jane exclaimed when we hit a bump. "You okay?" I called back to her.

"This is bumpier than riding a horse with an off gait over a rocky canyon," she said. "But this is more fun." She was grinning.

"Hang on to something," I yelled, as the ATV went slightly airborne after going over a dip in the landscape. The ATV bounced and rocked and shook over the ups and downs of the landscape, and my teeth started feeling loose in the back of my mouth. My jaw was sore from clenching it as I hung onto the wheel with both hands, holding it tight enough for my knuckles to turn white.

"Yeeeeehaw!" Jane called, in a great cowboy yell. It made me wonder what she'd think of roller coasters, if just a little rocky ATV ride was giving her a thrill. If she was still around next summer, then maybe I needed to save up the money to take a bunch of us to Cedar Point in northern Ohio, near Lake Erie. I'd bet some of the Wonderland folks would also enjoy it, as well as giving Allie and her mother a good day out. I'd stuff 'em all full of cotton candy and hot dogs and put them on the fastest, highest coasters I could find and see how much they loved it. I was sure Jane would, and I had a funny feeling a bunch of the rest of them would feel the same way.

Back to the task at hand, I thought. We sped across the park, and I barely noticed the beautiful rock formations. I'd have to add coming back to actually look at all of this someday, without a magical emergency, to my list of things I'd like to do someday. At the moment, we had to get to Jonah and Paul before anything else happened.

Aiden and the others were heading our way. Had they lost sight of Paul and Jonah, as well? They were driving as hell for leather as I was, hurrying to get there, their vehicle jumping and bouncing and rollicking.

We pulled up right behind the abandoned ATV Paul and Jonah had been in, and found Bert in the backseat, still wrapped up in his towel and blanket, sound asleep. He woke up with a start.

"Whozat? What happened?" he asked, still groggy.

I grabbed him out of the back of the vehicle, towels, phone, walkie-talkie and all, then handed him over to Mia.

"Bert, where'd they go? What happened?" I asked.

He yawned again. "Some lady showed up and told them to get out of the cart and follow her."

"And they did it?" Mia asked.

I saw one green hand come up and rub at one eye. "Well, yeah. She asked real nice." Another yawn echoed the first one. "They went 'cause she said 'please.'"

"Are you freaking kidding me?" I asked. "They knew we were watching for them. They didn't even try to signal us, or have you do something to signal us?"

He was already asleep again, snoring as he burrowed down into the towels in Mia's arms. She shook him and even tried pinching him, but no go; he was out cold. I'd seen him sleep like that before. Not much was going to wake him when he was out that deep.

Aiden and the others pulled up right behind us. "What happened? Where'd they go?" he asked. Pete jumped out of their vehicle, running towards the opening in the rock formation as fast as he could go.

I suddenly smelled peppermints and old books, strong enough to almost make me sick to my stomach.

"Oh, crap," I said. "Heads up, guys. Magic incoming!"

We all reached for weapons of some kind, without a clue as to what we'd be facing. I just hoped it was something we could handle.

I saw the purple shimmering haze of a portal, right where the rock formation opened up in front of us.

It was the biggest portal I'd ever seen.

Looked like we were headed into a magical realm. This time, however, we were taking weapons, food, and drink. I did not care if I was violating some kind of magical protocol. I did not care if I was going to piss off someone else. I was coming after my friends and I did not care at the moment what I was going to have to go through to get them back in one piece.

CHAPTER THIRTY-FIVE

Allie had Bert in her arms; otherwise we all stepped through the portal on our own power. Mia and I had the backpacks of supplies on our backs. Aiden and Pete had the crossbows and Jane had the shotgun loaded with rock salt. We stepped through one by one, into a barren, dry, desert-like landscape. The park we'd been in had more green and vegetation in it in a square foot than this place looked like it had in a square mile, ten miles, even.

There was a path, and it looked like it had been mostly abandoned other than the scuffling of what looked like recent footsteps. The wind was slight, but it was blowing, and it wouldn't take long to cover up those steps. I hurried down the path, following the footprints as fast as I could before they blew away.

"Look," called Mia, after a few minutes of hurrying and watching the ground. She was right behind me.

I looked up and saw her pointing, and followed her finger. She was pointing at a neighborhood of primitive dwellings carved into the side of some of the rock formations. They were barely visible until I stared long enough to see the window holes that had been carved into the rock. I followed the carving down, and spotted a stone stairway about a hundred yards from where we were standing.

"There it is," I called to the others. "Let's go."

We hurried to the base of the stairway, not even trying to be covert or quiet. Anyone in that housing complex in the rock would have heard us coming without even trying, but there were no heads popping out of the windows, no dogs barking, and no little kids crying or playing. We climbed the stairs, slowing down as we went.

Stairmaster, I thought. *Gotta get a Stairmaster and start exercising.* Why did I always think something like this during a magical emergency, and then never do anything about it until the next magical emergency? I hated running. I hated exercising. But I really hated feeling like I was an asthmatic when I had friends in harm's way more.

I was gulping for oxygen when we got to the first level, and started searching room by room for Paul and Jonah. All of us were somewhat winded except for Aiden. When I gave him a questioning look, rather than having the air to ask the question, he just raised an eyebrow and said, "What? I've been going to a gym, and jogging, and I push heavy carts of car parts at work. We've been doing more and more of this, and I figured I needed to start getting in better shape."

Get off my brain wave, I thought, as I nodded at him and kept going. There was a time when we'd practically been finishing each other's sentences, one of us able to pick up what the other was thinking without much effort. I didn't think we'd been able to keep doing it when we hadn't spent that much time together until the last week, but I'd been wrong before. We stopped for a second, and I took a swig from the now warm Gatorade in my backpack, swallowing the tart, slightly salty orange liquid in the plastic bottle. It helped me get my breath back.

Jonah and Paul weren't on the first level of rooms, so we headed for the steps to the next level, and we repeated the search. We kept going upstairs and searching rooms, and, of course, found our friends standing on their own, facing the back of the room, in a trance, staring at the floor.

"Jonah! Paul! Wake up!" I called, grabbing at Jonah's shoulders and shaking them. He didn't respond. I tried the same with Paul. No dice. I couldn't even shake Paul because of the size of his shoulders and chest. He didn't budge.

Mia tried with Jonah, up to and including kissing him on the lips. I gave her a look, and she shrugged. "What?" she said. "It works in some of the fairy tales you've had come up, and it's worked in some of the stories Dad had me read. It was worth trying, wasn't it?"

I had to give it to her; she was right. But I hadn't ever heard of an American story that involved waking up with a kiss, and that had been mostly what we'd been dealing with this time around. I didn't have the heart to tell her that, though. She'd had a decent point, and if it made her feel like she was doing something that might help, then I wasn't going to dispute her effort or her thought process.

Okay, so we'd found them. But we weren't going to be able to drag them down the stairs and back through the portal, especially Paul. So what were we going to do?

Aiden circled the room, looking for something. I left Mia and Allie to their ideas of how to check Jonah and Paul for magic, for a way to wake them up, and for a way to try to see what was going on. Pete slapped his brother in the face, but that didn't work either. I walked over to Aiden, looking in the corners.

"What are you doing?" I asked.

"I'm looking to see if there's some kind of salt or binding agent in the corners by the floor. If this is a spell, it seems to be somehow confined to this room, and maybe even confined to them. I'm trying to figure out if there's a circle or a rune or some kind of way of keeping this in. Is there some way that is keeping them asleep that isn't affecting us?"

He had one heck of a good point, but I thought he might be looking in the wrong place. While he searched the corners of the room, I started looking at their feet. Nothing was at Paul's feet, but Jonah's was another story. There was green moss right at the edges of his shoes, not a lot, but just enough to notice. And it was growing, although it was growing very, very slowly.

"Aiden, you gotta see this," I said, waving him over.

I still had Mia's keys with the penlight in my pocket, and yanked it out, shining it on the green, which was barely a shadow at his feet, but it seemed to grow a bit more with the addition of light.

"I guess there's not a lot of doubt, then," Aiden said. "as if we'd had a lot of doubt before as to where he came from."

"No doubt at all," said a voice coming from the doorway. "He's the apple heir."

I couldn't see who it was. The battery on the penlight, not much left to begin with, flickered and failed. The room wasn't letting in a whole lot of light and there were enough people in the room that I had no idea where the voice had come from at first.

"Who's there?" I asked, somewhat stupidly. "What do you want from our friends?"

The unknown voice didn't answer right away, and I didn't hear any of my other friends say anything else. When I looked around the room, it seemed my friends were in the same state as Jonah and Paul, some form of sleeping on their feet where they were upright, but not responding to anything.

Why wasn't I in the same state?

Before I could say anything, I saw movement around the sides of my friends, where they stood silently around the room. And then I realized I couldn't move anything from the neck down. I could talk. I could hear. I just couldn't move.

"You must be the Grimm girl everyone's been talking about. I hear things. The little girl who has everyone so worried that you'll upset the apple cart, so to speak." A long, slender leg with a bare foot slipped around Jonah, followed by a lithe woman who looked like she was in her early twenties. She was beautiful, with dark hair and classic, sculpted, Native American features. Who in the world was she?

"Call me Frog Woman," she said. "I'm wondering why you are in my lands and what you could possibly want from an old Indian woman who lives alone?"

CHAPTER THIRTY-SIX

How did she know who I was if she lived here alone, and what brought Jonah and Paul here? For that matter, if she lived here alone, where in the world was Babe? Why didn't I think of that when we'd first walked up to the cave dwellings? If Babe had been away from Paul, wouldn't he be huge enough that we'd have been able to spot him? Or had we missed the boat entirely?

I didn't have time for worrying about that at the moment. I had to figure out what we were doing here and how to get out of here.. "I'm sorry, ma'am, I don't know you. Can you tell me why my friends are here, and what you might want with them?

"I didn't bring them here, miss. They came on their own. I'm not sorry to meet your green friend, however, and there's no question he is the apple heir, but I did not bring them here," she said in a quiet, but sultry voice. I'd have called it a whiskey voice, kind of like younger Kathleen Turner.

"He doesn't know much about his heritage, ma'am," I said. "If there is anything you can tell him, I know he would appreciate it."

"Are you bargaining for a favor, miss?" she asked, her peculiarly light eyes sparkling. They were a lighter color than the medium brown I would expect from someone with a Native American heritage. In fact, as she passed in front of the window and turned her head, they looked ocean blue. Where in the world had she gotten eyes that color? I wondered, but that wasn't what I needed from her immediately.

"I am not bargaining at this time. I merely made a statement that my friend was adopted by a family without children at a young age. It was not easy to confirm that he was who he is, and we had a deadline to keep."

"A deadline?" she asked, seemingly surprised.

"Yes," I answered. "We had to have him here before the American Thanksgiving holiday. That's tomorrow. Why did you want him here before that time?"

"I didn't. They appeared on my doorstep, so to speak, and so I invited them inside. I saw the spark in the green one's eyes, and recognized it."

Wait a minute. If she hadn't set the deadline, then she wasn't the one who had Babe. And if she wasn't the one who had Babe, we'd been set up by whoever actually did have that ox. How much danger were we in with her? I'd never heard of her before. Or were we in danger? How did she know the apple heir, and how did she even know there *was* one in the first place?

"Ma'am, our friend here," I indicated with a tilt of my head toward Paul, "he had something he valued taken away from him, and a ransom note was left, indicating he should be at the Zion National Park's Zion Narrows by noon today, moving the deadline up twelve hours. We don't know why, or what they want, but what was taken from him isn't something easily hidden."

"I don't have anything hidden here. I did not take anything from anyone," she answered, and her words tasted like truth.

"Have you ever been to Minnesota? Ohio? Nebraska? Illinois?" I asked, naming the places where this journey had had weird magical stuff come up.

"It has been over three hundred of your human years since I've gone into the mortal realm and traveled east of the human marked Zion Park. I have not been in the Ohio Valley region since that time." She sounded sad when she said it, like there had been some reason why she'd left that area disappointed or heartbroken or something.

"If you don't mind, ma'am, I actually think someone has set you up," I said. I was becoming pretty sure on that point.

She waved her hand, and I felt my lower body start moving again, twitching from being so still. I ignored the twitching as best I could.

"Miss, what do you mean . . . someone has set me up? I have not seen many beings in my own realm in many hundred years. I've stepped over into the mortal realm only a handful of times, when it appears someone is close enough to risk stepping over into my own portal. I've closed up all but one, to keep my people from trying to come back here until I can get some things fixed."

"Frog Woman, if you've heard of me, then maybe you've heard

that I've tried to help out in other realms. Is there something I can help you with?" I asked. "Maybe we could trade a service of some kind for information, or for a way back to the mortal realm."

She shrugged. "I'll not keep most of you, but I must keep the apple heir. I've tried every magical means at my disposal to fix my land for my people to return, but my magic is not enough to fix the land that went barren under my watch. The apple heir must stay."

I sighed. This was going to be a long negotiation, then, because *damned* if I was going to leave Jonah here to save the rest of us. I owed it to Mia to get at least one of the men she loved home in one piece.

"I think if he had been asked, he'd be willing to help out, but he doesn't have a lot of practice using his abilities. It would take some considerable time and effort for him to help you, and so I think him helping you at all is a considerable boon."

She narrowed her eyes. "Are you under some impression I can't prevent you from leaving? Did you not feel the restraint I put on your body to keep you here?"

"I did. I'm not insensible to the idea you could keep us here against our will for years should you wish it. However, even forcing us to stay here would not necessarily get you what you want. We are, all of us, mostly human, which means we need to eat and drink and sleep and use the restroom and do all of those human-y type things that keep us alive. Keeping us here would require you to go to some expense to keep us fed and watered and awake, and, well, not smelly. So keeping us here would either cost you further or kill us. Neither of those things gets you the help you want without our agreement."

Frog Woman seemed to consider that statement. "I could torture you."

"And I've gotten myself freed from one situation where I was taken to and kept in a magical realm against my will. Rather than test our individual abilities to hurt each other, or to work against each other, why not see if we can work out an agreement where we both might benefit? I see no reason why you, why me, or my friends should be hurt." And maybe I should be taking more care in what I was saying. Was I all but daring her to test me? Too late to turn back now. "My own stepmother tried to keep me against my will, against the rules of her own court. And when she went back on her own word, and they ruled that she had to give me back, she tried to attack me. I won that battle. She still bears the scars I gave her in that fight. I will always live with regret that it had to turn out that way. Why fight when one can bargain? And as long as everyone lives up to their agreement, then all parties win in the end. No one wins when fighting starts."

She considered my statement. "My people have learned the hard way that fighting a better equipped adversary will not end in their favor. They have also learned, however, that not everyone who bargains does so in good faith. So while I would prefer this not turn into a fight of force, I don't know if I can trust you to bargain in good faith."

"I have no worries that if you had other magical contacts, they could and would tell you I have kept my word on all counts in my dealings in matters such as these. If you don't have a way to make such contacts, then I fear we're at an impasse. But let me propose again that we bargain. If I fail to live up to my end, we can fight. You have more magic than I do. I have other weapons and tools, and more people than you do. I don't know who would win. That doesn't mean either of us would win in the end." Please let her not test me on that one. We had weapons, true, but what good were they if we were all frozen to the ground? Then again, the fact she was even considering it told me maybe she couldn't hold us here like that indefinitely. I was counting on it.

Of course, there was also the possibility holding us here indefinitely would deprive us of the oxygen we needed to live. She only had to hold us long enough to suffocate us to death. I tried not to think of it; after all, I'd been breathing enough to speak even though she'd frozen my body below the neck. Maybe it didn't work that way.

"Ma'am, I think we can work out a deal, if you'll meet me halfway."

The silence between us stretched into a minute, then two. I didn't turn away from her, waiting for her answer.

"I think we can do business, at least for now," she said, waving an arm.

My friends all collapsed to the ground, their legs twitching from being frozen just like mine had. I heard a voice from the ground.

"What the hell just happened, and get the hell off of me!" It was Bert, wide awake and thoroughly annoyed.

Her eyes widened when he hopped out of the towel he'd been wrapped in.

Oh, dear. Frog Woman met our frog, who might have just thrown a monkey wrench into the whole negotiation.

CHAPTER THIRTY-SEVEN

She was transfixed by the talking frog as I tried to open negotiations. Finally, she stopped me from talking about a give and take, and informed me it would be better for her to tell me the background of how she came to be here.

"I have a very large problem and I'm not altogether sure how to fix it. Better to tell you the background and then ask if you have a recommendation."

I nodded.

"My people lived in these caves in the mortal realm. I cared for them. I was a guardian for them, keeping the water of the rivers and the creeks flowing at the right rate and flow by weaving baskets and rushes that dammed or let loose the water as needed to keep them safe and to keep their crops fruitful and their families safe. This went on for years. Then, suddenly, the water stopped flowing. My power was receding. My people tried to adapt, they tried to live, and then they gave up. The once fertile land that had sustained so many of our families would no longer keep us and hold us alive and people were dying. I watched, for several generations, as the land let us down. I have not yet figured out why the water disappeared. At this point, the land was still in the mortal realm. I yanked it through a portal, to preserve what was left of their heritage until I could find a way to restore the land to what it had been for generations."

I guess she'd never heard of global climate change. "Did you know what caused the water to dry up?"

"I did not." Frog Woman looked sad. "It must have been a trick played by Coyote, the trickster, but I never did figure out how he had done it."

I'd heard something of Coyote before, but I didn't know where. Had Dad done some project on it? I had no way to know at the moment. "So what did you try to do about it? I'm sure you tried to do something to change it."

She nodded, and motioned that I should follow her. She walked out of the room we were in, and headed down the stairs towards the ground. Why couldn't we have found our friends on the ground before we'd climbed all those stairs? At least going down was easier than going up had been, but she wasn't stopping in between levels. My legs felt rubbery as she kept going down.

Frog Woman got to the bottom of the stairs and turned back again to talk to me. I was still several steps above her. I couldn't respond just yet, being out of breath. She told me she had heard of a man in the Ohio Valley with the power to make things grow. She did not know how his power worked, but she felt that seeking him out would be important, and she wanted to see if he might work with her to find a solution. She had gone through her portal and had traveled to the Ohio Valley region, to find that he was only interested in spreading his religion and planting apple seeds.

"What was his name?" asked Aiden, although there was no doubt in my head as to who she was talking about.

"John Chapman," was the answer. She hadn't given up, and had asked if she could learn more about the apples he was planting and their uses. "I thought if I could learn more about his methods, then maybe I could use them to bring plants back to my own village, even if they were different plants than my people knew from before."

They had traveled across Pennsylvania, Illinois, and Ohio together, planting Chapman's apple trees, but she kept noticing that the climate was different than the land she'd wanted to learn to protect. Chapman was fast becoming a friend, but at the same time she was concerned she wasn't learning what she needed to in order to fix her lands and bring back her people. She kept asking him if there was a way for them to combine their abilities, and he finally, reluctantly, gave in. Together, they planted an orchard and the apples were grown to full size in twenty minutes, with Chapman encouraging the plants to grow and Frog Woman directing the water within the plants and within the ground to force the growth of the plant.

Frog Woman had been thrilled, hoping for the two of them to go back to her lands and use the newfound magic to rekindle the life in what small amount of plants remained, but Chapman refused. On the night she had planned to take her leave, they had toasted each other with Chapman's applejack, and took their leave of each other.

It was on her way back that she realized she was pregnant. As Chapman was a mortal, she knew her child would be mortal as well, and would not have an easy life in a land where no food grew and no water would flow.

"I left my daughter with the family that had taken me in. They were farmers, working with the land, and there was a stream nearby where my child would always have water surrounding her and running through the land. I knew I had made the right choice in leaving her when I got back and the land that was mine was completely barren. It would not have been right to bring her back here and see her starve to death."

Huh. I couldn't help but think of Aiden as she talked about her own half-magical, half-human child. Aiden was the only known half-magical, half-human being we had known of, but it sounded as if Jonah might be descended from another. I wondered if there was any way to find out what problems that child might have had as they grew up, and had children of their own, but that was a few hundred years in the past. But Jonah was living proof it was possible for someone with that kind of heritage to pass it on. I hoped Aiden was listening.

"Ma'am," Jonah started, then cleared his throat. "How did you know your child had a child? How did you know that the line continued? If you haven't gone west of the state line, then how did you know someone existed?"

She shrugged. "I have had some other friends since that time in the human realm. While I don't generally choose to cross that portal, I did meet people in the park who have helped keep me apprised of what was going on."

Jonah's mouth was hanging open. "You mean to tell me, that all that time I was living in a foster home, all the time I was alone, hoping and praying for someone to find me and adopt me, I had some kind of relative in this country?" He looked confused and a bit angry.

Frog Woman shrugged. "It was better if I left you with humans. Coyote has spent way too many years waiting and hoping for something he could use against me, something he could use as blackmail. I heard that you found yourself a wonderful family. Do you regret living with them?"

"Um, no." he said, looking down at his feet. "They were awesome. I wouldn't ever trade that away for anything."

"So I did make the right choice," she said, with a grin. "I left you with them because you were happy. Coyote was beginning to circle around again. He ended up taking one of my human friends and tricking them into telling them I'd had a child, and threatened to have them killed. I don't believe he would actually do that, but I stopped ever checking on you again. When he couldn't get more information, Coyote killed the human that had been keeping me informed. My friend refused to give him the information about where you'd been adopted, and Coyote couldn't find you."

Wait a minute. I was starting to think Coyote might have been working with humans and magical beings alike, and maybe had written the ransom notes to drag us out here. But what would Coyote have wanted with Jonah, and why drag us out here where we'd meet Frog Woman?

Except that we'd been an hour early to the meeting.

I was pretty sure if we'd been on time, we'd have never gotten inside the portal, and they probably had another plan for us, one we wouldn't like.

CHAPTER THIRTY-EIGHT

Frog Woman wanted to talk one on one with Jonah, and wild horses wouldn't have been able to drag him away from the sole living biological relative he had on this earth. As they spoke, I filled in the others on what had happened while they'd been frozen, and caught them up on my own guesses as to what might be waiting for us to deal with later. I thought I had the whole thing figured out, but there was still the possibility I'd missed something.

"Ma'am, I think we can probably come to some agreement here. We do wish to return to our lands, but I think our friend here might be willing to work with you on some magic to see what can come back to your land. I will not leave him here, however, because he can't survive here indefinitely, as the rest of us also cannot live here. If you allow all of us to leave, I would personally guarantee that he returns within the moon cycle to work with you on finding a way to bring back cultivation of some kind to your land."

She nodded, her eyes on Jonah.

His eyes were bright and wide-open. "That's fine with me," he said. "But you need to know that I don't know how this works all the time. I might not be able to do much to help you just because I don't know how."

She smiled. "I do understand. I believe we can work towards greater things."

I stepped in. "One caveat. I don't believe either of you should be working magic in the mortal realm. Any experimentation should be done here. I believe we can arrange some supplies for you to start working on experiments with plants. For the supplies, I think we should have another favor."

She narrowed her glance at me. "What do you wish?"

"I think we could agree to Jonah coming to see you once every month, for a period of twenty-four hours at a stretch, to experiment, to work on your magic, for the space of one year. But I also believe we're going to be stepping out of that portal into a trap. If we are, we may not be able to actually get Jonah back here to do so. I'd like to know if you're willing to help us see who's on the other side of the portal waiting for us, and to assist us in getting our friend's ox free from captivity."

Jonah nodded his head, eagerly. Good, I thought. I hated I was negotiating on his behalf without having talked to him first, but it looked like he was in agreement.

"Ox?" she asked. "Who in the world keeps an ox anymore? Your farmers don't use them to work the land, and the land here cannot be worked."

Paul meekly raised his hand. "I do, ma'am. He's a friend."

"Of course," she said. "The lumberjack. But why would someone steal your ox to get all of you to come here?"

"I don't have a clue, ma'am. I think they meant to use the threat of hurting Babe, that's the ox, ma'am, to get us here, and I think they meant to lure you into the human world. Are you weaker there?" I asked.

She looked at me thoughtfully. "No, but I did put it about that I was some years ago. I just wanted them to leave me alone, and I thought that if they would just stay out of my own little section of the universe, it would be enough. Apparently I was wrong, if they are using others to draw me out."

"Who did you tell this to?" Mia asked, finding her voice again. She'd been so eerily quiet this afternoon. But. I had so many other things in my brain that my worry for her was on hold.

"Knowing who was told might be the first step in figuring out the whole thing."

Frog Woman considered that for a moment. She turned her back, crossing her arms over her chest, and it was a long several minutes before she turned back around.

"There's a group of humans who I've dealt with over the last fifty years or so. They've seemed fairly organized and have stated they wish to preserve the original purpose of the land, and to bring the land back to whatever state it should be in. Their leader was fairly charming, and seemed to be very passionate about preserving the past.

I was quite taken by him, and I told him I needed help in guarding the portal to my lands, because I was weaker outside of the magical realms. I told him I needed human help to prevent others from coming to see me, because that way I wouldn't have to police the portal itself when I could be working on raising magic to fix the land."

Oh, crap. If the people who had really taken Babe had been the ones Frog Woman had been dealing with over the years, and they thought she wouldn't come to the portal, then they never would have thought we would actually cross the portal. Or would they? Were they waiting on us to come back out, an ambush, with Babe's safety still on the line? Or were they looking to capture her as well? I looked around my group of friends, and realized each and every one of us was remarkable in our own way.

I was the last living direct descendant of the Grimm brothers.

Mia was the daughter of Tobias Andersen, the human boogeyman to magical do-bad-ers, and descended from the same family as Hans Christian Andersen.

Jonah, as we'd learned this week, was in all likelihood descended from Johnny Appleseed.

Aiden was the only living half-human, half-faerie being, and his father was a member of the faerie high court, as well as one who played the political game well enough to call in favors to benefit himself and his son.

Allie was the daughter of the original Alice from Wonderland.

Bert was a human cursed into a frog.

The rest of our group? Paul Bunyan. Calamity Jane. Cordwood Pete. Legendary figures of American tall tales and history, whose lives and exploits were larger than life.

We were *all* individual targets. But put all of us together, and what did we have? A highly desirable group of targets, ripe for the picking. And if we were distracted by the loss of one of our own? Likely we wouldn't be paying attention to all the details we should be paying attention to, the kind of details that had saved my butt on more than one occasion.

So were Frog Woman's humans actually human? I asked if she knew for sure.

"I didn't sense magic around them, but that doesn't mean they were human. It just means they weren't using any at the time," she said. "They said they were human. Lying just doesn't happen between magical beings, so I figured they had to be human."

She was right and yet she wasn't; I'd learned that from my evil faerie stepmother. Magical beings *could* in fact, lie, but it was highly frowned upon. A single lie could be the basis for unseating monarchs, for toppling dictators, for serious, long-standing change. And magical realms weren't exactly known for embracing change. That didn't mean they couldn't do it. My stepmother *had* lied, and she had broken her promise, something even more frowned upon than lying, and the fact that she had done both had saved my life, and likely Aiden's, as well.

But humans could, and did, lie on a regular basis. Sometimes they got caught. Sometimes they didn't. Sometimes, they even got rewarded for that; just look at the politicians who got elected in November, and all of the campaign promises and mudslinging in the political ads. Never mind whatever the tobacco company CEOs made from covering up the dangers of cigarettes, or the promises of a public relations spin doctor saving the latest pro athlete from a scandal of some kind.

I didn't like it, but I was beginning to think that regardless of whether or not the people she was dealing with were exactly that, people, they had absolutely lied to her about their intentions and their goals.

And I had a bad feeling about that.

CHAPTER THIRTY-NINE

I quizzed Frog Woman extensively on the people she'd made a deal with to guard her portal. She truly had believed she was doing something good, by getting someone to guard the portal to protect her back. She'd been surprised to see two people standing right outside of her portal, looking at it like they'd known what it was, rather than the normal tourists and campers and backpackers. She'd immediately stuck her head out to see what they wanted; surprised no one was present to guard the portal itself from magical intruders. She'd recognized something in Jonah, and had hypnotized them by harnessing the water in their bodies to compel their behavior in the way that she wanted.

Neat trick, I thought, and filed it away for later. Maybe her ability with water, combined with Jonah's ability to heal plants, would go a long way to fixing things. The next thing I had to offer her was our assistance and consultation on coordinating their magics, but that would mean bargaining with Aiden's area of expertise rather than my own. I had to see what we might be facing before I made any further deals.

"Ma'am, do ya think ya can see through that there purple portal thingy?" Jane asked, taking the words right out of my mouth. "Be nice ta see what's waitin' for us on the other side."

"What she said." I grinned at Jane, who beamed. I got the feeling that even though she was rather rough around the edges, she was actually a gentle soul. I saw her look over at Paul, and, as I'd suspected, I saw a look of tenderness on her face. What was it about magical emergencies that seemed to foster friendships and romance? With that thought, I couldn't bring myself to look at Aiden, but I felt his eyes on me.

Frog Woman took a deep breath. "Yes, I can. In fact, I can see out better than I can see in, if I'm in the mortal realm. I used to be stronger in this realm than out there, because it was my own home base; but my powers are stronger in the presence of water, and there is more water in the mortal realm than there is in my realm."

So, did she just admit that *she* had lied to the humans about her powers? I raised my eyebrows at her.

"I know what you're thinking," she said, apparently reading my mind. "I didn't lie. Just like humans are more protected behind a threshold than they are out in the open, magical beings are generally more powerful on their home turf. That's what I told them, and that's the truth. I didn't tell them the presence of more water makes my powers stronger."

And that was where magical beings got away with it. They bent the truth enough so they could say the exact opposite and still not be accused of lying or of breaking a promise because there was enough truth behind the statement that it wasn't completely wrong. And, unlike the last time I'd caught a magical being bending the truth, this time, it was only bent, not broken, and this time, it would work in my favor.

"Okay, can you look out of the portal and see what's out there without them being able to see that you're looking?" I asked. "We need to know what we're facing before we step a single toe outside. Can we open this portal from this side?"

Frog Woman shook her head. "I sealed it so that I was the only one who could open it. I wanted to be able to work on my land without interruption or danger. I didn't want anyone bringing in anything that could pollute the land when I was trying to fix it, so I made it so that no one could come in without my allowing it. I brought in Paul and Jonah because I saw something in Jonah. Turns out, I was right, he is someone who might be able to help me."

And suddenly it became a whole lot clearer as to what was going on. "Follow me for a second, guys," I said. "I think whoever took Babe had some idea that you would be sent my way. I think we've been looking at this backwards from the beginning. Babe wasn't the real target. Frog Woman isn't even the real target. I think the real purpose of all of this was to get us all in the same place, at the same time, and find some way for us all to be either eliminated or put on display, I'm not sure which." I explained to Frog Woman what I meant. It wasn't like she hadn't pieced together who some of us were, already, and I was pretty sure the so-called humans who had tricked her were the ones that had taken Babe.

Aiden's jaw dropped. I was a little surprised myself; surprised he hadn't figured it out on his own. "You're absolutely right, Janie," he said. "I don't know why I didn't see it before. Paul, in some ways, that's good news. It means Babe wasn't the real target, and I doubt they'll do anything to him if he's the bait to get us into place. The bad news is that I think we're the ones in real danger."

"I apologize, Frog Woman. We brought metal into your realm with us. I know that isn't normally allowed." I thought for a second. "Wait a minute, I thought you said no one could get in unless you let them in?"

She smiled. "I allowed you into my realm when I couldn't figure out what these two wanted. I'm not sure they could articulate it, but I also don't think I was asking the right questions. They just told me they were looking for a friend, and that they were there to meet the person who had taken their friend. They asked about the Big Rock Candy Mountain, and I was curious. I let them in, and meant to freeze them, to still their bodies, to allow me to go look for what was going on. Then you came up, looking for them, and I thought I would get more answers that way. I understood why you had metal; you were looking to protect your friends. You didn't know me. You had no way of knowing whether or not I was going to hurt them. And I knew I could still the fluids in your bodies to prevent you from employing your weapons."

She sure had gotten more answers. And a whole heap of trouble. But, damn, she'd thought of a pretty good plan to use while she got those answers. I thanked her.

She stepped up to the portal, and got as close as she could without putting her face through, her hands splayed out on either side of her head, like a little kid looking through a knothole in a high picket fence. She watched carefully for a few minutes, before she pulled back and turned to report, "Six men with guns are searching your vehicles. Four more don't appear to be carrying weapons, but they are wearing what you call suits, and they seem to be very unhappy with the men carrying the guns. I recognized those men from the last time I dealt with the human group. They're some of the younger members of that group, and they've only been around the last fifteen or twenty years. There is one man, with long hair, also wearing a suit, who is smiling. He looked familiar."

"Can you describe him?" I asked, pulling out the gun from my backpack, and encouraging the others to start arming themselves. Allie put Bert inside of her zip-up hoodie and tucked the bottom of the sweatshirt into the waistband of her pants, keeping him hidden while also keeping him warm. Aiden and Jonah had the crossbows. Allie had the rock salt shotgun, and Mia and I had the handguns that had already been loaded with Tobias's special ammunition. If she thought men who had been around for fifteen or twenty years were younger, what would she think of us? Mia and I hadn't hit our twenty-fifth birthdays yet; we would in the next few months. Jonah and Aiden, well, they were only a year or two older than we were. And Allie was still a teenager. I didn't say anything. I didn't want to remind the immortal being how old she was.

"The man with the long hair? Well, his hair is gray and black, and it's tied back off of his face. It's as long as his waist, oh my," she stopped. "He's turning toward me."

We all waited, holding our breath.

"It's Coyote. He's the one behind all of this," she said.

Well, I was glad she knew who it was. Because we didn't have the time to do the research to figure it out for ourselves.

CHAPTER FORTY

S he filled us in, briefly. Coyote was her enemy, but not because he was evil. He was a trickster, constantly playing pranks and causing things to not go as planned. And he was constantly tricking her and her people out of the water they craved for their plants and their lands.

"He is tricksy and smart, and will always have another plan, and another, until you think he couldn't have another plan left," she said.

We had to go. There was no reason to stay any long than we already had. We were armed, fairly well rested, and had a magic user behind us. We would not get any stronger if we stayed; in fact, we'd likely get weaker once we ran out of food and water. Aiden and I agreed, without speaking, to step through first, keeping Mia, Paul, and Jonah behind us.

As we stepped through, we had the attention of every single one of them, staring back at us.

"Well, well, well," said the man with the long black and gray ponytail. "You must be Ms. Grimm. And if you are, then this has to be Mr. Ferguson. Word on the street is that the two of you are inseparable. I should have known you'd be together. Oh, wait. I did know."

I pointed the gun at him, and Aiden had the crossbow pointed as well, stepping just far enough out of the way for the others to step through behind us. I noticed a slight stumble to Aiden's step, and grimaced. He was completely coordinated in the magical realms, but he had two left feet in the human world. I realized he hadn't been nearly as bad lately, but I didn't have time to do much thinking about it. We were holding projectile weapons and pointing them at people who had the same pointed back at us.

As Frog Woman came through the portal right behind us, I saw Coyote's smug smirk change into a blank look of shock.

"You," he stammered. "You haven't come through that portal in fifteen years! Why would you come through now?"

She smiled, a long, languid, slow spread of a grin against his surprise. "I came through to keep you from your latest mischief, Coyote. You seek to trick others for your own gain, without regard to their wants or needs, and only for your own amusement."

His hands came up before him, and suddenly the air blossomed with a cloudy fog, so thick it was almost impossible to see through. I couldn't see past the end of the gun. I reached one hand out to my left, toward Aiden, with the gun still held high with my right. My hand landed on his elbow, which was raised with the cross bow, and he did not drop it. I felt the twitch of the muscle under my hand, and then he relaxed, as if the chemistry between us had surprised him, and then he'd remembered we were in the middle of something important.

I felt better for having my hand on him, to know he was right there beside me, and to know we hadn't gone anywhere. I couldn't see five inches in front of my face, but everything was fine as long as I could keep my hand on Aiden. And then, the fog started to clear.

Frog Woman came up to me and the fog began to lift. Her eyes had gone that watery blue again, the same color I had noticed when she had frozen us all in our tracks in her own realm. She must have harnessed the water in the fog the Coyote had set to confuse us. She had the water held in a bubble in between her hands, and she shoved it through the portal to her own realm.

"I do not believe in wasting that which would bring back our crops," she said. "It may not seem much, but every little bit helps."

It made me wonder if maybe Jonah and I should be researching irrigation systems when we went back. No matter what magic she might have, plants wouldn't do much of anything without water. And no matter how much she could manipulate water, one cannot manipulate what one does not have.

And right now, we didn't have a clue what to do next.

When the fog finally dissipated enough, I noticed our ATVs were still there, but the other men were not. There were, however, tracks from another set of ATVs, ones that led in a different direction from the ones we'd made on our way in. We loaded into our ATVs, with Bert demanding to get out of Allie's shirt, getting fractious and snappy with us until the dust started kicking up again from our movement on the open air vehicles.

I drove the lead ATV, following the tracks we found all the way to a parking lot on the edge of the park, not more than a couple of miles from the one we'd parked the Winnebago in when we'd picked up our own transportation. We found a park ranger getting out of his truck just as we pulled up.

"Hey, sir, can you tell me if you've seen a gentleman with a long black and gray ponytail, wearing a suit, walking around with about ten other men?"

He nodded at me.

"Can you tell me where they went?" I asked, following up on my earlier question.

"Don't know for sure, but they were in a van with a logo on the side. They work at Coyote Gulch Zip Line Tours and Americana Museum." The park ranger looked impatient, like he was late for work. I let him go without asking anything else.

"Well, at least we have a better location," I said to the others. "We need to find out what we're dealing with. I wonder if there are brochures anywhere, or a website we could check, or something like that. We really need to check things out a little better, if we can, before we run right into the fray."

We looked around, and sure enough, on the other side of the parking lot was a ranger station. Rather than descend en masse on the rangers, only Aiden and I headed to the station. The rest of the group went back to the Winnebago. Frog Woman seemed impressed by it. She kept saying the last camper she'd seen didn't drive itself, that it had been silver, and rather tiny. I almost wanted to tell her that there were still Airstream trailers on the road, but I didn't want to interrupt the fun the others were having, showing her all the amenities of the camper. I hoped they had enough room to actually show her everything. We had things packed in there pretty tight.

Aiden and I, on the other hand, walked slowly to the ranger station. It was the first I'd really been alone with him since that morning at Pecos Bill's cabin, the morning before Tobias died. The minute we were out of earshot, he asked me, "How are you doing with all this? You've done an incredible job of keeping us all on track, here. I hope you know that."

I shrugged. "What else is there to do? We can't just give up and go back. Paul would never get Babe back. Mia would never forgive herself for that; she would feel like her father's death did mean anything if we don't finish the job. Jonah would never get the information he wants desperately about his background. Even if he would never admit it, he's dying to know more about who and what he is, and who could blame him?" We walked up the steps, and opened the door.

The same ranger we'd stopped in the parking lot was behind an information desk, looking slightly bored. "Oh," he said. "It's you. What can I help you with?"

I asked, "What can you tell us about Coyote Gulch, the company whose logo you told us about on that van? We're looking for some things to do in the area, and that actually sounded interesting. What all do they have for groups? What about individuals? It's more than just shooting down a mountain on a zipline, isn't it?"

The ranger raised his eyebrow at me. "You're familiar with a zip line, right?"

I nodded. I hadn't ever actually been down one, but there were some in Ohio, and I'd seen the pictures of smiling people wearing helmets and literally zipping down some rope line from a higher point to a lower one. It looked like a lot of fun, and if I didn't have anything else pressing, I could see something like that as a good afternoon out for all of us, even the F.A.B.L.E.S. guys. We'd all been working awfully hard on getting the Wonderland folks set up, and we'd all been working so hard on trying to figure out what was going on with Paul, with Babe, and with Jonah. Maybe, when life settled down enough for us to have an off day, we needed to schedule something like that.

The ranger, of course, had no idea what I was thinking about. "Well, it's not a bad zip line course. There are others that are longer, or that might have a better view, but it's really not that bad. The true value here is that museum. Here, take a look." He handed me a glossy brochure.

Meet the real legends behind the tales! The true heroes, the true story behind the legends! See the real artifacts and know the truth! the brochure screamed, with comic book-like coloring and lots of exclamation points. I half expected to see the words "Pow!" or "Bam!" somewhere on the page, but they were missing. I leaned in, getting a little closer to read the fine print. There, in smaller letters, they were advertising a real blue ox, debuting in the Bunyan Barn, and being made available to the public for the first time ever starting Thanksgiving weekend.

Thanksgiving weekend. Huh.

I thanked the ranger, took the brochure, and we walked outside.

"Aiden, are you thinking what I'm thinking?" I asked.

He still hadn't fully processed what we'd seen. "Are they really that dumb? Is that what all this is really about?"

It sure looked that way to me.

CHAPTER FORTY-ONE

There were a million and one questions from the rest of the group when we got back to the Winnebago and explained what we'd found.

"I think we are all potential targets," I said. "There's not a single one of us here that wouldn't be interesting to the people running this establishment. We are all at risk."

They all looked at each other.

"I'm all ears as to ideas, guys. I'm a little worried about us just walking in there. I'm a little worried about what happens if we just go home. I think that if we leave without doing anything, they'll eventually come for us. It doesn't look like they are trying to hurt people, but if you look at the brochure, they are showing pictures of Annie Oakley, pictures of someone named Slue-foot Sue, and they mention Babe. It makes me wonder if these people are free to leave. And if they're not, what happens if we get caught? Will we be allowed to leave?"

Paul started to break down. "We can't just leave Babe there! I can't. I'd rather be locked up with him than let him live like that!"

Jane went to calm him, adding her own sentiment. "'A course we can't let 'em get away with it, but we can't just 'a go in there, guns blazin' and make 'em give us that ox, now, can we? I mean, wouldn't they call the law?"

She had a point. So what could we do to prevent becoming victims in Coyote's get-rich scheme?

We started batting around ideas. Going in guns blazing, as Jane put it, was likely not a good idea. We might now how to point a gun, and how to fire it, but without Tobias, we certainly did not have the training or the know-how to truly go Rambo on them. And that didn't guarantee us that any of us would make it out okay, much less that we'd get Babe out. So that left us with the need to find out more, to see what we could find out about the people who ran Coyote Gulch, and to see what we could find out about their operation.

We all piled into the Winnebago, and Aiden got behind the wheel. He hit the curb on the way out of the parking lot.

"Hey!"

"Watch out!"

"Be careful up there!"

All these statements came from the back passenger section, and Aiden apologized. I, on the other hand, was grinning like a loon. It had been a while since Aiden had truly done something clutzy, and hitting the curb, on the grand scheme of things, was really not all that bad. It reminded of me the old Aiden, the one who couldn't walk and chew gum at the same time, but had forgotten more about magic than any one of us actually knew.

We bumped our way back onto the road, and he turned to look in the rearview mirror with a sheepish grin. "Sorry, guys. Didn't realize I was that close to the edge."

They all started to complain about his driving, but I felt better now. He was acting more like himself. I smiled at him, and he seemed to relax enough to not hit the median in his effort to overcorrect from the curb.

Yeah, it would be a long trip if Aiden was driving, but it did give people some reason to take their mind off of the very strange situation in which we all found ourselves. I'm a big believer in stepping away and looking at something else when the problem in front of me seems insurmountable or too big to figure out.

And just like that, I had an idea. It would be stretching it to call it a plan.

"I think we've got to see what we can find out about the place, and then I think we need to see what we can find out about the person or persons, who own the business. I think we might then have ourselves an undercover operation, guys. I think we can actually do this," I said, and Aiden hit another pothole.

Mia looked at me, cocking her head sideways. "What are you thinking? We can't take any more time? How would we be able to know that Babe is safe? I mean, the meeting time was supposed to take place today; in about fifteen minutes as a matter of fact. After that, I don't think we've got a lot of . . . OW!"

The Winnebago bumped and jostled and Aiden grabbed the wheel with both hands as if he was afraid he was going to lose control of it.

In fact, he almost did. He finally brought us to a stop on the side of the road, just a few hundred yards down the road from the RV park at the Big Rock Candy Mountain, where we'd spent the night before.

"I think we've got a flat," he said. "Or at least that's what it felt like on the wheel."

Of course. And that was what had gotten us stopped before, at the campground where Tobias had met his end.

Wait a minute.

I glanced out of the windows at the front of the Winnebago, but I didn't see anything. I unbuckled my seatbelt, and now that we were stopped, I ran back through the camper, shoving people aside and looking out the windows. Finally, I saw it.

There was a coyote off in the distance, trotting away from us as if he wasn't in a hurry at all. Probably wasn't; we hadn't figured it out the first time, why presume we'd figure it out now? But I thought I had.

Coyote was behind everything. I was pretty sure he was behind the whole trip, from start to finish, that he'd maybe even have followed Paul around to see who he might go to for help. If he was collecting people with magical connections or backgrounds, or just enough of a connection to fool the touristy public, he must have thought he had hit the jackpot when Paul wound up at my house. Could he have landed this many targets without Paul coming to us? Probably not, but who was to say that that was the only goal.

The letter about bringing the apple heir had actually shown up well before Paul had tried to chop down the tree in my backyard. So, had they known about Jonah, or were they taking a shot in the dark?

I turned to Frog Woman. "Did anyone know of your daughter? About your relationship with John Chapman? Did anyone know you had a living descendant?"

She shook her head. "I don't know. I have told a few over the years, but other than the men at the Zion Narrows, I haven't told anyone."

And if the men at the Zion Narrows worked for Coyote, then of course he knew. And if they knew, would they have tried to do the research to track down Jonah? Or were they just using their knowledge of Frog Woman's child to try to capture another legendary person for their archive? I had a funny feeling they hadn't done the research, but had trusted to Paul's own tenacity and dedication to Babe, his desperation, to do the looking for them. And that was one gamble that had paid off.

So how to find out what they were actually doing in that place?

I was spinning ideas in my head of how I could get us into that place when there was a knock on the door of the Winnebago. I heard a muffled curse, and smelled a slight ozone burning snap to the air. I forgot Tobias had told us he'd had laid metal into the lining of the walls of the Winnebago. That meant the someone outside, trying to get in, was magical. I looked around the room. It hadn't kept Aiden out, who was half magic, but then, he'd been invited in. It hadn't kept Paul or Pete or Jane out, either, but they were the same, invited guests. Frog Woman, as well, fell into that category. But whatever was outside hadn't been invited, and I didn't plan to do so now.

There was no way I was opening that door.

CHAPTER FORTY-TWO

I opened the window over the kitchenette table, instead. I didn't stick my head outside, I'm not stupid, but opening the window meant I could at least ask what they wanted.

The man with the black and gray ponytail stood outside, wearing his suit. Rather than the coyote I'd seen off in the distance, he looked immaculately put together, as if he was headed to some corporate board meeting rather than knocking on the door of a beat up Winnebago on the side of the road. I didn't know what I had expected at the end of this journey, but Joe Q. Coyote in a power suit was not at the top of that list.

"Hullo, I'm looking for some friends who may be lost," he said.

"There's no one in this camper who knows you," I said. "What do you want?"

"Is that the Grimm girl?" he asked. "It's a pleasure to make your acquaintance. I've heard so much about you, and I've been looking forward to meeting you." He stepped towards the open window and away from the door.

I wasn't that worried, just yet, but my hands were still on the window latch. It wouldn't take much to slam that window closed again. If he truly could turn himself into a coyote, he could be a dangerous opponent, but I was pretty sure that even the most industrious of coyotes couldn't jump high enough to get to that window. If he tried, Aiden had a canister of table salt with the spout open, ready to douse him good, and Mia stood by with an iron wrench she'd pulled out of the tool box by the driver's seat. She'd whack him good if he reached even his pinky finger inside the window, and from the look on her face, she'd enjoy every minute of it.

"I can't say I share that sentiment, sir," I responded. "What do you want with us?"

"Why don't you come out here, where we can carry out a proper conversation?"

"Hell, no," I responded. "I'm not that stupid."

He laughed. "I never said you were, only that I'm getting a kink in my neck trying to talk to you. Why don't you be civilized?"

"Why don't you be realistic? We don't trust you. We have reason to believe you either wish to hurt us or imprison us. So why don't you tell us what you really want?" I asked.

"I'm immortal. I can wait you out."

"I've got a cell phone, the cops are on speed dial, and I've got AAA. I can have a tow truck, police car, fire truck, and ambulance out here fairly quick. Besides, as you've already learned, you can't get in here without an invitation, and we're not giving you one," I shot back. "Heck, we've got enough food and water in here for days, and we've even got a chemical toilet. We could sit right here on the side of the road and not have a reason to come out until we're good and ready."

"This is ridiculous," he said.

"I agree. So cut the crap. What do you want with us?"

I saw a couple of grins on the faces of the people inside. They were the kind of smile that told me that they were on the same page as me, the kind that told me they were all in.

He sighed. "I want to talk. Honest." Except he kept tapping on the side of the Winnebago, as if testing the anti-magic barrier or threshold, or whatever else Tobias had done to protect the place. It looked like Tobias had done a hell of a good job, because he wasn't finding a weakness.

"Bullshit," I said. "I'm sick of someone saying they just want to talk, or they just want some information, or they just want some other minor piddly thing. They might want that, true, but it's not the only thing they want. From what we've seen, it's not the only thing you want, either. It was you, wasn't it, who stole the ox from Paul?"

"Steal is such a strong word. I prefer borrowed to share with others."

"I don't care why you stole him. You stole someone very precious to a friend of mine. I think you were plotting to steal a person who is very precious to another friend of mine. And now, I think you're trying to steal us," I snapped. "So give me one very good reason why I don't call the police and ask them to send a SWAT team out here to save me from a stalker who is guilty of human trafficking."

"Because you would be exposing magic. If you call the human authorities, then I will have no choice but to attack the vessel you're traveling in. Whether you like it or not, sooner or later, I will succeed in breaching your defenses, and with a flat tire, there's only so far you can run."

He had a point; not that I was going to admit it to him. If he was strong enough, it would be like the attack the Seawitch had tried to level against my house a year or so ago; unrelenting, and one we could not win, and could not outlast.

"So what do you want?" I asked.

"I want you to come outside and talk to me. Just you, no one else," he said. "We might as well try to bargain our way through this stalemate rather than just bash each other with magic and weapons. And I assume that you have weapons, since you had them at the Narrows."

"Give me a minute," I said, and slammed the window shut.

Aiden was immediately shaking his head. "No, Janie. You can't do this. Please don't do this."

"I have to."

Mia tried. "I can't lose you, too."

I hugged her, hard. "I've got a plan; it's going to be okay. And if something goes wrong, then you get to unload on this guy."

She smiled. "Can't I just do that anyway?"

I shook my head at her. Even Paul tried to talk me down, but I wasn't having any of it.

We settled for having everyone armed to the teeth and bristling with weapons, posted at every window and opening available. I agreed I would open the door to the Winnebago, but not go outside unless and until it looked like I didn't have a choice. I actually felt a little better that they insisted on this. Despite my bravado, facing this guy down kind of scared me. I wanted a magic-proof vest, like the bulletproof ones police officers wore, but to stop a magical blast. I wasn't sure the threshold would actually hold in the Winnebago if Coyote started blasting us with magic.

I stepped to the doorway of the camper, and waited until the others were in position. Aiden had a crossbow aimed from the passenger side window, with the window cracked just enough to fit the bolt through and still see down the sights. Jane had taken the handguns back to the bedroom and was doing the same through the window back there. Mia had the shotgun filled with rock salt. And Jonah had the keys, sitting at the driver's side and ready to take off. Even if we had to drive off on the rim, the Winnebago would at least move. Allie had the cell phone in her hand, ready to call for the police if things went sideways.

We were as prepared as we were going to be.

I opened the door.

CHAPTER FORTY-THREE

Coyote watched with a smile as I opened the door, but he frowned again when he realized I wasn't stepping outside.

"Look, that wasn't the deal," he said.

"I wasn't aware that we made a deal. In a true negotiation, neither side gets everything they want. Both parties have to give a little. You get to actually see who you're talking to, but you don't get me outside of this threshold. I get to stay safer, and you and I actually have to talk, face to face. Believe me when I tell you this isn't my idea of a good time," I told him, crossing my arms over my chest.

"So how can I get you to understand?"

"Understand what? So far, all I've seen here is that you're willing to take what you want, without concern for what others want, or about free will. Have you been just taking things, so that you can benefit financially from exploiting them?" I asked. "It sure feels that way."

He shook his head. "We're in the business of protecting that which the human race cannot protect on their own. We have a facility that is safe for those magical beings who live in the human realm, and they can live their lives in peace."

"But not obscurity," I said. "I've heard about your museum."

"That's completely voluntary."

"Oh, yeah? What, you get them all to sign consent forms?" I asked, the soon to be lawyer in me peeking out a bit.

"Of course we did."

So, how does an ox sign a consent form? I wondered, but I left that one alone for now. "What happens if someone refuses to sign the form?"

"We can't take responsibility for someone who does not work to earn their keep. If they will not sign the form, we cannot guarantee their security," he tried to rationalize.

"So they agree to be exhibits in your living folklore and legend museum in exchange for your protection," I said, trying to sum up the arrangement as simply as I could.

He seemed to understand. "Of course. We have to keep everyone on the same page, or we risk everyone. If one person doesn't pull their weight, then technically, they are a danger to everyone else."

"And so you encourage conformity, punish non-conformity, and throw people out of the homes and security they know if they refuse to sign your consent forms. That doesn't sound like informed consent to me. Which, in the human courts, would make those waivers void, and unenforceable," I explained. "So how many of them are in real danger, and how many of them believe themselves to be in danger, because of the danger you yourselves have warned them about."

He bristled at that one, his eye taking on a yellowish glow as he got upset. "You don't understand. There has always been danger for those who are different. There is always danger for those who fall outside of society, the ones who are not in charge. I give them refuge."

"You give them the sand to bury their heads in, well past their own noses."

He was getting impatient. "Are you trying to tell me the human world is perfectly safe? There have been so many murders, so many rapes, so many assaults. How can we leave someone to the hands of the humans? Why would they ever wish to subject themselves to that?"

"Why would they bury themselves away? There are things in this world that make freedom worth it." I could do this all day. I'd done it with the Queen of Hearts, in Wonderland, although I hadn't known that the "queen" I'd been dealing with hadn't been the one actually holding the power on the throne. "How much have they missed, all while making themselves part of a sideshow exploiting their backgrounds, their abilities, their very beings, for you to make a buck?"

"Those 'bucks' as you put it, pay for them to be fed and clothed and housed."

"And how many of them would be able to contribute to society at large if they weren't hidden away by a wall of fear? We could go round and round all day without coming to a resolution. What do you want from us?"

"Why, I want to offer each of you a place to come and stay, a place to come and live free from the magical attacks you seem to be threatened with, a place that will keep you safe from all of the nastier bits of magic that keep turning your life upside down. The only thing we ask in exchange is that you work for us, that you become part of the show itself. The museum and the zipline close relatively early in the day, which means all of our employees are free to roam the grounds as they will after hours, and yet they know that as long as they stay within our walls, they will come to no harm. Can you say the same of your house in Ohio? Of your friends' homes? What about those senior citizens who come to your house all the time?"

He'd hired people to come to my house. He'd had them follow us. I was pissed, but he did have a decent point. What if we could live life free of magical emergencies? Would that solve the divide between Aiden and I? Would Mia have the time and space to live free of her father's death, and still have a life, or would she always mourn him if she was in a place where magic lived behind closed doors, behind lock and key, cowering from real world dangers just because they had a place where they thought they were safe?

I couldn't believe how easy he'd made it sound. "So, the people who come to stay with you, the ones who are somehow trying to avoid magic, or magical badness, what do you have them do for you? What power do they give you over them?"

He shrugged, stalking quietly closer to the open door of the Winnebago, as if looking to grab me should I step a solitary toe outside the threshold. He could stalk all he wanted, though, because I had absolutely no intention of giving him any way of getting to me short of an agreed negotiation. The other thing I wanted was to stall him. Sooner or later, someone driving by was sure to see a camper on the side of the road, broken down, and call for help, being a Good Samaritan. I just had to keep him talking long enough for that phone call to go through and someone to get dispatched to come to where we were sitting.

"They all grant me different things. It depends on what they are able to give. Different beings can contribute in different ways. I can't give you the same answer for each of them."

Somehow, I didn't trust his words, but we were quickly arriving at an impasse.

"What do you actually want from us, Coyote? I don't know what else to call you. It appears you've manipulated us from the beginning, getting us out here, and you apparently want us to be vulnerable to you, to your magic, or to your will. Rather than sitting here and playing twenty questions all day, can we just cut to the chase and see if there's something we can agree on? Because otherwise, we're in for an incredibly long day," I said.

He seemed a bit taken aback by my suggestion, as if he was looking forward to a long drawn out parlay of negotiations. "I guess I didn't think you'd be so direct."

I laughed. "You did enough research to want us out here and you didn't figure I'd get a little impatient at finally figuring out what was going on? Whoever you tasked with that investigation missed some pretty big details about my personality."

Coyote's mouth turned up in a slight wry grin. "Obviously, that's true. But what I truly want is for you to give my facility an opportunity. I'd like you all to come and see it. I think you might be tempted to stay."

Not on your life, I thought, but if going and looking at his 'facility', whatever that was, got us out of this standoff, and allowed us to figure out his game, get Babe back, and get on with our lives, I was open to it. Maybe not as open as he wanted me to be, but I'd listen.

"What's your plan? I assume you have one."

"What do you mean?"

"Give me some reassurance we won't be attacked, that we'll be allowed to retain our own free will, that we'll be free to return to this camper and leave on our own, and we'll discuss going with you."

He considered my proposal. We haggled a bit more, but ended up agreeing, at least temporarily, to a break in our negotiations. We agreed to go with him; he agreed to have the tire fixed on the Winnebago, as he was the one who had flattened it in the first place. We agreed to give him two hours of our time, to look over his facility and consider whether to stay, and he agreed that if we wished to leave, we would be able to.

We might have agreed to go, and we might have agreed not to take weapons, but I wasn't dumb enough to go without some kind of protection. I'd been through too many weirdo magical moments lately to walk blindly into something that could be a trap. We had rock salt. We had table salt. We had some metal. If we were leaving the relative safety of the trailer, then those of us with pockets were going to take a bit of a guarantee that we couldn't be magicked into agreeing to something we would never agree to on our own.

I thought it wouldn't hurt us to see what he was talking about.

We'd gotten ourselves out of deeper messes in the past.

I so should have known better.

CHAPTER FORTY-FOUR

Coyote whistled at someone off in the distance, and an old battered pickup truck showed up, with seats in the back, and a copy of the Coyote Gulch logo on the doors. It looked like a truck that used to convey zip lining tourists from one end of their zip line to another, or to travel around a larger park getting a guided tour. It made me slightly uneasy to get in the back, but I'd gotten him to promise, so I went ahead. It helped that we were in the back of a truck, rather than cooped up in a creepy van, like the one I'd sighted in the parking lot at the park.

Nothing says danger quite like a creepy van that looks like it should sport a "free candy" sign. No matter that van had carried their business logo, and didn't look like it had a lot of rust spots or holes, any van that doesn't appear to have windows in the back makes me think, "creepy van."

The truck we were riding in was an old work truck, but they had put wooden benches along the sides of the truck bed, and had wooden backs to the seats, so that we could sit fairly comfortably without worrying about falling off into the road. I leaned back against the wooden support and took a deep breath, letting it out slowly as I tried to calm the pounding heart in my chest. It wouldn't do for me to look even slightly nervous as we did this. I looked around the back of the truck, and met eyes with Mia. She seemed ready to do battle, the hard look in her eyes one I'd seen in Tobias's before a fight. Jonah seemed a little overwhelmed, but he held her hand and watched her carefully. He appeared more worried about her than whatever we were facing.

Bert sat in Allie's lap, quiet, but there was something to his expression that worried me. He seemed to be, like Mia, almost itching for a fight. Allie didn't seem to notice, watching the landscape go by. I wondered if she'd ever ridden in the back of a pickup truck before. It was a bit of a different experience. Aiden's eyes were squarely on me, but I couldn't tell what he was thinking. I hoped he was on the same page I was. I hated to risk all of us, but I couldn't bring myself to walk away when Babe was still missing and there might be other magical beings whose freedom was being severely curtailed. Much like I'd been unable to leave the situation in Wonderland alone, I couldn't really leave them to the mess they'd found themselves in without at least trying to help.

The others, Jane, Paul, and Pete, weren't really saying much, either, and I couldn't even begin to imagine what was going through their heads.

Of course, the hamster wheel running at hyperspeed in my brain was fascinating enough.

Jane hadn't really had much history of magic, but her reputation had risen to the level of Wild West legend due to the show she'd been involved with in her days traveling with her friend, Wild Bill Hickock. She'd talked a little about it, and it had reminded me of things I'd read about her in the past. She might not have had any magical abilities, but she sure commanded a lot of people who thought she was awfully cool, and if she was convinced to put on a show similar to her act from back in the day? How much could Coyote charge for a Wild West show with the real Calamity Jane?

How much would he charge for American school children to get their pictures taken with Babe, the big Blue Ox? Or Paul Bunyan and Cordwood Pete? What would he want to do whatever with someone descended from the Brothers Grimm, from Hans Christian Andersen, from Johnny Appleseed, or the daughter of the real Alice from Wonderland?

Of course, that was why Coyote had taken Babe. It was why he'd placed the ransom notes or had them placed, to get Paul to go looking for him, and to make him desperate enough to look for help. I'd started to gain a reputation for rescuing myself, and others, from magical emergencies and mishaps. Whether Paul was the true target, or whether we were, my friends and I had started to be known for solving riddles, talking our way out of problems, and otherwise resolving magical difficulties. I wasn't aware of anyone else doing such work. It would make sense to be sent our way. Did Coyote have connections in the magical realms? Had he planted someone who would point them in our direction? I wasn't sure I'd ever know that answer.

Either way, he was looking for the "apple heir"; so he'd definitely found out about Frog Woman's child who had been placed for adoption. Whether Frog Woman had told humans who worked for Coyote, or if the humans had learned of her child by someone blabbing to the wrong person, Coyote had learned that his old nemesis had a weakness. Could he control her? Gain access over her lands? Or was he just jealous? Another question that would probably never be answered; but no matter what, there was no way that I was going to let Jonah fall under Coyote's power if I could help it.

We bounced along in the back of the truck, and the pieces kept falling into place in my brain. Coyote must have planted the first two notes at Paul's house, in order to really stoke his desperation, and make him scramble for help. Once we'd actually gotten out here, he had to have a human step over our salt line to leave the third note while I'd been out for coffee. In a crowded campground, no one would have noticed a human just walking around as if they were looking for someone, or looking for the right campsite. All it took was waiting until someone was up and moving to know that the note would be noticed fairly quickly.

The truck pulled into a driveway that had a stone gable at the curve, with the words "Coyote Gulch" imbedded in the rock. The driveway was long and winding, probably at least a half-mile long, leading back to a stucco building designed to blend in with the scenery. If I didn't know better, I'd have thought this place was the kind of chi-chi spa my stepmother might have attended, for appearances sake, spending tons of money to have heated rocks put on her back and seaweed wraps around her toes.

Behind the house were hills and mountains, and I assumed this was where the zip line part of the business took place. So where was the museum?

The truck passed pulled up to the main house, and pulled around behind it. There were several cottages a few hundred yards behind the main house, and signs up saying the museum was to the left, and the zip line tours started further to the left. Eventually, we came up on a large, three story building, which had a big sign above the large double doors on the front that read, "Americana Legends Museum". The truck stopped, and Coyote got out of the front. We all started to climb down from the back of the truck.

There weren't any people around, but I assumed they wouldn't be busy, maybe even closed on a national holiday such as Thanksgiving. Even though the holiday was tomorrow, it was already evening, and highly unlikely that any tourists would still be walking around the place at the moment. Sure enough, a big sign on the door declared they were closed for the holiday until Saturday. I wasn't sure whether that was a good thing or a bad thing at the moment. On the one hand, I liked that there wouldn't be any collateral human casualties from whatever Coyote had planned, but on the other one, it also meant there wouldn't be anyone hanging around and asking questions that we might ask to call for help.

We all followed Coyote and the human who had been driving the truck into the building and into a large lobby. Large banners hanging from the ceiling announced the upcoming exhibit with Babe. I heard a choked noise behind me when Paul saw the signs, with screen printed images of Babe to draw in the crowds. Come meet a blue ox of extraordinary size, one with legendary proportions and mystical origins, read the signs.

But the signs also hinted at a larger display, a new upcoming exhibit with further American legends and artifacts and displays. Coming soon, they talked about more exiting and storied American legends, visiting displays, and interactive attendants. Were they talking about all of us? I didn't like how that looked.

Coyote began to show us around the museum, but it looked fairly deserted. He showed us Betsy Ross's chair, paintings of the Swamp Fox, Davy Crockett's hat, and other artifacts. It looked like random hodgepodge, except that the chair was still rocking slightly, as if someone had vacated it just seconds before. The area was decorated like a room that might have belonged to a Revolutionary War era seamstress, and there was a flag laid off to the side, with a bone sewing needle sticking up out of it. Davy Crockett's hat was sitting on a hat stand, but it was sliding sideways, as if it had just been stuck on the stand in a hurry. It slid off and landed on the floor with a soft sound.

Someone, or more than one someone, had been in the room just recently.

Coyote saw it as well, and turned to me immediately. I tried very hard to keep my face in check, to prevent him from realizing I'd found out we weren't alone in the building. I assumed it worked, because even though one eyebrow quirked up, he didn't say anything right away. After a few minutes, he sighed.

"Well, this is the museum. If you want, you can walk around, and take a look. There are some very fascinating exhibits."

I shook my head at him. "Before we do anything like that, do you mind if my friend Paul here sees his ox? It's been a long time, and I'm sure he'd like to make sure that Babe's ok before we do anything else."

"Certainly," he said. "Follow me."

CHAPTER FORTY-FIVE

Coyote took us down the hall past several other exhibits, showing Annie Oakley's rifles, Jim Bowie's knife, and other odds and ends of Americana. All of them looked like they'd been dropped in a hurry, rather than placed deliberately in a display case. I wondered if this was on purpose, but Coyote did not look happy as he looked around the museum.

"So, why build a museum like this, way out here, away from everything?" I asked.

"It's a good getaway, and we're near enough to draw plenty of business from the local parks and tourist attractions. The sale of tickets here has been enough, in past years, to fund the living expenses of a number of beings; ones who would not do well living in the human world of today. Many of them wouldn't even know how to conduct themselves in public anymore, much less how to hail a taxi, or search the internet, or even drive a car. Many of them have lived years longer than they were supposed to as humans, and to be honest, I'm not sure just how many of them would deal well with transition." He opened a large sliding door, and pointed. "Babe's in there. Don't take long. We still have much to discuss."

Paul rushed in and hugged Babe around the neck. As we all slipped inside, it was gratifying to see that Babe looked well cared for. He had feed in a feeder in front of him, still cool water in a trough, clean straw, and even a large beach ball that he was nosing around in the pen. When the ox saw Paul, though, he got more excited than a puppy who hadn't seen his master all day. If I didn't know better, I'd have thought Babe was excited enough to lick Paul's face and pee on the floor in over stimulated joy. Instead, Babe nuzzled Paul's neck and the big man hugged his friend, and it did my heart good to see them reunited. Pete finally came up behind him and indicated we needed to keep moving, as we were on a time frame to see everything, negotiate what we could, and get out and on the road as fast as possible. It was also interesting to note that Babe was still in a smaller size, as if Coyote had somehow maintained Paul's get-smaller magic.

Paul reluctantly stepped away, and even Babe seemed like he didn't want the big man to let go. "You're right, Pete. There's more to see, I'm sure."

Coyote nodded. "There is. In fact, there are people to meet." A woman in a long skirt stepped out of the shadows, and a man in knee breeches and tall stockings stepped into the light. The woman had a white lacy mobcap on her head, and she bobbed at us in a curtsy, a kerchief around her shoulders.

"This is Betsy," Coyote introduced us.

Betsy. It was Betsy Ross.

I never thought I'd be face to face with Betsy Ross.

Coyote was speaking, saying something that wasn't registering with me very well. "What was that?" I asked.

"Your reaction. It's part of why we opened this place, part of why we have offered sanctuary. How many Americans out there have heard the tall tales and legends and stories about different people in our history? How many of them would be just as star struck as you are with meeting the real person, or talking to an honest descendant of that real person. I'm saying wouldn't it be in everyone's best interest to consider that a place like this is in the legends' best interests?"

I understood the words coming out of his mouth, but I didn't like the idea that anyone, no matter their background and no matter their abilities, would have to hide, or trade away their freedom for a little bit of what I saw as false security. I didn't say anything, but I went up to Betsy.

"Are you here of your own free will?" I asked, softly. I didn't want her to feel like she couldn't answer, but Coyote's eyes were burning a hole in my back.

She looked over my shoulder, and I followed her gaze, to where she was watching Coyote. At a brief nod, she dropped her eyes, staring at the floor. "Yes, mum, of course I am."

Well, that sounded about as staged as a kindergarten Christmas pageant.

Others were standing at the back of the room. I had a funny

feeling I'd get similar reactions out of all of them if I pushed it.

I turned back to Coyote. "This is sad. You have here freedom fighters and American legends, showmen and patriots. Almost to a man, or woman, every single one of them was a go-getting, true hero, one that didn't back down from a fight. Their actions shaped what this country became. And look at them. They don't feel free to talk."

Coyote's eyes narrowed. "She just talked, didn't she? Besides, you haven't even seen their quarters, or the spa, or the in-ground swimming pool. How do you know they aren't living in the lap of luxury here, afraid you're going to spoil it?"

You know, he could be right. But I was looking at the back of the room, and I saw Davy Crockett, Daniel Boone, and Jim Bowie with their heads bowed, and I knew I wasn't wrong. These men hadn't bowed their heads to *anything* or *anyone* during their original existence. I would be *damned* if I would believe that they would do so during their magical existence.

Frog Woman and I had talked, while we had considered Coyote's offer in the Winnebago. She seemed to believe these people had all lived normal, human lives, but the telling of their exploits and their legends had turned them into actual legends; the magic of their notoriety had brought them a kind of magical existence beyond their human years. It wasn't something that happened to everyone, she thought, but ones who had truly gone above and beyond, had served a higher purpose, and had transcended a normal human life. Belief kept them going.

If that was the case, I could see why having a facility such as this would keep the belief going and keep them alive. I could see a purpose for it, but at the same time, would people keep believing if they saw what their heroes were turning into? Or were they passed off as actors? If that was the case, why did Coyote want them to stay?

He was getting something from them. The question was what, and I wasn't going to get that from any of them while Coyote was in the room.

"Lead on, Coyote. We'd like to see the rest, and the clock's ticking," I said. What else could I do? Maybe during a tour I could get one of the residents alone? I had to look for an opportunity. But I also had to get us all out of here before our negotiated time was up. How to do both? If I couldn't get them free, then the choice had to be to get us out. We could always come back and try to free the others later. It didn't look like anyone was in mortal danger.

And then, I saw it.

There was some sort of cage, off in the darkened corner of the cavernous room. I hadn't seen it before, because of how the dim the lights were. I realized we were barely a third of the way into the room, and it looked like the lights were purposely dim, and only on in the section of the room we were in. Off in the distance, past the pen where Babe was kept, was the cage. If I hadn't been looking, I would never have seen it, or I would have passed it off as equipment piled up in the back, like in a storeroom or a barn.

I walked towards it, with Coyote trying to keep me away. My friends followed me, and the eyes of all those who lived at Coyote Gulch watched as I headed straight for the cage in the back.

There were three sitting inside, silent.

What could they possibly have done to have gotten thrown into a cage? And if they were in a cage, it leant more credence to the idea that the others were also not here voluntarily, that their consent was not freely given.

One gentleman inside the cage was clearly Native American, with a feather in his hair and a chest plate that looked vaguely familiar, like I'd seen it somewhere before. He was an older man, but the set to his jaw made him look like he'd been a force to be reckoned with in his day. Another was a woman in early pioneer garb, in her mid forties, who looked highly pissed. She wore a necklace, but it looked like . . . were those alligator teeth? The third person, a young man with broad shoulders, wore a vintage baseball uniform and cleats, a flat topped turn of the 20th century baseball cap on his head.

There was something about each and every one of them that had me wondering who they were. I was supposed to know who they were, wasn't I?

CHAPTER FORTY-SIX

J ane started tugging very insistently on my sleeve. I brushed her off the first couple of times, but she wouldn't quit. I turned to her. "What?"

She pointed at the Native American man. "That's Sitting Bull. We was in Bill's Wild West show together. Most stubborn man I ever met. Can't imagine he'd put up with somthin' like this if'n he didn't feel he had to."

But was he actually putting up with it? He was behind bars, after all.

I turned to Coyote. "If people are here by their own free will, then why are they in a cage?"

He didn't seem to like what I was asking. "That's not part of the tour, Ms. Grimm."

"I don't really give a shit." I stalked over to the door to the cage, and tried to test the door, but the woman inside stopped me.

"Miss, you don't wanna touch them bars. We've tried. There's some kinda magic on 'em."

She sounded a lot like Jane's frontier accent, but not quite; she had a twang to her speech Jane didn't. I wondered where she was from, but didn't ask. I also didn't touch the bars. I had no problem with that.

Coyote kept trying to talk me into looking at the hot tubs or the beds with the six hundred thread count sheets. I kept looking around the darkened room and thought, *these people don't care about the sheets, or the hot tub, or the spa.* So how to get them all out of here?

I shook my head at the three people behind bars. I didn't currently have a way to get them out, but I didn't plan to leave them there long.

"What do you get out of them being here, Coyote? What is possibly worth all of this?"

He shrugged, as he pointed the way out of the back storage room with the cage and with Babe. "This place makes a mint. It keeps them alive. And some of them have untapped magical abilities that they don't even realize they have. They are beholden to me because I keep them safe from harm. It's a great symbiotic relationship."

No, it wasn't. He showed us the residences, the places where the people stayed when they were not at the museums, and they were actually pretty nice. They had huge beds, covered with down bedding, central air, private hot tubs, and a private chef provided all of their meals. There was a tennis court, and a shuffleboard area, a place to throw horseshoes, and a community hall, where they could all gather for dances and bingo if they wanted. In short, the place kind of reminded me of a high end retirement community. I wondered if that was where he'd gotten the idea.

It wasn't my idea of retirement, and it wasn't what I thought the people who were here would have thought of for their twilight years. I'd go nuts if all that was left was going to a museum, playing shuffleboard, and hiding from the world. I had a hard time believing the others weren't feeling much the same way.

There had to be another reason. As we walked, I pulled Frog Woman aside. "Does Coyote get some kind of boost to his power by having the others here, or is he just trying to have more power under his own control?"

"He doesn't gain power from others, but he is very clever. He's a trickster, and gains power over his own ability to control others through his own machinations. He is, for some reason, controlling the other's abilities, and keeping them under control by whatever agreements he has made with them. The key to breaking his control has to be in how he structured those agreements."

My brain swirled as he kept up the tour, showing us the minor conveniences and the material comforts. Time was clicking away, though. I needed to figure a way out of all of this, and I needed it to happen quickly.

As we circled back around to the museum, I waited until we were back in the presence of some of the other residents before I made a statement about needing to use the facilities. In truth, I did need to pee, but I locked eyes with Betsy Ross, trying hard to signal to her to sneak out to meet me.

Coyote didn't bat an eye, telling me to go down the hall, around the corner, and into the second door on the left. I nodded at him, and headed that way as the rest of the group headed to the next exhibit. I ducked into the hallway, and waited.

Betsy had caught my signal, and she joined me shortly thereafter.

"I've got to ask, ma'am. What did Coyote promise you to get you to stay, to be a part of his museum? Has he got something on you, or the others?"

She nodded, briefly. "Look, he's tricked us all here, but it took more inducement for some to get them to stay. Coyote made us think we were in danger, and then promised us all kinds of safety. I don't believe any of us were in actual danger, and some of weren't even out in the public eye to be in danger in the first place. I never really went out. I just stayed in, sewing flags that I sold to the souvenir shops in Williamsburg and Philadelphia. I was content; didn't really want for much. Coyote showed up, and stayed for a while, telling me I was a target; that I was such a symbol of American pride I was a target for terrorists. I didn't believe him. And then my front door was set on fire and foreign symbols were painted on the windows. He promised to protect me as long as I only sewed flags for his souvenir shop, and as long as I was a part of his museum, I'd be safe. I was scared, miss. I don't know how to get out of it."

"And the others?" I asked. "All the same?"

"Mostly, he's stolen something we can't live without, or he's been able to trick us into forgetting tragic events and then slowly letting us relive and remember them again. The ones in the cage are ones he hasn't been able to break, or ones he is holding to keep others compliant. There's got to be a way out of this. He keeps telling us he'll allow us to be hurt, or he'll hurt the ones we love. The woman in the cage is Sally Ann. 'Thunder Ann' Whirlwind Crockett. Her husband and his friends are very brave, and they've given up their lives before for freedom, but they can't bring themselves to put her at risk. Casey, the man in the baseball uniform, keeps trying to rally all of us to rise up against Coyote, but I think that's just because he's sick and tired of being known for striking out. Sitting Bull is the most stubborn man I've ever met. Coyote has made him forget and relive the deaths of his family over and over and over and the man still won't do what Coyote wants. He knows they're dead, and he won't go along."

"What does Coyote make you do?" I asked, whispering, and hoping that Coyote wouldn't double back and look for us.

"It's really not that bad. We're part of the museum. We work the grounds. We spend time together. But we cannot act against Coyote, or he says he will withdraw his protection. Whether we agree with him or not that we're in danger, we believe he will endanger us or our loved ones if we don't do as we are told."

As much as I was glad she was explaining this, I had guessed much of it. And if they were so scared of him, then why was she telling me all of this? I asked her as much.

"Well, we're all kind of at the end of our rope. And we've all heard of you, Ms. Grimm. We heard about what you did for the people in Wonderland. We've heard how you have handled yourself in many different situations. Coyote started saying he had big plans to expand, that he was going to bring you and all of your friends here, so he could control big magic in the mortal realm, and so that the magical realms would take him seriously. That's when we knew we couldn't let him get that kind of power. It was not an issue when it was just us, but Coyote wants to trap you here, he wants to trick you into agreeing to stay, and then hold you here with your promise."

"What did Babe, the ox, have to do with any of this?" I asked. I had to see if I'd guessed correctly.

"He was part of a manufactured danger, a made up emergency to get you involved. He wanted Paul, that's true, and anyone else he might be able to get. He wants all of you. And he'd hoped to snare Frog Woman, his old nemesis, as well. He was chortling to himself the other day, rubbing his hands together like some old time villain from the moving pictures, convinced that his plan was working exactly the way he wanted it to, but then you got to the Narrows before he did."

I grinned a bit at that. I liked that I might have thrown a monkey wrench in his plans.

"No," she said. "That's not a good thing, because Frog Woman might not have gotten involved if you guys hadn't had a chance to talk to her without him. He wanted the apple heir so he could lure her out.

Instead, he has *both* of them, and they've come onto his property voluntarily. Don't you understand? He wants to control all magical beings in North America, and because she came out, he's got her, and all of your friends, and at least one of your friends has ties to other courts. He'll try to leverage that, too. There's only one being in the country that he hasn't tried to control. He's rounding up everyone. He's saving that one for last."

"Who is he saving?" I wanted to know. Maybe I could get to them, to warn them.

"Tobias Andersen," was the answer. "But now that his daughter is here, Coyote will have a plan to bring him in line as well."

Except that Tobias was dead. Apparently that news hadn't gotten out yet. Was that something we could use to our advantage? Maybe. But either way, it was comforting to know Coyote did not appear to have had a hand in his death. Maybe it really was just a fluke accident.

I wasn't sure that Mia would feel any better about that.

CHAPTER FORTY-SEVEN

While I was gone, I went ahead and used the facilities. It wouldn't do to have to ask for another break while we were in the middle of a negotiation or other long debate about possibly freeing everyone. And I'd hate to feel like something as important as another's freedom was somehow put in jeopardy by the needs of my bladder.

Betsy had left me to the ladies' room while she snuck back to avoid being noticed arriving with me. My own brain buzzed with ideas of how to handle Coyote and his machinations. I was not going to let him stay in charge of these people, and I needed to get the rest of us out of here. It was no surprise he wanted to use Jonah against Frog Woman, Babe against Paul and Paul against Pete. Was Jane part of that equation, as well, or was she of further use against Sitting Bull? I wasn't shocked that he wanted to use Mia against her father; it was what her father was afraid of most. And use Aiden against his father, likely, to gain access to the faerie realms and their power. But how would he get them to agree?

Me.

Of course.

My relationship with Aiden hadn't been a secret, but apparently the news that we'd broken up was. The joke, I guess, was on Coyote. But I did believe that Aiden still cared. He wouldn't want me hurt, when I'd brought him back from Wonderland and insisted on getting him the care that saved his life. Mia was my best friend, and she'd just lost her father. Of course she'd try to protect me.

And I had working relationships so far with the Snow Queen and with the Wonderland courts, working through diplomatic relations with both to keep humans safe and to negotiate safe passage for others.

I was valuable, not just for who I was related to, but also for what I'd built up in the amount of time I'd been working on the magic stuff.

Damned if I was going to let him get his way.

I marched down the hallway, toward the same back room. Coyote was acting like a bored tour guide, but those sharp eyes of his didn't miss much. "Ah, Ms. Grimm, welcome back to the group. And now that you are all together again, the terms of our agreement have changed."

I narrowed my eyes at him. "Since when?"

"Since the two hours we agreed on have expired."

There was no way that had been two hours. I had a hard time believing it, but I looked at the watch on my wrist, and it did say that the two hours had gone by.

"So, you have us here. What do you want, Coyote?" I asked.

He raised his hands, and I felt the cool push of his power brush against my skin. I smelled that same stale peppermint and dusty book smell of magic, but it didn't do anything to me.

"Huh?" he said, tossing a stronger wave of magic.

Bert yawned, in Allie's arms. "You dumb, stupid, crap for brains. You're a slack brained, low brow Neanderthal, a magic slinging skunk weasel. You antiquated addlepated magic-less monkey. You think we aren't ready for that?"

Coyote went red in the face, and I thought steam would come out of his ears. "I thought I told you no metal. It was part of our bargain. How dare you bring such items into my home, into my lands!" He snarled at us, and I giggled.

I think it was the giggle that got to him worse than anything else.

He lost it, and started slinging magic at us, yelling and demanding that we do something, that we follow his orders, that we respond to his commands.

I pulled the plastic sandwich baggie of salt out of my front pocket. The others did the same, pulling the salt out of their pockets and wherever else they had hidden them. We'd been carrying plenty of salt on us, divvying it up between multiple bags, so that no one person had one bulgy bag that might be spotted.

I hadn't known if we'd be patted down, and we weren't.

Allie walked over to Coyote, and began pouring a small line of salt beside him. Frog Woman and Mia and Jonah each walked up and continued the line, encircling him with salt and holding him in place. He tried to escape at one point and Mia punched him in the face, knocking him back enough to keep him inside the salt circle.

"Salt isn't enough to completely block my magic," he cried. "You cheated. You just wait. Word will get out that you broke your word, and the reputation that you've been so carefully building will be in the dust. You have no idea what you're dealing with now!"

I laughed.

He stopped his rant at the sound.

"Coyote, you are a smart individual, but you are nowhere near as smart as you think you are. You have a lot of people here, whom you believe you are freely bargaining with, and that they support you. They do not support you other than to protect themselves from dangers that you have manufactured. You have the wife of one of the men in a cage to ensure his cooperation and that of his friends. It's not a hard line to figure out you were going to do the same for Paul Bunyan; you took Babe, his ox, in order to get him here and subservient to you."

His jaw dropped.

I figured I'd leave out the rest. There was no reason to drag everyone into this. We had been hired by Paul, after all. We'd leave it there for now.

"Coyote, all of those things that you are threatening to take away from me, I've won by being very, very lucky, and very, very smart. You did not say 'no metal.' You said 'no weapons.' We have abided by that agreement, to the letter of the word."

"There's no way that's true!" he howled.

The others joined me, from the edges of the room, Davy Crockett, Daniel Boone, Betsy Ross, Annie Oakley, and all the rest. We all stood in a ring outside of the salt circle, as if we were all waiting for Coyote to do something really stupid. He reached out, trying to throw raw magic at us. The ones who lived here at his property staggered a bit, but the salt circle kept the magic from doing much of anything else to hurt them.

"How are you doing this?" he demanded. "What weapon did you use?"

I reached into my other pocket, and the others that had come with me did the same; well, all except for Bert, who didn't have pockets. I pulled out a handful of Tobias's homemade bullets, the ones that were jacketed in iron.

"Guns don't kill people," I said. "Bullets do," and dropped the handful of bullets onto the floor. My friends did the same, reinforcing the salt circle with the iron in our pockets that had been protecting us from his magic.

I really wished I'd had a camera to take a picture of the look on his face.

CHAPTER FORTY-EIGHT

There was much celebrating and much hugging going on amongst the others as Coyote finally sat down inside the salt circle, holding his head in his hands and crying softly. As the link to items he'd enchanted was broken, the door to the cage sprung open, and the woman inside ran into the arms of her husband. Casey, the one in the baseball uniform, sprang out, and grabbed the wooden ball bat that lay in the opposite corner of the room, swinging it back and forth and loosening shoulders that had to have felt cramped from not being used. Sitting Bull stepped out, and with a great deal of dignity, thanked me. I saw the look on his face. If Coyote had been torturing him with visions of his long dead family, then it was no wonder that he looked tired. I could tell the man needed no reminder of their deaths, but how much longer could he have held out?

Paul jumped the gate and hugged Babe around the neck, introducing the manically happy ox to Calamity Jane and reminding him of his brother, Pete. The three of them looked extraordinarily happy together. I hoped they'd stay together.

Word spread quickly to others who hadn't been in the building. The others seemed joyous and excited, and Frog Woman contrived a way to move Coyote into the magical cell he'd held others in, sealing the cage with magic of her own. Coyote didn't really resist, however. He looked like he'd been broken in the confrontation we'd had.

As the others whooped and hollered and danced and celebrated, some of them faded away. Those that did were ones whose lives had been cut short, and their deaths were part of their legend. Sitting Bull was one of those, and he indicated no regrets, stating that he'd see his family soon, as he faded. The others that remained didn't let the good-byes stand in their way of a celebration.

They brought out food and drink and offered me all kinds of things in thanks, but I declined. Paul was paying for my services, after all. There was no need for anything else, and no matter what they said or did, I was tired. As crappy as my own life was, it was beyond time to get back to it.

Aiden's eyes twinkled at me as the hubbub started to settle down. He squeezed my hand. "You did well, Janie. No one could have done it better."

I thanked him, sincerely, and accepted the hug he gave me, but wondered if this was the last magical victory we'd have together. That was the part of my crappy life that would come flooding back when we went home. I'd finally have to have that discussion with Aiden, the one I'd been avoiding, the one where he finally cut himself out of my life and went his own way, to find someone new.

We agreed to spend the night with the people from Coyote Gulch, and began to discuss with them what the next step might involve.

"You might open the place yourselves, with tourists coming in. You've already got the advertising that Babe is here. That kind of belief is something Coyote already did the legwork for to bring in the crowd. That would bring in money that might let you pursue something else down the road," Allie offered.

She had a good point.

It was an already established business, with an already established promotional base. There were already groups booked to come in for the holiday weekend. It could totally work.

"Or, once you get past the initial weekend, you could turn this into a spa. You know, for the magical set. For people like all of us, who are connected with magic somehow, but who need some time to themselves, where they can be themselves, without worrying about being exposed. You could just run the zip line. There are a lot of possibilities," I said.

Betsy and Annie Oakley shook their heads. "There's no one here who knows how to manage a business in the mortal realm. We wouldn't know the first thing about how business works these days. I'm not sure this is a good idea, unless you, Janie, or one of your friends, would stay behind and teach us how."

I'd be damned if I was going to leave any of them behind. "Sorry, guys, but we can't stay. While we do appreciate the sentiment, and we are willing to help as much as we can, we do have real life issues that we can't ignore forever in our own lives." Including that painful conversation I knew we'd have when all this was over, but I shoved that thought back.

Paul scratched under Babe's chin, and said, "I think I'll stay, if that's all right. I know a bit about modern business, because I've negotiated some royalty contracts. We can do more of the same, and I know a bit about taxes and modern business necessities."

Pete and Jane immediately agreed to stay as well. Jane, at least, had experience in the Wild West shows with her friend Wild Bill Hickock, and had talked at length with him about the needs of the entertainment business. Pete wanted to put the past behind him and try to rebuild a relationship with his brother.

After several hours of long discussion, it was agreed that Frog Woman would stay as well. She was lonely, and did not want to go back to her lands on her own if there was a way to start making connections with others, including Jonah. He didn't let her offer to come back to Ohio with him, though, which I thought was impressive.

"Look, I do appreciate the opportunity to know my roots, ma'am, but I don't know you. You don't know me. We've agreed on a mechanism to start working magic together over the next year, once a month. Let's get to know each other better before we talk about anything else."

Frog Woman didn't really have an argument for that. In some ways, I think she felt a little relieved, after centuries of mostly self-imposed exile.

Mia sat by herself, off to one side, watching everyone dispassionately. I went over to check on her. She smiled at me as I sat down beside her.

"You okay?" I asked.

"I keep thinking that Dad would have loved this, that he would have loved to have been here, and he would have stayed to help these people. He would have wanted to spread them out to protect them, and close this place down, keep them all on the move to keep them safe, but that would absolutely have been the wrong move. He did just that with Mom and me. I understand why he decided what he did at the time, but we've done a lot to make the world a little bit safer. So did he, without knowing it. I think he knew his way wouldn't work anymore. He'd be happy about all of this, I'm sure. And he'd want to be part of the changes. I wish he could have been."

I wrapped my arms around her, and hugged her tight. "You'll be back here, I'm sure, with Jonah, from time to time. I'm sure you can help as much as you can to be part of the changes. I think your dad would like that."

She smiled back at me. "He would."

After a long night of talking it was all decided. Aiden, Jonah, Mia, Allie, Bert, and myself would make the trip home alone. The others fixed the Winnebago and brought it to us, letting us get a good night's sleep before we left for home. Sleeping in a comfortable bed and taking a hot shower did a lot for each of us, but the others would be fine.

The real question was whether we would be just as fine when we got home.

CHAPTER FORTY-NINE

M ost of the drive back was fairly quiet. Aiden and Jonah did most of the driving while Mia and I started the heavy duty studying scramble for next week's exams. Aiden insisted on driving straight through with us rotating drivers through the night rather than hitting an RV park or campground. I felt disappointed and relieved at the same time; disappointment that he seemed eager to end the last week we'd had together, but relieved because I was definitely ready to start sleeping in my own bed. As much as I'd enjoyed time with my friends over the last week, I was looking forward to spending time with them in my four bedroom sprawling Victorian style house rather than in something as confining as a Winnebago.

We pulled into the driveway of my own house in Ohio just before dinnertime on the Friday after Thanksgiving. We all piled out of the Winnebago, bleary eyed, bladders about to burst from the final hurry to get home, and knees wobbly from the cramped confines and amount of sitting. As we hurried inside, bringing in backpacks and bags and sleeping bags and cycling through the bathroom, it took me a few moments to realize that the house smelled incredible.

"What's going on?" I asked.

Aiden looked at me, rather sheepishly. "We missed Thanksgiving in our hurry to get home. I called Mom yesterday from a payphone when we stopped for gas and told her when I thought we'd get here. Smells like I timed it just right." He sniffed, sighing at the aroma of his mother's cooking. "I hope you don't mind, but I asked her to fix Thanksgiving a day late and in your kitchen. I figured no matter where everyone was headed after we got home, we could all use a hot, home-cooked meal."

It smelled heavenly. I dropped my bags in the entryway and followed my nose into the kitchen. Doris was pulling a giant turkey out of the oven, and the center island in the kitchen was covered with food: candied yams, homemade stuffing, oyster dressing, green bean casserole, scalloped potatoes, buttered corn, and five or six of Doris's famous pies were laid out, waiting for us. Harold was in the kitchen, helping Doris leverage the massive bird out of the oven.

"Thanks so much for doing this, Doris," I said. "It's a wonderful idea."

Stanley sat at the kitchen table, next to an older woman in a wheelchair. It had to be his wife, who had been dealing with some serious health issues the entire time I'd known him. I'd never met her before, but I was glad she was up to getting out of the house. Stanley was beaming. I smiled at her.

"I'm Janie. It's really nice to meet you."

She smiled back. "I'm Edna. I've heard so much about you."

Before I could say anything else, Aiden grabbed my hand and dragged me out of the kitchen

"What was that for?" I asked. "Isn't that kinda rude to your mom? With a turkey like that, she's been in the kitchen all day."

He took my other hand, holding both of them together in his own in front of me. "It is, but she'll understand. Janie, I need to apologize to you. I've been so wrapped up in my own drama, thinking magic was ruining my life, that I didn't realize how I was hurting you."

"Aiden, I . . ." I didn't know what I was going to say, but I couldn't stop myself from interrupting him.

"Shut up and let me get this out," he said, clearing his throat. "I've thought and thought about how I was going to do this, and I didn't know how to do this while we were in the midst of a magical emergency. I didn't want to distract you, or me, or anyone else, until we were all safe, home, and behind a threshold, but we're here now, and I refuse to wait any longer."

Oh, God. He was going to break up with me right here in my own dining room, with a houseful of people. I couldn't help it. My eyes teared up, and I swallowed hard, trying to keep from breaking down until the conversation was over. I wasn't sure I was going to be able to pull it off, but I was glad he'd thought enough to wait until we were safe, and I'd have the last week as a good memory to carry me through the hard weeks ahead of dealing with losing him.

He looked down at our hands, held together between us, and

didn't see my struggle. I kept thinking it couldn't be easy for him, either.

Aiden cleared his throat, again. "I am sorry that I've put you through so much indecision. I'm sorry I've hurt you. I've never known anyone like you, and you don't deserve how badly I've treated you."

Here it comes, I thought, and took a deep breath.

He let go of my hands and started digging his pocket. What was he doing? Had I left something in the camper? Whatever it was, he dropped it, and something dark bounced and skittered across the floor. Panic flashed across his face. Both of us scrambled after it. He came up with it first.

"Janie," he said, still on his knees, opening the dark thing he'd picked up off the floor.

As I turned back to him, I didn't see it at first.

It was a ring. In a box.

It was a diamond.

And he was holding it up to *me.*

I have no idea what my face was doing, but I probably looked like I had been smacked with something blunt and heavy. I was shocked.

"Well," he said. "Say something, please."

I opened my mouth, and nothing came out. I closed it and tried again. Nothing.

His face fell, taking my silence as a no. He started to get up from the floor, and I thought he looked completely crushed.

I certainly hadn't meant that.

"Aiden," I said, glad that sound was coming out again. "I was convinced you were working your way up to breaking up with me. I've been, well, girding myself for that conversation, for the idea that you were leaving my life for good. You've taken me completely by surprise. You've got to give me a minute to process this."

He held out the ring again. "I want you, Janie. I want all of you, no matter what comes next. Whether we have magic in our lives or not, regardless of where we end up, no matter what we learn about our friends, and it doesn't matter about anything else. I just want you. My life is empty without you. I thought I needed to work on my memory, and that I needed to be alone to do that. I was wrong. I just need you."

I reached for him. "Yes, Aiden. I'll marry you." That I'd say yes to him wasn't really in question, because I felt the same about him. I wanted to know that we'd be tied together forever, in magical emergency and not, in daily monotony or homeownership or family squabbles or whatever else might be on the horizon.

He'd picked a perfect ring for me, just enough glitz to make the inner girly girl squee, but simple in design, not enough to be overwhelming on my hand. He'd picked something that would look perfectly respectable on the hand of a lawyer who needed to impress others without being showy or ostentatious. I wrapped my arms around his neck and kissed him, hugging him tight and thanking my lucky stars that I'd been wrong.

I could handle being wrong in that direction all day long.

ACKNOWLEDGEMENTS

Special thanks to . . .

Ray Westcott, my husband, my best friend, and my biggest supporter, for all the love and encouragement. I would never get this much done without you.

Daniel Westcott, for reminding me of the concerns of teenagers on a daily basis

Alvin and Karen King, the best parents in the world, because they're mine

Eugene and Sandra Westcott, for showing me constantly that I hit the in-law lottery in the best way possible

Bert's biggest fan, Mary Jane Woodruff, for being such a wonderful supportive grandmother.

Skyler, Desi, Sierra, Ambrosia, Marah, Anna, Savannah, Joran, Blake, and Kenley, for being the best nieces and nephews in the world . . . again, because they're mine.

My friends and cheerleaders, Sara, Sarah, Steve, Rebekah, Rebecca, Andrea, Amy, Breanne, Michelle, Ashley, Erin, Erin, Chris, Audra, and all the rest, for listening to wild plot conjecture and understanding the insanity of a writer.

James Barnes, Kathy Watness, Melinda Timpone, and all the rest at Loconeal Publishing for taking on the series and helping me to make it shine.

AUTHOR INFORMATION

Addie J. King

Addie J. King is an attorney by day and author by nights, evenings, weekends, and whenever else she can find a spare moment. Her short story "Poltergeist on Aisle Fourteen" was published in MYSTERY TIMES TEN by Buddhapuss Ink, and an essay entitled, "Building Believable Legal Systems in Science Fiction and Fantasy" was published in EIGHTH DAY GENESIS; A WORLDBUILDING CODEX FOR WRITERS AND CREATIVES by Alliteration Ink. Her novels, THE GRIMM LEGACY, THE ANDERSEN ANCESTRY and THE WONDERLAND WOES are available now from Loconeal Publishing. The fourth book, THE BUNYAN BARTER, will be available in 2015. Her website is www.addiejking.com

www.ingramcontent.com/pod-product-compliance
Lightning Source LLC
Chambersburg PA
CBHW071302250626
47159CB00004B/1273